Forever Lately

A Regency Time Travel Romance

Book Two of the Forever in Time Series

Linore Rose Burkard

LILLIPUT PRESS
Dayton, OH

This is a work of fiction. Names, characters, places, and incidents are products of the author's imagination or are used fictitiously. Any resemblance to actual persons, living or dead, or to events or locales, is entirely coincidental.

FOREVER LOVELY: A REGENCY TIME TRAVEL ROMANCE
Book Two of the Forever in Time Series

Copyright ©2023 Linore Rose Burkard

Published by Lilliput Press, OH

Library of Congress Control Number: TBA

ISBN: 978-1-955511-23-0 (ppb)
ISBN: 978-1-955511-06-3 (ebk)
Burkard, Linore Rose
1. Fiction—Romance, Time Travel 2.Romance, Historical, Regency 3. Time Travel—Romantic

Cover Design by *100Covers*

Printed in the United States of America

Praise for the *Forever Lovely*

In *Forever Lovely*, you'll be immersed in a love story that spans two very different eras but can't be broken.... You find adventure, love, family, friendship, and sacrifice in a way that makes you want to just *keep reading*.
Samantha DeWitt (Rivera) Readers' Favorite 5 Star Review

It was wonderful! Time travel gone askew... Wonderful second in the series. Entertaining and fun while being a quick read. I couldn't put it down.
Joyce Reavis, Reviewer

Burkard never disappoints with her Regency love stories, and this one is no exception. How to move between centuries without disturbing the time continuum is handled deftly in this fast-paced three-day whirlwind that never slows. Will there be a 3rd book in this series? I'm already waiting!
Gerald E. Greene

Oh, my! The twists and turns and traveling back and forth in time kept me so engrossed, I read (this) in record time. I could see this becoming a movie or television series. Highly recommend!
Author Donna J. Shepherd

Such a sweet, clean, time-travel adventure! Easy to read even if you didn't read *Forever, Lately*. Love this author and I can't wait to see if there's more to this series!
Lindsey DeLost, Goodreads

A charming time-travel romance! An intriguing story about the importance of love and sacrifice in any time period. Don't miss reading this delightful tale!
Elizabeth Allan, Bookbub

Come! Get swept away! Ms.Burkard does a great job blending (two time periods) into a lovely story that will entertain and inspire you.
Deb Mitchell, Bookbub

And Praise for the Series

A writer of historical fiction travels back in time—and into the world of her characters. An enjoyable and dramatic era-spanning love story.
Kirkus

Spot on with entertaining language and engaging plot twists. Clean fiction at its very best! A must-read.
Lisa McCombs, ReadersFavorite Blog

Eccentric characters, well-defined period details (have you been to 1816, Ms. Burkard?) and a rollicking plot, Linore Rose Burkard takes us on a fast-paced, unpredictable journey that leaves the reader breathless until the very end!
Janice Dick, Author, *Eye of the Storm*

This is such a good book. Pure Magic. It's the best Regency novel I've ever read!
Kristen Malone, Historical Romance Writer

The plot is intriguing…
The BookLife Prize

Move, over, Poldark! Julian St. John is our new English heartthrob! The fun is on with Burkard's cast of mismatched, mischievous characters. I highly recommend this read!
Lisa K. Simonds, Author, *All In*

I just read the first chapter. Wow, what a stunner! Going back to read chapter two right now.
Dana McNeely, Author, *RAIN*

I loved this book! Romance, magic, mystery, and time-travel, all rolled into one delightful story to keep you turning the page!
Jody Blair, Reviewer

It is part of the human condition,
and a recurrent feature of human history,
that what we find is not always what we were looking for,
and what we accomplish is not always what we set out to do.
Wilfred W. McClay

Chapter 1

New York City, Present Day

"Upon my soul, that was extraordinary! Excuse me, sir, but my legs have gone weak!"

Miss Margaret Andrews held heavily to the arm of Julian St. John, who had brought her through time from 1819 England to the 21st century. Unlike St. John, Miss Margaret had never travelled through time before. The effect left her breathless.

They were to contact her elder sister Clarissa at Dove Cottage in America so that Margaret could see her for the first time in three years. It was that long since Clarissa had gone to the future and chosen to stay.

St. John patted Margaret's arm. "You'll recover in a moment," he said with the voice of experience, but there was something in his tone that made her look up at the face of her tall relation. A gentleman of vast good looks and taste, St. John was studying their surroundings with a scowl.

Impossibly tall buildings towered over them, nearly blocking the sky from view. Strange equipages of fascinating shapes and colors crawled in the street in a slow, noisome parade, while other discordant sounds permeated the air. Foreign and unidentifiable, the racket accosted Miss

Margaret's 19ᵗʰ-century ears in ways that the busiest thoroughfares of London never had. The equipages looked clean, even pretty with their rainbow of colors, but hadn't improved much for speed, she thought, watching them trickling along like recalcitrant dogs on leads, in stops and starts. The roads were smooth and free of mud, however, which seemed a wonderful improvement. Yet Mr. St. John had told Margaret that Dove Cottage, their intended destination, was in a quiet countryside in Maine. She realized they had arrived in the wrong place, which accounted for his frown.

"Where the devil are we?" he muttered, blinking rapidly to get his bearings, and looking nearly as flummoxed as his young charge. The tallit, the divinely mystical shawl that powered his dizzying leaps through time, had always brought him to Dove Cottage. After Clarissa had torn it in two, he and his wife Claire were able to reach the cottage together, each using one-half of the shawl. But this was a bustling metropolis, not the quiet retreat in Maine.

Turning to Miss Margaret he said, "Something has gone amiss. We must return to the past and try again. I have no inkling where we are, but we'll never meet your sister here."

St. John had agreed to bring Miss Margaret to see her elder sister only after much cajoling and pleading. Margaret claimed that since Clarissa had changed places with Claire Channing—who was now St. John's wife—it was only just that he should allow her to clap eyes on her sister one last time.

It was Claire who first discovered the tallit was magical, enabling time travel when drawn across one's chest. It had transported her from Maine to 1816 England quite by accident, but as a result, she and St. John had fallen in love. Clarissa, who wanted St. John for herself, accidentally discovered its qualities after tearing it in two in a fit of rage. Eventually, she and Claire agreed to trade places in time. Clarissa assumed Claire's identity as an author in the 21st century, while Claire happily joined St. John in the past permanently to be his bride.

The switch worked out fortuitously, for Claire and Clarissa, to both their surprise, were distant relations (born two hundred years apart) but near twins in appearance! Even their names were similar. But the similitude ended there— St. John loved sweet Claire, yet had only ever tolerated the scheming Clarissa.

Ideally, Claire would have brought Margaret to the future, sparing St. John the trouble. She was very near her lying-in with their first child and would have been glad, she said, for 21st-century "obstetrical" support. But she no longer had an identity here, and St. John insisted, moreover, that she mustn't dare risk the trip for the baby's sake.

Neither Claire nor St. John knew Miss Margaret's real hankering was to accomplish far more than visit Clarissa. Her elder sister, after all, had never been an affectionate sibling. Quite the opposite. What Miss Margaret really wanted was to see the many inventions she'd heard about, such as the analytical engines that St. John assured her surpassed the best upper-class libraries, and even college and university libraries, for riches of information. And the new-fangled devices that allowed people to speak to each other from anywhere in the world! She was simply mad to see these things.

But above all else, hidden in her heart of hearts, was the secret quest to settle her destiny. She had given it much thought, recognized her fate would be that of a spinster in society, and concluded she must go to the future to find some small invention to bring back and claim for her own. How else could she secure her comfort beyond her father's lifetime? For, upon his passing, his fortune would descend to a distant cousin due to the cursed law of primogeniture. It was unthinkable that she could depend upon the heir treating her generously, a virtual stranger. So, despite good pedigree (including that Lady Ashworth, a marchioness, was her relation) her reputation as a plain bluestocking, or bookish bore (as the nastier members of the *ton* liked to put it), would never go away, respectability and family notwithstanding. No, she was destined to secure her own comfort in the world, and if it meant borrowing a future invention to do so, then so be it.

Besides, Margaret *longed* for recognition. Society granted her a modicum of respectability but never true acceptance. They would grudgingly squeeze her onto their invitation lists—but she would be last on the train of couples for dinner, a wallflower at balls, an outcast in a crowd; in short, a magnet for disdain. Becoming an inventress would change everything!

Or nearly so. It would not make her desirable to the opposite sex; but to this, she was reconciled. With none of Clarissa's beauty or charisma, Margaret knew she must use her brains to make her way. Indeed, her earnest prayer every night was that the Lord would provide her with the opportunity to do just that, to make a splash based on merit. A proper invention was all she needed. And coming to the future was her best hope to find one.

Unbeknownst to him, Mr. St. John himself had given her the idea for he'd "invented" handy leather straps that helped secure passengers in carriages (called "seat belts" in the future, he said) which had already saved countless lives. The Regent was wild for them and had them installed in each of his multitudinous equipages. His example, as usual, set high society on a mad dash to follow and do likewise. St. John was suddenly not only wealthier than before but welcome at Carlton House and Brighton Palace as a genius of England with the veriest stars of the *beau monde.*

Like St. John and his carriage straps, Margaret's invention would serve society while earning her a place in it.

"Come," St. John said just then, pulling her from her reveries. "We'll return another time, after Claire's lying-in."

Margaret's heart sank. The biggest ball of the season was to take place just before everybody left London for their country estates in two months. Everybody who was anybody, that is. Margaret had hoped to have a name for herself by then. If they left now, gone was her hope of gaining notoriety, of blessing society with a new-fangled device, of being *a social success at the ball.*

"Please, sir!" she cried. "We have only just arrived! Do not say you cannot spare me but a few hours. And recall that I have not yet seen my sister. We *must* stay if I am to see her."

He shook his head. "You have not seen her for three years. A few months longer is no tragedy, surely."

Margaret's mind darted in various directions like a mouse trying to escape the claws of a cat. Cannily she said, "Seeing her was only one of my goals, sir. I *long* to observe this fascinating period." She looked around and spread her arms. "The future! I pray you, do not deny me!"

Miss Margaret could be winsome when she was passionate. St. John hesitated. A sudden onslaught of foot traffic engulfed them, moving past like water around river rocks. Margaret gawped at the strange clothing, her eyes widening with amusement. Women showing their legs! Other women in pantaloons! And all with an appalling lack of proper bust support. Men without stockings in scandalously short –were they poorly tailored breeches? — showing *their* legs! Margaret was no prude nor excessively prim, but a flush rose to her cheeks.

Many passersby noticed their 19th-century clothing with a gleam of interest or a smile, but no one stopped or inquired, and the massive volume of pedestrians continued to sweep by in a nearly unbroken tide.

"Lud! I am all astonishment!" Her father forbade her from using the exclamation 'lud,' claiming it was not ladylike, but it escaped her lips now. She laughed as she gripped St. John's arm. She was often amused by society when surveying the ghastly apparel of some of its members at a ball or rout, but this level of ghastly was utterly unprecedented. "I own I could stare all day," she said, still rather in awe of how indecent some were.

"I warned you," St. John said. "Few people have a shred of taste with regard to clothing in this century. Try not to gawp." He spied a metal signpost, motioned at it, and said, "Come."

Picking her way through the moving crowd, Margaret reached it first and read aloud when he joined her, "Red Zone. Tow and Fine $185 minimum." She turned to St. John. "We are in Red Zone, wherever that is."

He shook his head. "The sign is for carriages, er, cars." The flood of pedestrians was slowing to a steady trickle, and he turned to take in more of their surroundings. Behind them stood a long, grand, Palladian-style building upon a raised terrace. Above the arched entranceways flanked by columns were engraved the words: "THE NEW YORK PUBLIC LIBRARY."

"New York!" he exclaimed. "Little wonder it's so much busier than Portland."

"A library!" sighed Margaret in an altogether different tone, as though they'd stumbled upon the pearl of great price. The dignified Georgian building had three sets of steps, a plaza, and three arched doorways. Two huge stone lions on their bellies sat regally to both sides, as well as a huge stone vase, fountain and stone benches. It looked stately and wonderful. Eagerly she asked, "Will they let me peruse the books, do you think?"

He scowled. "There's no time for that. I promised you *one* day only." His plan was simple: contact Clarissa at Dove Cottage (formerly Claire's home in Maine). With luck, she'd be at her husband's ski lodge close by already. If not, they'd take a spin in the Jaguar kept there expressly for his use while they waited for her to fly up in a private plane. Once she arrived, they'd all have dinner in Portland, and then he and Margaret would go home again to South Audley Street in Mayfair. He would be back well in time for the birth of his first child, as the doctor assured him just a day earlier that the baby showed no sign of emerging just yet.

It was a neat plan. Miss Margaret would no longer plague him to see her sister or the future. He would enjoy the spin in the Jaguar, though 'twould be better with Claire beside him, and all would be well. Except they hadn't arrived in Maine, and his plan could not be followed.

"You did promise one day, sir, one *whole* day," replied Margaret, still eyeing the library as though it were Aladdin's cave. And it was, for among its treasures she could surely find her invention and bring it home and then embark upon the delightful prospect of making a wave in society. Her heart swelled at the thought.

St. John frowned. "If I must, I'll take you to a library in Portland, but we're in a different state—the Colonies have states, recall—and the one we want is Maine."

Margaret smiled indulgently. "They are no longer our colonies, sir," she said, thinking how old St. John must be to refer to them as such.

St. John, of course, knew this but liked the comfort of the old nomenclature.

Two women stopped before them. "Excuse us." The speaker looked Oriental, and Margaret stared curiously, having only seen one other Oriental woman in the flesh in her span of eighteen years. The woman turned to her companion. "In New York always some people are in costume. I must get picture. Such clothes! Such pretty lady! So handsome gentleman!"

"Pretty?" exclaimed Margaret under her breath. "She wants spectacles, I think!"

"May we take photo, please?"

"Photo—a pho—pho-to-graph?" exclaimed Miss Margaret, her eyes sparkling with excitement. To St. John she said, "Claire told me about pho-to-graphs! I own, I *adore* the idea of a photo-graph!"

The lady laughed heartily. "Actors, too! Brava, brava!" She edged in between St. John and Miss Margaret, and the companion clicked the photo.

Miss Margaret asked, "Is that all? Is it done?"

"One more please," said the lady, smiling. Then she switched places with her companion, and another click ensued. When they peered into little hand-held devices, one held hers up for Margaret to see. And there she was, an image of her bespectacled self and St. John, right before her eyes! St. John scowled with his usual mien, while Margaret's face was frozen in an expression of fascination. "Lud!" she exclaimed.

It was all she could do not to snatch the lady's device so she could keep staring at the miraculous likenesses.

"But you do not smile!" said the lady.

"Should one smile?" asked Miss Margaret. Every portrait she had ever seen gracing the walls of homes, whether modest cottages or wealthy estates, showed people staring somberly out. Rarely did one see a smile.

The women laughed and admonished St. John and Margaret to smile, then took more pictures. St. John managed to soften his scowl, while Margaret dutifully grinned, though she felt absurd. She covered her mouth when she saw her smiling face. "How gauche!" she exclaimed. The ladies laughed, thanked them heartily, pressed something into Margaret's hand, and walked away, chatting happily.

Perplexed, Margaret stared at the green paper in her hand. "Is this—a banknote?" Her face cleared, and she giggled. "Sir, they have given me *money!* They think we are in *trade*, the photo-graph trade!" She rubbed her lips together. "My word, papa would have apoplexy if he knew!"

"Do not let it concern you; things are different now." He took her arm and turned her toward the building. "Come, let's find a quiet spot and try again." He led her to a recess behind the fountain where they were not in plain view.

Margaret turned to him with glowing eyes. "Sir, this is the most diverting adventure of my life! If I may only explore this library, I will never plague you to take me here again." She looked starry-eyed at the building as if it were the Celestial City.

But the Jaguar waiting in Maine was calling St. John's name. And, while he enjoyed reading as much as the next man, he did not relish the thought of spending a day among books. He said, "We may have difficulty getting home since something is amiss with the tallit. What if it has gone awry? I suggest we try it at once. With any luck, we'll arrive in Maine, contact your sister, and while we wait for her to fly up, I'll take you to the Portland library. It will dazzle you, I assure you."

He took her by the elbow, but Margaret's face fell. Searching for some straw to cling to, she pouted, "You promised to show me an analytical engine." A woman walking past stared, but they ignored her. "I daresay there are none at Dove Cottage."

He offered his arm and walked them to the far side of the pavement where it was quieter and then withdrew his half of the tallit from a pocket. They had long ago discovered that, no matter how large the tallit was when in one piece and unfolded, the two halves had an amazing capacity to shrink when folded to fit in a pocket or reticule. It was one of its mysteries. "Clarissa has a portable analytical engine," he informed her.

Margaret's eyes widened. "She OWNS one? She owns one of those marvels?"

"As do most people of this day, only—I keep forgetting—they call them computers. Or er—laptops."

Margaret glanced down at her stomach region. *Lap*tops?

"Come, come, where's your half of the tallit?"

With pursed lips, Margaret produced the item from her reticule. "Oh, but wait," she said. "Do you suppose I could take photo-graph making back with us? Imagine society hearkening to *me* to get their likenesses made without having to sit for an artist! They will save time *and* expense."

He frowned. "No." St. John had studied the progress of inventions over time on one of his Maine visits. "The process cannot be easily transferred."

"Given time, I could study it," she replied in a subdued tone.

"We did not come to indulge ambition."

Pulling out his half of the tallit, he said, "Shall we? I warrant my wife will rejoice at our return—"

"Or my sister at our appearance in Maine," she said glumly.

She held up her half of the shawl, admiring the edging of embroidered lovebirds. The tallit was a special Israeli prayer shawl which, as Claire had discovered, had time-travelling capability. Not knowing its power, Clarissa had one day torn it in two in a fit of rage. But this led to the discovery that two people could travel together through time, each with one piece. Claire and St. John had done it many times. Claire had sewn up the ragged edges to make two neat halves, but her work wasn't nearly as lovely as the lovebird design bordering the rest of it.

Margaret gave a sigh to be leaving without a glimpse into the great library but raised the tallit near her bodice. "I'm ready, sir."

St. John held up his half. "Together, now. At the count of three."

Margaret moved closer to take his arm. This time she'd be ready for the loss of balance.

He counted, "One...two...three." Each pressed their half to their chest, but nothing happened. St. John blinked and shook his head. "Let's try that again." When again nothing happened, he said, "Perhaps if we wrap it about our shoulders and cross the ends."

They did as he suggested, but still there was no roaring sound in her ears, no dizzying motion, no temporary darkness as had happened earlier. She turned large eyes up to St. John. "What has gone wrong, sir? What shall we do?"

He shook his head, his lips compressed, then rubbed his chin. "Try it again, as tight as you can."

Margaret carefully drew her half of the shawl about her shoulders, pulling it tightly, watching as St. John did the same. He'd done it this way many times with Claire, Margaret knew, to visit this century. He enjoyed the occasional spin at top speed in the Jaguar, while Claire enjoyed visiting her home state and century. The tallit had always brought them through time—surely it must do so for her and St. John now.

Only it didn't. When the last attempt failed, the cold truth niggled at Margaret's brain.

They were stuck. They were stuck in New York in the 21st century.

Stand fast! Look brave! Then none will guess
The fear you feel but won't confess.
Thornton W. Burgess

Chapter 2

They were trapped in the future. Margaret's heart did a flip, a horrified flip. She was aghast at the thought of being separated forever from her home and life and world. But her heart flipped again, this time with dawning satisfaction. Although they were stuck, she felt sure the condition wouldn't be permanent. After all, Claire and Mr. St. John had travelled to the future and back at least a dozen times and had no difficulty returning. Surely whatever hindered them now would be resolved. But until then, she had time to explore. To find her invention!

Julian rubbed his chin. "Apparently the tallit won't allow us to leave. There must be some purpose in our being here." His brows furrowed. "But we aren't meant to stay—or our clothing would be contemporaneous. When Claire came to the past, she was dressed perfectly for our time, and your sister, when she arrived here, was dressed in keeping with this time."

Margaret nodded with growing excitement. The tallit was giving her the delay she needed to find a proper invention, some small thing that would make a big difference in her day. "Please, sir, as we cannot leave, may we explore the library?"

"I need to contact your sister. I just realized—she has apartments in New York! How pigeon-headed not to think of it sooner." He paused. "But how to reach her?" He normally contacted Clarissa once he'd arrived at the cottage through a landline she kept there, the telephone being a most convenient future innovation. But here he had no phone and would have to procure one.

Margaret pleaded, "*After* the library, if you please!"

He shook his head. "I have no inkling how long it shall take to find her. We'd best get started. And I believe she said something about leaving on an international book tour this month. Let us hope she has not gone already."

Margaret rolled her eyes. "Oh, let her go on her precious book tour! She has no use for me in any case, if you recall."

He frowned. "Had I not thought you *pining* to see your sister, I should never have been constrained to leave Claire with her lying-in so close." e stared at her. "Did you not say you *longed* to see her?"

Margaret swallowed. "I did, yes, but now I'm here—" she looked toward the library— "I only want to explore this place!"

His lips firmed. Margaret knew that look and her heart sank. St. John was a decisive man. When he'd decided upon a thing, it was done.

Surveying his young companion, St. John felt sorry for Miss Margaret. She'd been abused by Clarissa most of her life until Clarissa disappeared into the future; and now, home with only an ailing father, she spent her days playing nursemaid while he did little more than complain that he wanted her elder sister back. Claire had tried to take Margaret under her wing in society to raise her consequence, as had Lady Ashworth. They removed her spectacles (despite her objections) and dressed her in the latest modes, but the efforts of both served only to convince older women that Margaret was impertinent, and younger ones, a boring bluestocking. Most young ladies wishing to secure husbands for themselves behaved accordingly, speaking little or fawning, if necessary, while Margaret was known to have embarrassed young men by knowing more than they did—upon most any subject of conversation. The consensus was that Miss Margaret Andrews was not at all 'the thing.'

Well. If she cared not to see her sister, why should he press her? "Right then, we'll do a walk-through, but quickly," he said.

Margaret thanked him so effusively that it brought forth a mild frown on his handsome features. "Recall, I said *briefly*, if you please."

As they climbed the steps to the main entrance, Margaret surveyed the stately structure. "Aside from how tall buildings are now, architecture has not altered significantly, has it?"

"The classical style is still superior," he agreed, looking up at the marble building. A stream of pedestrians was exiting ahead, and many gave looks of curiosity and admiration as they passed. Margaret stared in surprise at the admirers, for she was not accustomed to such reactions. No one back home ever looked at her admiringly except for her pet pug, Homer.

"They appreciate our well-tailored clothing," she said to account for it.

"I would prefer they take no notice of us," he replied, "as we do not wish to be a spectacle." But Margaret stopped before the revolving entrance door in astonishment, which caused a backup of traffic. The doors went completely around before St. John pulled her in beside him and then swiftly out at the right time. Margaret giggled, her eyes brimming with mirth. "A door that moves in circles!" she exclaimed. "It seems a hazard, does it not?"

They were now in a grand entrance room, with the title "ASTOR HALL" engraved in the stone wall. "Candle lamps!" she declared in surprise, staring at two ornate, enormous marble standards, each with about a dozen long tapers burning in gilt or bronze-covered sconces. She'd been told about electricity and hadn't expected to see candle lamps.

Ponderous marble stairs lay at each side. "Shall we begin at the top?" Margaret asked. St. John surveyed the steps. "If you wish. Only recollect we cannot dawdle."

On the third floor, they entered a tasteful foyer with dark wood wainscoting and paintings. Moving them on, St. John led the way into a tremendous reading room. Margaret halted to admire the sheer enormity of the place with its ceiling of painted murals of sky and clouds.

"A very pleasing prospect," she said approvingly. "And only look at the books!" Like all bibliophiles, the sight of endless books filled her heart with excitement.

Reading tables spanned the length of the room in two long rows. Margaret noted that those on one side were interspersed with reading lamps, while the other side held odd, box-like things. She questioned St. John, who explained that these were the famous "analytical engines." She breathed in deeply, filled with joy at the prospect of experiencing the use of one.

She adjusted her spectacles to better see the titles on shelves as they slowly walked past. When they'd traversed the perimeter of the room, her thought was that she must find a way to return and linger in this place. And then something caught her eye—a studious-looking, bespectacled young man at one of the tables, wearing a topcoat and cravat. "Look!" she whispered. "He is properly dressed!"

St. John's brow rose. "In our fashions," he acceded, "but with ill taste."

"Nevertheless," she said, gazing curiously at the stranger, "I wonder at his reason for it."

At just that moment the young man raised his head, stretched his neck, and looked around the room. Blonde-haired with neat sideburns, he seemed a thin sort of person. When he saw St. John and Margaret, he nodded politely with very blue eyes—*very* blue, she noted—but with nary a hint of surprise at their costume. His nod was impertinent, Margaret knew, since they'd had no introduction, but she couldn't help the little smile that escaped her. She, too, was considered impertinent. St. John moved them on.

"Are you not curious?" she whispered. "Why he copies our fashions?"

"No." And that was all the response she got.

He offered his arm, which she soon realized was for the express purpose of hurrying them on. But she pointed up and said, "Look—a mezzanine." It was lined with more shelves and books. "May we go up, please?" He nodded.

From the mezzanine, she got a better look at the young man without his noticing. He wore a dark blue topcoat from which a light-coloured waistcoat peeked out below a prominent but poorly tied cravat. Whether he wore breeches or pantaloons, boots or shoes, could only be guessed. As they walked on, she watched to see if he would glance their way. He did, and, catching her eye, had the audacity to wink! She looked hurriedly away, secretly a little pleased but surprised at such impudence.

After the mezzanine, they went on to the ornate "Public Catalog Room." Then they passed reading rooms, offices, and even an art exhibition. From Margaret's quick perusal from the doorway—for that was all St. John would allow—the art looked appallingly bad, like something children would create.

A few minutes later they turned into a lonely passageway. There, ahead of them, with his back turned, was the blonde-haired man! She could now see he wore breeches and black shoes. He had well-shaped calves. He turned into a room with a sign jutting out overhead and shut the door behind him. Margaret took note of the sign: "The Pforzheimer Collection. Room 319." How she wished to explore it! She longed to know what it was and why that young man was interested in it. She also longed to know why he was dressed in gentleman's clothing of *their* day. As they walked past the room, she regretted that she'd never know the answers to her questions.

"We have traversed the third floor," St. John said. "Let us find the staircase."

"Perhaps..." She pointed back at room 319. "We might explore there before leaving this floor?"

He looked toward the room. "If I mistake me not, your interest is in a person that room contains, not its shelves."

"No, I assure you!" But her voice was weak, and a blush of mortification gave her away.

He took her by the elbow. "Another time, perhaps."

Margaret's face fell, but she obediently allowed him to lead her away. They rounded a bend. Looking ahead, St. John said, "It strikes me that the reason we couldn't leave was due to our being out in the open on the street. Here is a quiet landing on the stairway—no one in sight. Let us try again."

Margaret said glumly, "But I haven't really seen anything; we just browsed."

"You'll see wonders on the computer." Pulling out his half of the tallit, he said, "If Dove Cottage fails us and we return home, as I said, I'll escort you here another time, or Claire will."

"But I long to see the analytical—er, com-puter. And Clarissa has one, so we must go to the cottage."

He nodded. "Ideally, we shall. I warrant Clarissa will have the patience to let you explore on her device."

Margaret almost snorted. Patience was not something Clarissa was known for. She drew her half-tallit from her reticule. Sighing, she raised it to her bodice. "I'm ready, sir."

"At the count of three. One…two…three." Both pressed their half to their hearts, but just as before, nothing happened. They tried it about their shoulders, but this too, was equally without success. St. John's lips were compressed, his brows furrowed. His dark good looks never failed to impress Margaret, who found him quite the most handsome man of her acquaintance, but she could tell he was troubled.

"The tallit seems to be exerting its will over ours. Lady Ashworth maintains it has a 'divine directive,' if you recall."

Miss Margaret recalled. Great Aunt Ashworth, who was Lady Ashworth, had come from the future with the tallit long before Claire had, before Margaret was even born. She was Mrs. Grandison, then. But once she fell in love with the marquess in the past and married, the shawl vanished. Much later, Claire, her granddaughter, found the shawl right back in Dove Cottage, which is how she ended up using it and fell in love with St. John.

At first Claire hadn't been certain about staying in the past and Lady Ashworth tried to prevent her from leaving by *burning* the tallit. But mysteriously, the shawl returned to Claire of its own accord with no ill effect from the fire. It was indeed as if it had a mind of its own. With a fresh ripple of excitement, Margaret hoped it was following that divine directive now for *her* sake, by not letting them leave New York. She was meant to find an invention, she just knew it!

St. John said, as if confirming her thought, "It has us here for some purpose, but I haven't a clue what that is. Or how we shall discover it."

Margaret swallowed a guilty smile. She thought she knew, but time would tell. No sense informing St. John he might be stuck in the future on her account!

Chapter 3

"Come along," St. John said curtly.

To Margaret's delight, he did not head down the staircase. "I'll show you how to use a computer right now, as I need to find out where your sister lives here in New York."

"But isn't she at the cottage?"

"Probably not. She wasn't expecting us. She uses a private plane from New Jersey—not too far from here—on the rare occasions when she's met us at the cottage. But with a book tour coming up, I doubt not but she's here in the city. The question is, where exactly?"

"And a com-puter can tell us where?" she asked, wide-eyed.

"I don't know. But let's find out."

Back in the reading room, they were extremely disappointed to find that every single computer was in use.

"I do not wonder at it," murmured Margaret. "If I could, I would plant myself before one for as long as possible."

"Not all of them were in use earlier," St. John observed. "Perhaps if we return later, we can try again."

"May I see Room 319 in the meantime?" Margaret asked.

Minutes later, with her heart beating strangely, they opened the door and entered a rather small room, circled entirely with books, shelves and more shelves. There was a cozy sofa, side table with a lamp and a sofa table, but to her disappointment, the young man was nowhere to be seen. The room was empty save for its books and furniture.

Curious about the "Pforzheimer Collection" in any case, Margaret perused the shelves. To her astonishment, the books were uniformly comprised of critical works about female writers of the 18th and 19th centuries.

"My word!" she exclaimed, her dark eyes large and round. "These books are concerned with *women!* Women writers!"

St. John, examining a shelf across the room, nodded. "As you say. This century is not nearly as misogynous as ours."

"How encouraging!" she said, holding a book up to her heart. "Imagine, a whole room dedicated entirely to literary females! I begin to think I was born in the wrong era. Perhaps there is a place in this time for me as there was for my sister."

St. John looked up from his book. "I do not recall you having an interest in writing."

"Clarissa never did until she switched places with Claire. Perhaps I can develop it as she has."

He shut the book in his hands. "Perhaps we should find lodging. I recollect, from an occasion with my wife, that a good inn will have a computer room for its patrons."

"Indeed!" cried Margaret, struck with wonder, and instantly amenable to the idea of securing rooms. It meant St. John was resigned to staying and that she had time yet for her purpose of discovering an invention. If he had not accepted their being stuck, he might have insisted upon trying, again and again, to get home. And what if one attempt should work? No, Margaret was not prepared to return. She prayed that Claire's baby would stay put, however, so that St. John wouldn't miss the occasion of the birth.

He led her down the marble stairs and from the stately building without her voicing a single complaint. She would have time to return, she was sure. The thought that they might be trapped in the future *forever* gave her pause, for, if that happened, what would Papa do without her? And did she really *wish* to live in this century when people had no taste and life was noisy and busy? What appeared as a great opportunity and adventure could become instead a tragedy. Especially for Mr. St. John! He would miss the birth of his child!

With that thought, she realized they *must* return, for he was a family man now. And she wasn't prepared to leave her life for good—she wasn't like her elder sister who had not looked back, it seemed, after discovering she could do well for herself in this century. No, despite her lack of success socially, Margaret enjoyed life, even the dinners and balls where she was largely only a spectator. She could predict who had set her cap at whom before an evening ended, and she relished her acumen for presaging the outcome of these romantic aspirations, whether the lady would end up a bride or in a "decline," a slough of despond. Nine times out of ten, she deduced correctly.

At the edge of the steps, St. John stood deliberating with narrowed eyes at the flood of pedestrians. Margaret stared too, but the novelty of the strange fashions was fading and the press of foot traffic no longer amusing. The thought of being stuck in this world perpetually was eroding her sense of adventure, stripping the scene of its diversion. Moreover, she found herself huddling against St. John as people brushed past, rudely not bothering to steer clear. She was relieved when he tucked her arm securely within his, patting her hand reassuringly. "Come," he said and then, moving forward quickly, they joined the river of humanity.

They passed a young man with short white, spiked hair. "Did you see that?" she hissed, looking back at him. "The whitest hair I have ever seen on a young person! And it stood straight on his head like pikes. What could be his malady, do you think?"

"Call it the ailment of modernism," St. John said sagely, not greatly surprised due to his past experience with the century.

Margaret spied an oncoming lady who sported more skin than clothing. "Do not look, sir!" she cried, jumping to put herself in his path to block the view. He halted and let out a breath of laughter. The crowd split smoothly around them like a coach taking a fork in the road, never stopping.

"You must know," he said into her ear as if he were about to impart some deep secret. "Besides lacking taste, fashion in this day has no shame. Fear you not; I am accustomed to it."

They went on to the corner of Fifth Avenue and East 41st Street. "What are those lights?" she asked.

"Red means stop; green means go."

"But there—that—that's a hand!"

A man beside her gave her a look of incredulity. His eyes wandered to St. John's face but, encountering an icy glare, he hurriedly looked away. The hand turned green, and the river of people surged forward, pushing them along.

"A trick of electric lights," he explained.

They walked a few more streets and, while Margaret could not feel completely secure at crossings, she learned that safety was in following the crowd and clinging to Mr. St. John's arm. Meanwhile, she was able to gawp to her heart's content up at the tall buildings, and ahead at the dense bustling sea of humanity hemmed in at the pavement by an astonishing array of horseless carriages in such vivid colors! She craned her neck here and there for better glimpses of unknown wonders or paused to peer into shop windows filled with odd, modern clothing or baubles. Slowly, her sense of adventure returned due to the sheer novelty and mystery of it all.

Fantastically huge, many-wheeled coaches in the street suddenly blocked her view; then, to avoid walking beneath scaffolding built over the pavement (that neither could feel secure beneath though others walked under the metal menace unscathed) they found themselves crossing the avenue north to south. They had to cross back when more monstrous scaffolds appeared. When they had soldiered on in this fashion through the bewildering landscape for at least a mile (Margaret was sure) they stopped to admire a huge cathedral. Reading a sign, St. John said, "Saint Patrick's."

"Anglican, no doubt?" asked Margaret.

"Doubtful," he replied, having learned better.

People were coming and going through its triple doors, and Margaret could not resist peeking inside. At the entrance, while a steady line of people came and went, she paused, utterly awestruck. "How noble!" she whispered.

St. John too, was stretching his neck to take it all in, but he said, "Come, we'd best not dally."

"One moment, please!" Margaret surprised him by dashing into a pew, sitting down, and bending her head. Seeing her in a pose that could only mean prayer, he sat beside her.

After a minute she raised her head. "It cannot be wrong to pray for guidance concerning the tallit. It seems we are in a predicament."

He nodded. She did not mention that she'd asked for enough time to accomplish whatever purpose she was meant to. They joined the foot traffic once again. Moving on, ahead they saw an establishment with three flags waving above its windows.

"Look!" Margaret cried. "Our flag! Here, in New York!" But her face dropped in the next instant. "Only conceive of it—putting our flag right beside the French! Whatever possessed them?" Cartier's was a lovely Georgian edifice, but because of the French flag, Margaret walked by stiffly.

Her eyes remained large and round as they continued in their search for lodging, but the pother and clamor of the streets, the endless flurry about her, made her feel quite small and eager for quiet. They passed tall street stalls with pictures of food pasted all over them, making her stomach grumble. They had traversed at least ten city blocks when St. John said, "This is absurd. Why have we not noticed a single inn?"

He motioned to a pedestrian. "Excuse me," he said politely. "Can you direct us to a traveler's inn or hotel?"

The man looked St. John up and down. "Nice costume." And walked on.

St. John asked a passing woman, who looked around. "Where are we? Oh, 29th Street. If you go a block that way and turn right," (she pointed back the way they'd come) "you'll find the Carlton. On Madison Avenue," she added.

Margaret's brow rose considerably. St. John thanked her, and they turned back. But she called from behind them, "I think it's called the James, now!"

Margaret exclaimed, "The James. But did you hear? It was the Carlton! Was it a new Carlton House? Did the Americans copy the prince's palace?"

St. John chuckled, but assured her, "No such thing, or Claire would have told me. I warrant it's an inn, not a palace."

When they arrived about fifteen minutes later, he said, surveying the entrance, "The building is not without character, I grant." But when they entered, he surveyed the spacious area disapprovingly. "This is nothing next to the Regent's house. I fear it was but a shabby use of the name."

"I've not been to Carlton House," said Margaret, "nor do I expect to have that pleasure, though I have seen newspaper illustrations."

He paused to fish out a small, flat, squarish-looking object from his waistcoat pocket. "Claire and I use this wherever we go. It belongs to your sister, but she allows us the use of it. When a signature is required, you'll have to sign her name." With a rare grin he added, "I'm afraid I do not look like a Clarissa."

"Thank God for that!" she said. Then, looking at it with perplexity asked, "What is it?" She took it from him and turned it in her hands.

"A card of credit."

She looked up at him, blinking. "What is it credited with?"

"Money."

Her brows rose. "How much money?"

"As much as we need."

Margaret smiled. "How propitious."

"I'll explain how it works later if you like," he said. "For now, just know that Clarissa pays the bill. She's richer in this time than I am in ours."

"Richer than *you*?" she asked, astonished. "My sister? A woman? My word! No wonder she never came back."

They entered the lobby—Margaret enjoyed the revolving door this time—and he led them toward the front desk.

"What do I do with it?" she asked under her breath. "How do I make it give us money?"

His eyes sparkled. "We do nothing but hand it over."

At the counter, St. John asked for two neighboring rooms.

Surveying them, the man smiled. "You're here for the JASNA Conference."

"Pardon me?" said St. John.

"You're Janeites, right?"

St. John scowled. "I assure you, we are no such thing. We are proper Christians."

The clerk's expression changed to one of alarm. "No, sir, I meant—for the conference. You are part of the Jane Austen of North America Conference, right? I've been checking-in members of your group all day. You're not the first to come in costume. What is the name, please?" He swallowed and kept his eyes on the analytical engine in front of him.

Margaret had stopped at several inns and posting houses in her time but found this exchange baffling. After a moment, the man, still looking at the computer box in front of him, and pressing little flat buttons with letters on them, frowned. "I can't find that name, Clarissa Channing. Is that the name you registered with?"

"Registered?" asked St. John.

"For the conference," he said. "With JASNA?" For the first time, he looked uncertain.

"I cannot say," said St. John.

The man nodded and looked very intently at his box. "I'm afraid your name isn't here. All I have are two Empire State view suites with king beds. I can't give you the JASNA price on them."

"No matter," said St. John. "We'll take them."

"Oh." He seemed pleasantly surprised. He reached out his hand. "Will that be credit or debit?"

"Credit," said St. John, who nudged her. "The card, if you please."

Margaret's mind was spinning as she wondered what an empire state view was, and what did he mean by 'king' beds? Richness, she supposed. But she hurriedly produced the card and watched in silent fascination as the clerk took it and did something with it, then gave it back to her. Shortly he handed her two cards in paper sleeves. "Thank you for staying with us. Enjoy the conference!" He paused and then offered with a little grin, "To be honest, I've never read Jane Austen, I'm sorry to say."

St. John looked at him impassively for a moment. "Well, hadn't you ought to catch up?"

"Yes, yes, I'll do that!" he seemed embarrassed. "Which book should I start with?"

The time travelers hesitated and looked at each other. "The first one, of course," said St. John. As they walked off, he hissed, "Who in the blazes is Jane Austen?"

Chapter 4

Margaret had no clue who Jane Austen was but stopped short, pressing Mr. St. John's arm. "My word!" With a raised brow, she pointed at a sign but could not bring herself to read it aloud for it said, "Sex, Money and Power in Jane Austen's Fiction.'" Wide-eyed she turned to him. "Lud! I never heard of her, but I daresay I must look up her books while we're here!"

"I think not," he said with an amused but tolerant look her way. "Your papa would have my head were I to allow it," he said, basing his opinion solely on the headline beginning with "Sex."

She stopped him again as they passed a table with books for sale. "Wait! I've read that book, *Emma*! I adored it. Jane Austen wrote it?" She saw *Northanger Abbey* and *Persuasion*. "I've read these too," she exclaimed, only this year! I don't recall Miss Austen's name, but what a lark! To think, there is a conference in her honor!"

As he moved them on, she added thoughtfully, "I do not recall there being anything of, *you know*, in them. They were quite delightful."

St. John stopped before two wide doors with no handles. A few other people were standing around as if waiting for something. "Why are we standing here?" she asked, lowering her voice.

"You'll see," St. John said, but he couldn't suppress a short grin. "Think of it as a moving staircase—without the stairs."

She stared at him in perplexity. "Why would a staircase move? Where would it go?"

A man nearby cleared his throat and kept his eyes carefully turned away. Two others looked at each other and then back at Margaret. She realized she must sound befuddled to them. A whirring sound was heard behind the door, and then it opened—by itself! Three people stepped out and St. John led her in while the others boarded. She looked around in amazement thinking, *we are in a closed box*. She watched while various numbered buttons were pressed, and then she gasped and flew against St. John's side when the box moved, much to the amusement of the others. One smiled and said, "Real acting! You're part of the JASNA group, aren't you?"

Her remark was directed at Miss Margaret. "I believe we are," she answered uncertainly. The woman laughed. "Oh, that's great! I didn't expect you'd be in character. Such wit. That's cool, really cool."

Margaret shot a glance at St. John, but the woman hadn't done. Surveying Margaret from head to toe, she said, "Your costume is *wonderful*. Where did you have it made?"

Margaret hesitated, torn between pleasure at being admired and astonishment at such impudence. Asking a perfect stranger where she'd got her gown seemed somehow improper. She looked down at her gown to remember its origins and then said almost reproachfully, "I bespoke it at Clark and Debenham's, Cavendish Square. The fabric, however, came from Pall Mall."

The lady gazed at her admiringly. "You're from England. That explains it. Your seamstresses are well versed at making good English costumes, I expect."

"Our *modistes*, are," Margaret corrected her punctiliously. A seamstress was the modiste's assistant who did much of the hand-stitching but had nothing to do with the design of a gown. Hadn't every woman ought to know that?

By the time they reached the 15th floor, the others had exited. "*Such wit*, that woman said, though I believe I said nothing worthy of that description," Margaret mused.

He made a small grimace. "In addition to having neither taste nor shame, today's population has precious little wit. I don't wonder she thought your remark notable."

Compared to the usual inns and posting houses of her day, Margaret had never seen anything so commodious as her rooms. "My word! All this space to myself?" she exclaimed, as she walked throughout the rooms. In the bathroom, she stopped and stared. She wanted to say, "*This* is the necessary room?" but good breeding prevented her. She peered at the sink, the shower, then walked to the closed seat and opened it.

St. John saw her and walked in, saying, "Excuse me, but this will help you." He demonstrated a flush. Margaret was not overly missish, but she turned and went back to the main room without a word, her cheeks reddened. Suddenly, she noticed the window and, gasping, made a beeline toward it. But she stopped about a foot away and steadied herself. The view made her dizzy!

St. John came over and looked out at the city with her.

"My word!" she said, wide-eyed. "This is New York City? I knew from the street that it was vast but I never dreamed of this!" Again, she had to steady herself as she gazed at the sparkling, towering buildings, a forest of gleaming steel and stone giants. She'd never before been so high upon the earth except for a brief holiday in the Lake District when she was only eleven.

They stood looking out as though the buildings were thick outcroppings of stalagmites that had erupted from some magical cave, glittering in the late sun like crystals. "It's actually quite beautiful," murmured Margaret, still staring wonderingly.

St. John turned to her. "It is impressive. But now that we are truly safe from prying eyes, I suggest we give the tallit one more try." He moved away from the window.

"Please let me explore these fascinating rooms first!" she cried.

He motioned with a hand for her to look around, but she watched as he found a small black box with drinks and other things and took out a bottle of water.

"Is that cold?" she asked.

St. John handed her one.

"*Cold* water! Claire talked about this once." Smiling, she tried to remove the cap but had to watch carefully as he took her bottle and unscrewed the top before removing it. She took a long swig and then, staring at the bottle, exclaimed, "I adore the cold box!"

"They call it a refrigerator."

"Refrig—horrid word. But how immensely convenient that would be for cook!"

"Come, come," he said, holding up his half of the shawl. Margaret frowned. She kept the water in one hand but obediently held up her half and pressed it against her bodice.

After a few seconds, he frowned. "Well, we haven't tried exchanging pieces." They did the exchange and again held the halves in place over their hearts.

When nothing happened, Margaret only sniffed as if to say, "Well, that's that."

St. John said, "You are not vastly concerned, I see."

Margaret shook her head. "No." But her face scrunched into thought. "Unless we are trapped here *forever,* I must think I am meant to have an adventure. Something the likes of which would be impossible had I not come."

St. John was relieved at Margaret's attitude for her sake, but where she lacked concern, he had plenty to grip his heart. He'd only found Claire three years ago and their marriage was still in its infancy. The thought of not being present for the birth of his first child he could bear, though it would disappoint Claire. But not going back at all? It was not to be thought of!

He moved again to the window and turned thoughtful eyes upon the city. "There is no need to lose heart," he said, though Margaret was in no danger of that at present. "Happily, Clarissa is here, and we will have her assistance." He turned to face her. "When we manage to find her."

Margaret said, "I will be happy to see my sister after so long, but if Great Aunt Ashworth is correct about the tallit exerting a divine directive, I daresay it does not depend upon having her help."

St. John shook his head. "Nevertheless, we will find her. God forbid that we are trapped."

She considered the matter, removing her spectacles to examine them for smudges. "I own, I do feel dread at the thought. Papa will suffer horridly if I do not return." She looked up at him with her large, dark eyes. "But I have scarcely any other claims on my life, sir, aside from you and Claire, and Great Aunt Ashworth." She put the glasses back on and with a glance toward the window said, "I could abide exploring this city and seeing more of the world as it is now. Women have greater opportunities in this century! As you know, I am called a bluestocking at home, a wallflower, and utterly ignored. Soon I will be considered a spinster, an *ape leader!* In short, I have no prospects at home that cannot be equaled here or possibly *exceeded.*"

"No prospects? A spinster? What are you thinking? You are hardly out of the schoolroom. I assure you, your prospects will increase. I have seen you change already from what you were a year ago. You are sure to be married and a happy mother of children sooner than you think." He gazed at her fondly. "*And* become a well-respected member of society."

Margaret, as she listened, looked first doubtful, then wistful. Softly, she asked, "You have seen a change in me?"

St. John spoke gently. "Without your spectacles, you put me in mind of your sister, a noted beauty who is almost as lovely as my Claire."

Margaret looked struck.

He continued, "Beauty runs in your family with more certainty than fortune."

"Beauty!" she looked away. That was coming it too strong. Now she knew that Mr. St. John was only being kind. She had long ago reconciled herself to possessing nothing of Clarissa's charms. If she'd changed in the past year, it was only her hair, which had slowly darkened from plain brown to almost black—much like Clarissa's. And her cheeks, perhaps, were smoother than before, the bust of her gowns, fuller. But still, she was plain old gangly Margaret and had nothing of the feminine mannerisms, the grace of deportment, that made men look admiringly when Clarissa entered a room.

"You are but eighteen," St. John continued. His lips firmed. "You have no conception as to your prospects yet; do not give up prematurely."

She smiled sadly. "You are kind, no doubt——."

"I am *right,*" he said severely. "And as for being trapped here indefinitely—I think not. We must accept, however, that the tallit—by divine providence, if you like—has a reason for keeping us here." His expression darkened. "We have only to discover what that is. But I am loath to stay, and we must fathom it out soon."

"The birth of your child."

"Indeed. I must be home for it. I gave Claire my word that I would stay with her." He folded his half of the tallit and tucked it neatly into an inner waistcoat pocket.

"That was generous of you, sir. I daresay most men wouldn't dream of being present, and Mr. Wickford, so Lady Ashworth says, finds it incomprehensible that you plan on it."

He turned, stroking his chin in thought. "I did not say I relish the thought. But Claire assures me that men of this day are 'involved' with their children's births."

Margaret smiled wanly. "A splendid idea, that. They ought to know what women suffer!"

He looked thoughtful but said, heading to the door, "I am off to find a computer. I must needs find your sister and think on our situation."

"Wait!" she cried, with more feeling than she'd meant to express. "Allow me to accompany you. You must teach me how to use this analytical engine." She ran to retrieve her bonnet and reticule. "I am sure to learn a great deal about this modern world and its fascinating gadgets." With rising hope, she realized that this very day might be the time when she would find her invention! Something she could study quickly and take back with her. Upon their return, she'd make her fortune and way in the world. (And really, she supposed they *would* get back. Or why had they not appeared in contemporary styles as Clarissa had when she came to the future? Claire had explained it all to her. How the tallit outfitted one for the time they were meant to live in. Just as Clarissa wore modern clothing when she came to the future, Claire had likewise appeared in perfectly modish gowns when she visited the nineteenth century.)

She went to the refriger-thing, the cold box, to keep the water cold until her return. Peering in, she stated, "There is more than water here, but nothing like a proper meal."

"Indeed. We have not procured one, yet."

She looked over at him curiously, suddenly noting the emptiness of her stomach. "Speaking of which, how is the food in this century?"

Minutes later the two Regencians were among the stream of pedestrians on the pavement, having agreed to find a place to eat.

"You are receiving a great deal of admiration, sir," Margaret said, endeavouring not to laugh. She had always found it enjoyable, how women admired him, for she cared for St. John. Claire's appearance at the ball that fateful night in 1816 had delighted Margaret, for Claire had quickly arrested the attention of Mr. St. John. She was the first lady who seemed capable of winning his heart, and since Clarissa, her unkind elder sister, wished to win that heart, Margaret rejoiced that someone might cut her to the chase. Clarissa did not deserve such a man.

He said, with a little smile, "I perceive that you are an object of interest as well; and if I mistake me not, the looks coming your way are also admiring."

She grimaced. "They admire my gown, no doubt, because, as you say, they have no taste. This is but a common walking dress, nothing out of the way at all."

"There's nothing common about it here," he returned. "But you seem to enjoy the illusion of being unattractive."

Margaret swallowed, not daring to look up at her companion. "That is because I am," she said in a low voice. St. John, whether because of the noise on the street or how low her tone, did not hear her. But the memory of Clarissa's words from years past rang in Margaret's mind.

There were many occasions when Clarissa had reminded Margaret of her unsuitability for marriage, but one stood out. Margaret had borrowed a tortoiseshell hairpiece with two pearls from her sister without her consent, to wear that evening at a dinner party. She'd hardly ever been allowed to attend dinner parties but on this occasion Papa had said she could. Wanting to look her best, Margaret borrowed the small bauble. But when Clarissa saw her wearing it, she'd sneered that no adornment could hide Margaret's plainness or her lack of feminine charm, that the schoolroom was her proper sphere, not the ballroom. "I can scarcely conceive of your being my sister at all," she'd continued, "as you bear no resemblance to me."

Moreover, Clarissa had emblazoned on her brain that she was gauche, skinny, and dull. "Little wonder," she'd once said, "the patronesses bade you wait to enter Almack's; they would as soon admit you as a housemaid."

Margaret found her refuge in books and studying. But seeing her often in the library, Clarissa frowned at her one day. "How long will you prefer reading above all? Books," she said, "are your only companions. No man wants a bluestocking for a wife." Thus, Margaret knew that future spinsterhood was inevitable for her. It was a stroke of bitter irony that now Clarissa was making a success of herself as an author! She who had used to despise much reading.

They stopped to peer in an eatery window. In the street, car horns beeped, and near their feet on the pavement, three grey pigeons pecked at small crumbs on the sidewalk. The hum of activity was already becoming customary. Putting her face closer to the window, Margaret said, "I believe this is an Inn, sir, and provides suppers." But St. John pointed across the wide, busy street. In a few minutes they crossed and entered Brava Pizza.

"What is pee-za?" she asked.

"Pizza," St. John corrected her, "is a simple dish, rather like a hot cheese sandwich with no top." To her doubtful look, he added, "You'll like it."

As they strode to a booth, curious looks came their way from other patrons. Margaret confided, "They are not accustomed to patronage by the upper class."

A waiter approached, set down curious utensils and two bills of fare. Margaret examined her fork, frowning when it bent. "Upon my word! Do they not use real cutlery today?"

"You'll grow accustomed to it," St. John said. He explained that plastic was the sad modern substitute for better things, including cutlery. Margaret studied her fork again, wondering if it might serve as the invention she needed. But an image of Lady Ashworth, struggling to pierce a side of roast quail with the flimsy utensil flashed across her mind. No, what sane person would choose it over good silver, if given a choice?

When the waiter returned, St. John ordered for them both. Margaret was grateful to find that service was speedy for she hadn't realized how hungry she was. But she stared at the enormous round pie of melted cheese when it arrived with some puzzlement.

"This," said St. John, "is quite good. And it can be eaten with the hands."

"With the hands?" Margaret's eyes widened, but she smiled mischievously. It was perfectly improper, she was sure, but she never minded being improper in harmless ways. She detested the stifling proprieties of polite society such as one that forbade you to eat any dish upon a table save what was to your right or left—unless a servant brought round the others. Elsewise, you could admire them at the far end of the table but not touch them.

She picked up a "slice" as St. John called it, folding it in her hands exactly as he was, and took a bite. St. John watched her expectantly.

After fighting with a mouthful of stretchy cheese, when she could speak, she said, "Rather good. I think I could grow accustomed to it." She swallowed and smiled.

On the way back, they passed a dress shop where plastic models in the window wearing floral dresses smiled vacantly out at nothing. Margaret halted before one. "Why is this painted statue smiling? Do they take its photo-graph?"

"They're not statues but another kind of plastic," St. John said. But he turned to her. "Should you like a modern gown? We don't know how long we may be constrained to stay in this century."

Margaret looked doubtfully at the specimens in the window. "I cannot imagine feeling properly clothed in any of these."

St. John peered up at the store's name, *The Well-Dressed Woman.* "Come," he said. As they entered it, he added beneath his breath, "Keep in mind that whatever we buy may vanish by morning if you're not meant to stay."

Margaret knew what he referred to. Claire had spent a small fortune on modern clothing for St. John from Brooks Brothers only to have it vanish once he used the tallit. He'd been wearing the new clothing until he returned home to 1816, whereupon he found himself in his usual gentleman's attire. When he returned to the future only minutes later, the new clothes did not return with him. He was in his 19th-century garments. Claire still wondered where in the universe the tallit had seen fit to send $2,000 of Brooks Brothers "duds."

"Did you not say Clarissa will pay for it?" Margaret asked. "I can bear the risk of it vanishing in that case," she said, her eyes glittering with amusement. "I daresay she owes me this; only think of all the abuse I have suffered at her hands!"

Margaret was giggling with amusement and still wearing her Regency clothing when she left the store with a large shopping bag in her hands. "The clerk who helped me seemed dazzled by my short stays," she said, much amused. "And she called my chemise a slip." With a little frown she added, "Besides speaking to me as familiarly as my equal."

St. John only smiled wanly. His shock at modern styles and the lack of class consciousness had faded, but he could certainly understand her sentiments.

"And to think, I had to sign Clarissa's signature—a *woman's*—and not yours, to use that card of credit. In that respect, I like this century."

They stopped at a store called City Outfitters (on the recommendation of the clerk) to buy St. John modern attire. After browsing a few racks, St. John asked a store clerk, "Have you no clothing suitable for a gentleman?"

The man blinked and then waved his hand. "This whole section is for men."

St. John said, "For the working class, it appears. Where is your section for gentlemen?"

An hour later, they boarded the elevator at the hotel. Margaret had only to keep a hand lightly upon St. John's arm now for the trip up. St. John seemed deep in thought. When they reached their rooms, he told her that if she wished to change into her new clothing before they located an analytical engine, er, a computer, she might do so now, while he retired to his room and did likewise.

About twenty minutes later he returned. Margaret did a delighted once-over of his new look. "My word, sir! You make even this fashion look modish." He had managed to find a pair of black stretch chinos, a paisley patterned short sleeve shirt, ankle socks and a pair of Perry Layton black tassel loafers—all for less than $375. Having only one previous experience shopping for men's clothing in the 21st century at Brooks Brothers, he'd whispered to Margaret as they left, "Little wonder the clothing is vulgar. The prices here are evidently meant for lower class pockets."

But at her praise, he grinned and bowed. "You do no disservice to today's mode, either," he said. She'd chosen the most modest gown she could find, a short-sleeved summer frock that reached her ankles.

"Happy you did not choose pantaloons like the majority of women today."

Margaret bristled at the thought. The idea of showing her legs was entirely odious, pantaloons or not.

"And now, to business," he said. "Besides finding your sister, Lady Ashworth spoke of purchasing the tallit from Israel. Let us see if we can bespeak new ones from there with the help of a computer."

"You can bespeak something from Israel—using an analytical engine in New York?" She shook her head, smiling at the wonder of it.

He nodded. "You will adore this device. You can read books on it."

Her brows went up. "How is that possible?"

"They hold compressed libraries."

Margaret was breathless with anticipation. On the ground floor, they learned that the hotel did not have a public access device.

"Do you know where we may find one?" St. John asked politely.

"If you look on your phone," the clerk said, "you should be able to find an internet café within walking distance."

St. John didn't blink. "Be a good man and look it up for us, won't you?"

The man hesitated. "One moment, please."

While they waited, Margaret whispered, "Sir! We can go to the library. There were many there if you recall!" Although she was wild to know what these analyzing engines were like, it seemed a blessing to her that the hotel had none. For now they must return to the library, and she could explore room 319, where secretly she hoped to see that young man again.

"There's one on East 20th Street," the clerk said, watching the black box in front of him which Margaret deduced was an actual analytical engine. "That's probably the closest." He continued reading and added, "Wait. There's a coffee shop right here on Park and Madison that may have public computers. And another on Park Avenue South."

"A coffee shop," Margaret repeated. "Hardly a proper sphere for a woman," she added regretfully.

The clerk stared at her in surprise. St. John said, turning aside to her, said, "Coffee shops are no longer the domain of gentlemen. They are leopards of a different stripe here, I assure you."

The clerk cleared his throat. "Actually, I'm afraid coffee shops will only have a lounge like we do where you can use a laptop, but I don't think they provide one. Your best bet is the internet café on East 20th—or the library.

At the word 'library' Margaret smiled. "Precisely," she said.

But being confident you are right is not the same as being right.
Steven D. Levitt

Chapter 5

The café was not far, and to both their relief, accepted the card of credit. He pulled up a chair for Margaret and soon logged on like an expert using the provided password. After watching and studying his every action, Margaret went to an adjacent cubicle and logged on for her own "explore." Her heart hammered with excitement at everything she saw, and soon she had clicked upon dozens of links, reading voraciously.

St. John did a search for "Israeli tallits." Many links led to stores that sold the shawls right there in the city, but these he deemed suspect, doubting a New York shop would carry a time-travelling hand-made shawl. He entered "tallits from Israel," and came up with the same list. When he put in "Israel—makers of tallits," finally links came up for locations in that country. He searched through as many images of their wares as he could find, but nothing similar to the lovebird design could be found. And all the shawls were from manufacturers; had not Lady Ashworth told him she had purchased her shawl directly from a woman who made them by hand? Even if she sold her wares to these manufacturers, how would he know which one might have special, time-travelling quality? And what if there were no other tallits with the power of slipping through time? If only he could speak to Lady Ashworth.

The two were lost in following link after link for hours, until the surrounding cubicles were abandoned, and they were told it was closing time. St. John had not ordered a tallit. As he explained to Margaret, how could he know which to choose?

They were hungry again and decided to eat before returning to the hotel. But as they left the establishment, she was dazzled by the brightness of lights all around! Street lights, shop lights, windows lit behind curtains, traffic lights. She could see other people so well, even at this late hour! And how many were about! Foot traffic and street carriages, as if it were day Lighting had certainly improved! Claire had not told her about all the improvements of the modern age as she felt it would only feed Margaret's appetite to come to the future—but she'd mentioned electric lights. It was just as she said.

After choosing a restaurant, they were led past seated patrons to a small table at the end of an aisle. Women glanced at St. John and then looked again, admiration freezing on their countenances. Margaret stifled a smile and felt pride when he drew out a chair for her before taking his seat. Claire was a blessed woman, no doubt about it. Though, not, perhaps, at the moment. She could be in childbed any day, even right then if the doctor had been wrong about the timing! Margaret had to remind herself that, in a way, Claire's labor was long past. All of them—their whole 19th century lives, by normal standards of time, were over! She must not think about that. She was here in the present, and Claire was there in the past—would be there, when they figured out how to return to her—and that was also "the present"—just a different one.

St. John cleared his throat while nodding toward her menu.

"'Tis a paltry menu," she said, seeing that the meat entrees were only beef and chicken. Why, at home, she thought, they might have goose, capon, partridge, pheasant, duck, pigeon, plovers and turkey. Shrimp and lobster were listed as seafood, but she gave an inward snort (outward snorts were prohibited to ladies) for seafood at home might be oysters, mussels, jellied eels, crab, salmon, herring and sturgeon. "They keep a very middling table," she added.

St. John nodded. "Nevertheless, you must choose."

Despite the lack of variety, the names of dishes made her curious and she ordered three appetizers, understanding them as a first course, four entrees, (much to the surprise of the waiter), four sides, and "vanilla coke" (purely out of curiosity) as well as "peach infused tea." St. John did not, alas, allow her a glass of wine, though she reminded him she had downed spirited negus upon two occasions, once at a ball and once at a Christmas festivity, and neither had caused inebriation.

After the waiter had taken her order, he turned to St. John, who said "That will suffice, thank you." The waiter nodded and was off.

Margaret grinned. "Have I ordered for both of us?"

"You've ordered for a small army," he said, smiling. "I should tell you that supper here, particularly when eating out, is not what you are accustomed to at home. People generally choose one appetizer, if any, and *one* entrée, and they eat it entirely."

Margaret gaped at him. "They eat the *whole* thing? How vulgar!"

He stifled a chuckle. "Which is why they only choose one. Your four entrees will be served together, not in courses. In this day, unless you find a restaurant serving 'buffet style,' you can't pick and choose from an assortment like you do at home, where servants take care of what's left for your cold lunch on the morrow. What's more, it's too costly to eat in that fashion here."

Margaret stared, digesting this. "So much for progress," she said dryly, but her eyes brightened when the drinks were served. Both were "excessively sweet," she said at first, but by the time they had eaten and were ready to leave, her glasses were empty.

She'd eaten only a little of each entrée, for supper at home always had at least three courses, often more, and one must never fill up too soon. But she was glad, when it came to it, that Mr. St. John had helped consume the repast. With a smile, she accepted the waiter's astonishing offer to package what was not eaten, for St. John reminded her of the amazing cold box at the hotel. And then she ordered dessert. After all, Clarissa, never a generous sister, was footing the bill.

When they were back at the hotel, they saw a sign in the lobby with a large arrow that said "JASNA: Music," with a singer's name, and "Soprano."

"I adore a concert," Margaret said.

They followed the sign and for the next ninety minutes greatly enjoyed music of their own day. The singer interspersed the songs with information about Jane Austen, such as whether she likely knew the tune, or played it herself on the pianoforte, and so on. Margaret saw a few people dressed in styles of her day and looked eagerly to see if the man from the library was there, but saw him not.

They ducked out of the room quickly at the end and took the elevator upstairs. It had been lovely to forget about their dilemma during the music, but now St. John stopped at the door of her room before going to his own. "Where is your piece of the shawl?" he asked.

"In my reticule."

"Allow me to come inside for one minute. There's no harm in our trying once more to get home. You've had your day's adventure in the future, what you were promised. Perhaps now it will work."

They went inside and he turned on the lights—which Margaret admired with shining eyes. But she drew the shawl from her reticule and came and stood before him.

"Do not be cast down," he said. "Claire will bring you another time."

A look of doubt swept through her dark eyes, but she said, "I'm ready, sir."

Minutes later, nothing had happened, though they'd tried it across the chest, about the shoulders, and over their heads like a scarf. They remained in the room looking at each other.

"Give me your half," St. John said.

She gave it, looking at him questioningly. He held it up to examine it side by side with his, but the edges of both pieces, the ones that had been torn and ragged until Claire mended them, flew together as if by some powerful magnetic pull. With a furrowed brow, St. John held once again a single shawl, the edges seemingly reunited! There was a seam where the tear had been like an old scar from a wound, but it was one shawl again.

They looked at each other in wonder. "What does it mean?" Margaret asked tremblingly. For with one shawl, only one person could time travel.

Gently St. John tugged at it. "They *cannot* have reunited," he said. He tugged harder—it was essential to keep the pieces separate if they hoped to both get back. Margaret watched in consternation.

He pulled harder, exerting more and more force until finally it came apart again, the ends falling like burst balloons.

"Astonishing," he said.

Margaret nodded, her mouth slightly agape. "Astonishing, indeed. Pray, keep the pieces apart, sir! It may become inseparable if you do not."

He stared at the two halves in bewilderment.

"Have you never seen this phenomenon before now?" she asked.

"I have not." He went to return one half to Margaret, but suddenly the two ends flew swiftly together again, determinedly, like irresistible forces. He tugged to separate them again but knew the resistance was too strong. "We may cut it, I suppose, if we dare, but it wants to be one piece again." He shook his head. "As fantastical as that is."

He sighed, held it up, and then, turning to Margaret, gave her an inscrutable look.

"What is it, sir?"

He didn't speak, but in a slow, cautious movement, staring at the tallit as though it were fragile and might break, he pressed it against his chest—and vanished.

To reject is easy; to be abandoned, terrifying.
Angela Mi Young Hur

Chapter 6

"Nooooo!" The cry left Margaret's lips as a hollow, dull fear spread through her body and her legs went weak. She gazed into empty space where St. John, only a moment ago, had stood. The excitement she'd felt at staying in the future disappeared right along with him, leaving only dread in its wake.

He'd *left* her! It was one thing to be stuck in a strange new century *with* St. John; he, at least, had some experience living in this time period and was older, wiser, and would protect her. But to be stranded in the future without him was quite another thing. She felt utterly lost and insecure.

While her mind spun cartwheels, she paced the room. There was no need to panic, she told herself. Mr. St. John was an honorable man. He would return. She continued pacing, gathering her thoughts. He had gone back to 1819, no doubt. And if he could go back, he could come forward again. That was the important thing, wasn't it? He'd check on Claire and then return, probably in minutes. He would linger only long enough to ascertain the safety of his wife in her confinement, but then he'd come back for her.

She tried to relax. She put the leftovers into the cold box, but then paced more, waiting, waiting. She drew aside a curtain and gazed at the city at night, a wonder of lights and color—but she could scarcely find it diverting now. She wished she had her own analytical engine—she liked that name so much better than 'computer,' which was difficult to remember—for suddenly she wished very much to find Clarissa.

Thinking of Mr. St. John and all she knew and loved more than 200 years away, filled her with acute homesickness. She felt so terribly lonely that she considered going down to the front desk just to assure herself that other people were about. But St. John wouldn't approve of her going about alone at night. She thought of the beautiful, enormous library within walking distance. A long walk, perhaps, but nothing she couldn't accomplish easily. With that thought, a faint ripple of excitement, trickling softly from within her like a hidden spring, nudged away a measure of her distress. If St. John delayed his return, she would have time to explore to her heart's content. She could return to the Pforzheimer Collection and perhaps run across that mysterious young man who dressed in their manner. Even more importantly, she could find her invention, for she was sure to go home eventually. She just didn't know when.

She thought of the long hours she'd spent in her father's and Lady Ashworth's libraries, growing acquainted with their collections. Neither of those were anything to this modern library, she was sure of that. And with the analytical engine, she would easily study how civilization had progressed with new gadgets and choose one for her purposes. She'd been so dazzled by headlines at the 'Internet Café' that she had hardly begun to search that out.

Except she must find Clarissa first. Despite her elder sister's past cruelty, she was Margaret's only connexion now, her only anchor in this new world.

As the minutes ticked past, she wondered if Claire's baby had arrived, or if she was being delivered of their first child right then! (In the past reckoning of time, of course, which was mightily confusing.) Mr. Wickford, the physician, had said just the other day that surely there was a week, perhaps two, before the delivery. St. John only agreed to take Margaret to the future because of that assurance. Mr. Wickford had added that one could never be *certain* when babies would decide to come, but he ended upon the words, "I am confident, however, sir, that this little one is not sufficiently ready."

Why had they journeyed to the future shortly before the birth? Clarissa had informed St. John on his last trip that Dove Cottage was to be sub-let for most of the year. She'd married Adam Winthrop, and as his wife, finally agreed to allow his family's business, Bavarian Mountain Ski Lodge, the use of it as a rental. The ski resort was posh and lucrative, and the cottage had been given a "facelift" (she said) to match the Bavarian theme of the lodge.

For the sake of Claire and St. John, however, Clarissa had reserved two weeks a year for the cottage to remain empty. This was when they could safely time travel to and fro, for they always arrived at the cottage in the present until now. It wouldn't go well were they to arrive while a patron of the resort was in residence; and so they had worked out exactly which days, in 1819, corresponded to the reserved days in the future, and thus had come this week.

If they hadn't, Margaret would have had to wait a full six months for another opportunity, and she doubted that St. John, as a new father (which he would be by then) would wish to leave his family and make the trip for her sake.

Only everything had gone awry. They had not arrived at Dove Cottage, but New York.

Guiltily, Margaret realized Mr. St. John would not have chosen to come just now had she not wheedled and cajoled him into taking her. She'd even used her sister as an excuse, which was dishonest. Though she hadn't seen Clarissa for near three years, she was hardly heartbroken about it. There were moments when she missed her. Papa often lamented in company that his "best and handsomest daughter" was sadly gone. For his sake, Margaret wished she would come back. For his sake only.

How was Papa faring, she wondered, now? Claire or Mr. St. John, she hoped, would have the presence of mind to send a messenger with word that she must be excused from attending him as she was stopping with them for the night. Normally she read to him from the prayer book before bed. She felt sad at not being there for him, but Denny would do it in her place. Mr. Denny had been their butler all her life and was, she thought, fonder of her father than even she. Papa would be taken care of.

And at least St. John had returned home. He was no doubt with Claire right now, whatever the stage of her lying-in. It was only right that he see his wife. And then she remembered he'd said Lady

Ashworth might have an explanation regarding the shawl. If St. John had called upon Lady Ashworth, that could take an hour or two—or longer.

She resigned herself to spending the night alone with no St. John nearby. She took the few pieces of reading material in the room, removed the modern dress, and slipped beneath the sheets in her chemise. She wanted a toothbrush but hadn't thought of it earlier.

She read every word of the literature, all about the hotel's "policies" and "amenities," eateries in the area, and extraordinary entertainment options. If she lived in New York, she doubted she could ever grow bored.

She shut the bedside lamp off with some trepidation, but when light still came into her window from other buildings, she relaxed. In fact, she settled into the mattress, which seemed a deal softer than hers at home, and felt strangely peaceful. What was it? Perhaps that there was no father to constantly summon her for his endless needs, no servants to oversee or direct, and no great aunt to lecture her on decorum or being amiable to the tiresome young women in their social circles. Slowly her plight felt less and less alarming. She realized with growing anticipation—*this was it! This was her adventure!*

She must welcome it bravely. If the thought that she was alone in a new century nibbled at the edge of her mind like a mouse eating crumbs in a cupboard, she must shut the door on that thought with a slam. It was *exciting* to be on an adventure, she reminded herself. As she drifted off to sleep, she remembered, too, that she was not utterly alone—she was still God's child—and He was with her. Nevertheless, the prayer on her lips was, *Dear heavenly Father, bring St. John back!*

And as she fell asleep, the word, '*alone,*" floated into her mind and settled there, leading her like a raft over a waterfall to an inevitable crash below. She dreamt of being on the crowded streets without St. John's reassuring presence. But as she said boldly to the mysterious man from the library (who suddenly appeared, to her delight), "No amount of foreign customs, poor taste or ill manners shall get the better of me. I assure you, I am equal to it!" She pulled out the little card of credit and held it up to where it glinted in the sun like a gold nugget.

When she awoke, she remembered the dream in detail. She remembered that St. John had vanished, leaving her all alone. She hopped out of bed to check her reticule for the card of credit. Had she given it back to St. John? But no, there it was, just as she'd dreamt! Out loud, to the walls and the empty room, she said, "So what if I *am* alone? I assure you; I am equal to it!"

Chapter 7

No sooner had she made her declaration that she was equal to
her current situation and its challenges, than Margaret remembered
that Mr. St. John may have returned! Hope filled her heart. A
gentleman would not disturb her sleep, so she'd have to dress and
go to the next room to find out. She'd wear the contemporary frock
to be less conspicuous.

But there was no new frock! St. John had warned her that it
might vanish, but she hadn't believed it would. She had no choice
but to wear her day dress again. It was modish, but not, alas, a
morning gown. Then she recalled that no one in this clueless
century, thankfully, would know the difference. How strange that
they had made such advances as the analytical engines, cold boxes
and elevators, but had regressed in terms of fashion.

Without Betsey, her maid, it took long and frustrating minutes
to get dressed. She had to wrestle the gown—fastening the back
bodice buttons before putting it on, for she couldn't do it afterward,
and thereby nearly tearing it. In the end, she had to leave a middle
button undone. Day dresses weren't meant to be fastened by the
wearer! Finally she smoothed it down and hurried to put on her
half boots.

Going to the next door, she knocked as loudly as she dared.
"Mr. St. John! Mr. St. John? Are you there?" Her heart was torn
between sinking at his absence or rejoicing for it. She was excited
at the thought of exploring the huge library but could not help
worrying, *what if he never returns?* Still pondering, she returned
to her door. Locked! She hadn't thought to bring that little card
with her; doors weren't supposed to lock by themselves! Her
reticule was in the room, and the card of credit inside it. And her
bonnet! This she felt as a grave loss. A lady seldom ventured into

society during the day without one. Good thing she had at least put on her half boots. The question was, what to do now?

When the tallit whisked St. John from the hotel room, he was relieved to find himself in his own library on South Audley Street, just as he had always found himself after time travelling. At least *that* hadn't changed. He heard a deal of hurrying footsteps in the corridor and muffled voices in urgent tones. Quickly he folded the shawl, put it in the drawer of a table against the wall, and hurried out.

"Sir!" Two maids stopped in their tracks, staring at him in shock. "Heaven be praised!" cried one. "The mistress feared ye were gone, sir."

"I was. Where is she?"

"In the bedchamber, sir. With the doctor!"

He started down the corridor. "What happened?" he asked, throwing the words over his shoulder. One of the maids, scurrying to keep pace, said, "Why, 'tis her time, sir! Her pains began a few hours since."

A shiver, a foreboding, something of discomfort, passed through him. That he was about to be a father seemed of less importance than the ordeal of his wife giving birth. They had discussed sending Claire to the future for the event, but what if, by some fluke, his son or daughter could not return? It was too horrible a thought. Claire agreed to risk childbirth in 1819 rather than face that possibility, for she too found it as repugnant and unthinkable as her husband.

His long strides had him at the door to the bedchamber in record time. He hesitated. Mr. Wickford had said the pains shouldn't begin for a week or more. "Send word to Lady Ashworth."

"She's 'ere, sir, inside, with the mistress."

"Very good." He turned the knob and hurried in. *Thank God he'd been able to get back in time.* Miss Margaret was no doubt suffering frights without him, but what could he do? She was safe in a hotel room. No worries there.

At his entrance, Lady Ashworth rose from a chair beside the bed. "Julian!" she cried, with a beaming face.

"Oh!" Claire cried from the bed. "You're back!" Her face was rosy with excitement, her beauty undiminished. She might have been enjoying a carriage drive. Her dark hair shone, and the healthy glow of being "in the family way" brightened her cheeks, though in her eyes he detected a shimmer of fear.

"My love, of course," he said, going quickly to her side and grasping one of her hands between his own. He would say nothing yet of the trouble with the tallit.

The doctor had been at the window but now turned. Julian said tartly, "Happy I'm back, as you said the lying-in would not occur for yet a week or two."

The man was unfazed. "God decides these things, sir. I'll have a word with you, if you please."

St. John kissed Claire's cheek. She said, "I'm so glad you've come! But go ahead and speak to Mr. Wickford. Tell me everything he says. He tells *me* nothing. Physicians of this day seem to think women incapable of understanding anything!"

St. John hadn't released her hand and he kissed it again. "Are you well?"

"Yes. Go. It isn't bad at all, yet." But she winced as soon as she'd spoken, and St. John stood and watched her endure a brief paroxysm of pain. With another kiss to her hand he said, "I'll just have that word with Mr. Wickford." She nodded and smiled bravely.

He followed the physician into the corridor. Mr. Wickford said, "The child's earlier than expected, sir, but I see no call for alarm."

"Do many come early?"

Mr. Wickford, a balding, bespectacled man, nodded. "They do, sir, yes. As I said, no need for alarm. Knowing you are home will be helpful to your wife, however. Please stay in the house."

"I'll stay right here," he said.

"In the corridor? That's hardly necessary."

"In the room."

The doctor's lips firmed. "'Tis quite irregular, sir. I do not recommend it."

"My wife wishes it."

Mr. Wickford frowned. "She *thinks* she does, sir, but she'll be much relieved if you do not witness her pains, believe me. It can be rather harrowing, I assure you."

"No doubt," said Julian. "But I must stay unless Claire gives me leave." He made a move to go back inside, but the doctor touched his arm.

"Sir, before we return—your wife refuses to take laudanum." His disapproving tone was exactly that of a frowning headmaster dealing with a recalcitrant student. But Julian's memory shot back to a discussion between him and Claire. She had said, "Laudanum is a depressant. It will exacerbate my labor, not help it."

"It will decrease your pain," he'd said.

"And pass to our baby! No, thank you. I will not have it. Be sure not to allow Mr. Wickford to give me the smallest drop!" St. John's research in the future had confirmed this idea, that a drug given to the mother would indeed pass to the baby, and so he hadn't remonstrated.

Julian's look, while Mr. Wickford awaited his response, was pensive. "That is her prerogative."

"Sir," he said with scarcely disguised disgust. "She suffers more than necessary without it. Will you indeed allow her to make this ill-informed decision when it concerns *your* child?"

"She understands it does nothing for the pains when they come."

"Well; I believe it does. But if not, it would relax her, sir, *in between* the pains."

"It must be Mrs. St. John's decision," he said, trying not to lose patience.

"Begging your pardon, sir, but your wife is no physician. You must allow me to judge—"

"No laudanum, under any circumstances," interrupted Julian, icily.

With compressed lips, the physician said, "As you wish. But do you really insist upon staying? Husbands are never present at these things. I fear your presence will only agitate your wife. You needn't feel an obligation."

"Lower-class husbands are often present for the birth of their children; I do not see why we in the upper class should be any different." Indeed, Claire had pressed this point upon him, as well as the fact that in the future, husbands were expected to remain with their wives. The doctor opened his mouth to object, but St. John added instantly, "I am entirely of a mind to stay, sir. I promised her."

The man grimaced. "I am not accustomed to having a husband look on."

"I will stand aside and not disturb you in the least," returned Julian.

Mr. Wickford bowed his head unhappily but said nothing. He'd just about had enough from these peculiar St. Johns. Especially the wife, who insisted he wash his hands with soap and water before every examination, as if that could accomplish aught!

Back at Claire's side, Julian wished to speak about the tallit, but with the doctor and a maid in the room, he dared not. But she motioned to him, so he leaned his head in. She whispered, "I begin to wish I could go to the future and straight to a hospital."

"But then you must go alone, or one of us will not come back. The tallit only accommodates two. And as for that..." his words died off as he did not wish to disquiet his wife. But he could assuredly not allow her to use the tallit, for now it seemed that even *two* could not time travel at once. The baby could be left behind, or Claire. Either was unacceptable.

She sighed. "If only I had assurance that all three of us—you, I, *and* our child—could make it back. They know so much better what to do if there's a difficulty in my day."

He tried to add a note of levity by saying, "Only think of Mr. Wickford's consternation if you suddenly appeared with our baby without having required his assistance to deliver it!"

She nodded, but then gave him a curious look. "I own I am relieved you are returned, but where is Margaret?"

"I had to leave her rather abruptly."

Claire stared at him. "Do you mean, she's still there?"

He nodded. "Yes—"

"Oh, with Clarissa, of course. I hope they are enjoying the reunion."

Julian left it at that, not wishing to correct her. He would tell Claire precisely what happened as soon as things settled down after the birth, but not now. She had enough to deal with at present.

Dr. Wickford approached with his watch in hand. "It's been seven minutes since your last pain," he said frowningly.

"Is that a problem?" asked Claire.

"They were only six minutes apart, earlier," he said. Looking at St. John, he added, "Your presence is not helping matters, I fear, sir."

Claire stifled a laugh. "His presence makes no difference as to that!" she exclaimed. "But it helps my peace of mind to have him."

But the minutes between the pains began to stretch out further. One faint pain would come, then cease. Eventually another, faintly, faintly, but none so strong as before. Finally, they stopped coming altogether. After an hour, Dr. Wickford came from his perch near the window and, begging their pardons, put his two hands about Claire's swollen belly, palpating gently. It had appalled Claire earlier when, in lieu of a stethoscope, the physician had used what appeared to be a rolled-up piece of paper against her belly to hear the baby's heartbeat! How slow science was! Now, as he tried nudging the child manually, he asked, "Is there pain?"

She shook her head. "No."

His face was scrunched in concentration.

"Ow!" said Claire, when the babe suddenly kicked.

"I felt that too," said Mr. Wickford. "Good." Satisfied, he withdrew his hands. Then, collecting his medical bag, he said, "I don't believe your child will be delivered today." He put back a pair of forceps and shut the bag. "I've seen this happen before. False parturition, we call it." He bowed. "I live not far, as you know. Summon me at the soonest return of pains." Turning to St.

John he added, "Take no journeys, sir. The birth is certain to be quite soon, possibly in the morning." He bowed again and left the room.

"I've read about this," Claire said. "Labor starting but stopping. They're called Braxton-Hicks contractions."

"Do they come back?"

Claire nodded. "In many cases, they do. But they can occur weeks before a delivery." St. John thought of Margaret, realizing he might need days in the future to figure out how to get them both back. How could he do it, never knowing if his wife was to begin birth pains in earnest?

He kissed her forehead. "You need to rest."

"As do you," she said, softly. She stared up into his eyes, enjoying his nearness. "'Tis after midnight. Since Margaret is safe with her sister, stay with me, darling."

He nodded. "I shall. Only I will speak to her ladyship first. I have hardly greeted your grandmother."

"She's been with me since this morning. She has the best guest room," Claire murmured.

Lady Ashworth, as if reading his mind, motioned to him, and he went to her in the far side of the spacious room where she sat beside a table with two burning tapers. She looked at him questioningly. In a carefully lowered tone she asked, "Did I hear that you left Margaret in the future?"

Keeping his voice equally low due to the presence of a maid, St. John quickly told Lady Ashworth how the tallit had gone awry. They'd not arrived at Dove Cottage as expected, but New York City, and now Miss Margaret was still there. He hoped she might have an insight as to what was afoot or an idea of how they could both return, seeing as how the tallit had rejoined itself together.

She stared at him in consternation. "Indeed! This is unexpected." After a moment her face lightened. "Did Margaret appear in modern clothing?"

"No. We both kept our usual style."

A sigh of relief. "Thank God for that! She must return, then. I cannot say I comprehend the workings of the tallit, but I do know this much: if it meant for her to stay, she would have appeared in modern clothes, just as Clarissa did when she arrived in the future. And when I arrived here, I was dressed modishly, for I was meant to stay in this time." Lady Ashworth's features, still fine for her age, and with whispers of the beautiful woman she'd once been, were firm with confidence.

"Does nothing occur to you?" he asked. "Something, perhaps, that you learned when you first acquired the tallit? Where in Israel did you get it, by the by? I may need to visit the place."

"'Twas many years ago," she replied doubtfully. "Well, many years in the future, to be precise." She hesitated. "I suppose we need a second shawl for Margaret. What else could it mean? When you return to New York or wherever you end up, find the street market in Jerusalem using the Internet."

"The—ah, the computer?" he asked. "I tried. I found plenty of tallit-makers but nothing hand-crafted. What was the name of the market?"

At this, Lady Ashworth's dignified face puckered into a frown, the fine wrinkles of papery skin about her eyes and mouth settling deeper. Even the grey curls about her forehead seemed to frown. "I do not recall it having a name. A woman sold me the shawl." Her face lightened. "Miriam would know! Miriam Avraham. You'll have to look her up."

"And tell her what, precisely?" he asked, with a curl to his lips. "That your shawl enables time travel but it's got stodgy and stubborn and one of us is stranded out of our time, and we need another?"

Lady Ashworth cried, "Naughty boy! All you need say is that Mrs. Grandison sent you for a shawl identical to the one I bought when I was with her. I was Mrs. Grandison, then. She'll remember." Her face softened. "And give her my best regards. She was a dear friend. I miss her!"

"And if she asks about you?"

The older woman shook her head. "You'll think of something satisfactory to say, sir, I'm sure."

He nodded. "Well. If that is the only thread we hang by, I'll find her. Margaret and I both must get home."

She gave Julian a look of consternation. "Indeed. Margaret must be at her wit's end." Her look changed to one of speculation. "Unless our gel has decided 'tis just the sort of situation she should enjoy. You know her alarming taste for misadventure." She sighed fondly, a little smile at the edges of her lips. But then her face sobered. "Until the method to get you both back is discovered, I suggest you trade places with her. I daresay you can better handle the challenges of the 21st century, though she is an intelligent gel."

"But then *I* would be stranded in the future apart from my wife and son."

"Or daughter," Lady Ashworth smiled.

"Or daughter," he allowed, with a glimpse toward Claire. She appeared to be sleeping soundly. Without awaiting a reply, he continued, "No, I depend upon finding that street vendor to secure a second shawl so we may both return to where we belong. In the meantime, Margaret has pluck to the backbone enough; I won't abandon her, but she will not sink into despair."

"I suppose that's true enough. But be sharp about it, sir. If Margaret were to vanish like Clarissa, it would be the death of her father. When you hadn't returned by 9 o'clock, I sent word that she's stopping here for the night. But old Mr. Andrews is bound to summon her home. Though he pines for Clarissa, the truth is that Margaret is a great comfort to him."

"I comprehend that," he assured her.

She leveled serious eyes upon him. "Show me the shawl."

"I left it in the library, in the drawer of the first table against the east wall." He paused. "Curiously, though it is one piece again, it still folds up to a very small size."

"One of its many mysteries," nodded her ladyship.

Since Claire was already asleep, he hurried with her to the library. Lady Ashworth was full of curiosity. She hadn't handled the shawl herself for years.

A footman sitting sleepily in the corridor came to attention. "Shall ye want a fire, sir?" he asked, when he saw their destination.

"No, no, nothing," said St. John. He went to the side of the room where he poured a drink. Lady Ashworth declined the offer of joining him, instead going eagerly to the table against the wall where she opened the drawer and pulled out the tallit.

She held it up and examined it, her face at first curious, then pensive, then sentimental. The mark where it had been torn was evident, but just as Julian said, tugging at it did not separate the pieces. Suddenly tears pooled in her eyes. Holding the shawl put her strongly in mind of her own time-travelling days, of how she had first ended up in Regency England from Dove Cottage. Her experience had not been far different from Claire's, only instead of putting her in the path of St. John, it had put her in the path of Richard Loudon Everhill, Marquess of Ashworth. They'd fallen in love swiftly. The marquess was older than Lady Ashworth—Mrs. Grandison then—by a decade, and a widower. He hadn't expected to marry again.

And no one expected that he would marry a widow lacking fortune and family or engage a barrister to make an extraordinary exception to the law and leave a great part of his wealth and estate to Lady Ashworth. There was no heir, for one thing, so male primogeniture had no claim to it. But such cases often resulted in the crown assuming possession of the estate. Lord Ashworth's foresight prevented that.

A tear made its way down her cheek. Richard fell ill only two years after the wedding. He never ceased to tell her that she'd made his last days on earth the happiest he'd known. His first marriage was arranged, his wife a childlike woman who could never take her place in society as a hostess or entertain guests properly for the marquess. He'd remained unmarried for ten years before meeting Mrs. Grandison, and his biggest regret, he told her often before his death, was that he didn't have ten more to spend with her.

She must conquer her sensibilities and useless grief. She lifted the tallit like a handkerchief to wipe away the tear before St. John could see it. Unfortunately, she held the shawl too close—and a few moments later, after the loud whirlwind and blur of time travel surrounded her and filled her senses, she was no longer in St. John's library on South Audley Street.

She was in a bustling metropolis. *Oh, dear.*

Life takes us to unexpected places. The future is never set in stone.
Remember that.
Erin Morgernstern

Chapter 8

St. John turned with a glass to his lips in time to see Her Ladyship vanish. He swallowed with narrowed eyes. This was no time for Lady Ashworth to play at time travelling. He needed to get back for Margaret's sake. He'd no notion the old dame would take it into her head to use the shawl. Scowling, he sat down to wait. He'd finish the drink and hope she'd have the sense to return by then.

Hadn't she accepted that her time-travelling days were over? She had said as much. After marrying the marquess, the tallit had vanished, she'd said, leaving her to live in the past, and she was happy to have it so. She believed her marriage was divinely ordained, just as it was for Claire, who found the tallit back in Mrs. Grandison's old Maine cottage and through it had met and married him. It was vexatious that the marchioness had used the shawl now.

When the minutes ticked past and she did not return, he conjectured that she intended to find the Jerusalem Street market herself. Perhaps this was best, as she knew who and what to look for, and could procure the special tallit they needed more speedily than he. Besides which, he'd be home for the birth of his child.

What else Lady Ashworth might hope to accomplish, he knew not. But where had the recalcitrant tallit taken her? If she'd arrived at Dove Cottage, there was nothing she could accomplish for Margaret from there. And if she arrived in New York City as he and Margaret had, she would hardly be likely to find the girl. New York was teeming with hotels, and he hadn't told her the name of theirs. Surely, if that were the case, she'd recognize this and return momentarily.

But finally, he made his way back to Claire. If her ladyship had indeed set out to find a second shawl, he could be waiting a very long time—days, even weeks. What oppressed him was the thought that *he* had brought Margaret to the future, that she was there by herself, and therefore it must be his responsibility to bring her back.

But without the tallit, his hands were tied. All he could do was wait.

Feeling half-dressed without a bonnet or her spencer, Margaret took the elevator—she quite enjoyed it, now—and hesitated in the lobby to look around. She knew she must have slept in, for hunger beckoned. She had meant to eat from the cold box, but now could not. Happily, she recalled that inns always offered a public breakfast and went to search out the dining room.

All she could find was tea and coffee. She often had only coffee and toast at breakfast (which Papa disapproved of, saying tea or chocolate was more appropriate for young women). Papa had coffee too but always wanted eggs and sometimes pork. But no toast at all? It was a shabby business, to her mind. Then, she saw the restaurant.

She hesitated at the doorway, suddenly remembering she didn't have her card of credit. She went back and made do with a cup of coffee after first watching how a middle-aged man poured himself a cup—and left without paying. Her first sip was so startling she stopped full in her tracks—so strong! But she must make the best of it. The cup seemed made of paper, but was sturdy enough, thankfully.

Not knowing what to do with herself afterward, and seeing others help themselves to a newspaper from a stack in the lobby, she took one, and walked out toward Madison Avenue. She would go to the library, find a quiet corner, and read the paper front to back, every inch of it. She hoped to learn a great deal about this century. Or maybe she'd go straight to the 3rd floor "Pforzheimer

Collection." With any luck, she'd get another glimpse of the man dressed in their fashions. But no sooner had she gained the pavement when she stopped in surprise. There was a large group of people milling about, many dressed in clothing of her day! The conference group, she realized. They were mostly in pairs, chatting among themselves.

"Hello!" cried an older woman, coming smilingly toward her. She wore a green patterned gown and dark spencer. The ribbons of a bonnet hung loosely about her shoulders, and her hair seemed rather messy. "I didn't see you yesterday or this morning."

"I'm er, just arrived," Margaret said awkwardly.

"I'm so sorry you missed this morning's breakout sessions. Last night's too—they were wonderful! But I'm glad you're here now! What is your name, dear?"

Margaret's discomfort was acute. "Miss Andrews."

The lady's face wrinkled in concern. "Andrews. I don't recall that name. But are you alright?"

"I, er, I left my card—er, key card—in the room, along with my bonnet and reticule."

The lady smiled conspiratorially and took her arm. "Oh, we dare not go abroad without *those* vital necessities, eh?" Margaret wouldn't have been surprised had she poked her in the ribs. "Come, let's get you a new key," she said briskly. As they walked, she asked, "Has your partner arrived, dear?"

"My—my partner?" What on earth was she suggesting?

"Your companion for the conference. I believe we placed everyone in pairs."

"Oh, er, he—Mr. St. John unfortunately was called away."

"Mr. St. John?" Her brows furrowed. "I don't recall that name, either." She stopped mid-stride and cast a wide-eyed expression upon Margaret. "But this is perfect! I mean, I'm sorry for your disappointment, but the fact is, I have a young gentleman who is also alone and who also happened to join us only this morning! May I introduce him? You can keep each other company. Is that all right?" Turning towards the milling crowd she called, "Mr. Russell! Oh, Mr. Russell!"

Margaret saw a glimpse of a top hat coming their way.

The woman turned back to Margaret. "Your no-show makes two, you see. But if you and Mr. Russell don't mind pairing up, I'm very happy that now we'll still have an even number of couples. That makes it so much nicer for the ball."

A ball! thought Margaret. How propitious.

The top hat had moved on. Instead, a blond-haired, bespectacled young man came and stood and looked quietly at Margaret. He wore the fashion of her day, breeches with a white shirt, a tasteful waistcoat and jacket. His cravat was tied nicely. Their eyes met and he gave a little smile. Margaret's heart jumped—it was the blue-eyed man she'd seen at the library!

She stifled a smile. "Hello."

"Hello again," he said, smiling more broadly now.

"Oh, do you know each other?" the lady gushed joyfully. "Wonderful!"

Just then someone called, "Sue! Sue! Over here, please! We have a question for you."

The woman smiled. "That's me they're calling. Mr. Russell, if you don't mind, Miss Andrews needs a duplicate room key. Will you accompany her, please?"

"Of course," he said. His gaze upon Margaret was gentle.

"If you need me, please don't hesitate," she added, squeezing each of their hands once and then hurrying away.

Margaret took a breath—what was she to do now? They evidently mistook her for a member of the group. The young man nodded and held out a hand. "Stewart Russell. Pleased to meet you."

Margaret stared at his hand for a moment for he did not seem to be asking for hers, but wished her to take it. How friendly of him. She did so. "Miss Margaret Andrews, pleased, likewise."

He smiled, glancing at his hand, and then gently extricated it. He had a very nice smile.

"You're British?"

"Yes. And you are er, a New Yorker."

He chuckled. "I am, now. I'm living here while I earn my doctorate. I'll stay, of course, if I land a great job." He flashed a smile and motioned her toward the front door of the hotel. It was a lovely smile, but she was sorry to learn he was there to "land a job." It meant he was in trade. How nice it would have been to meet an independent gentleman with means. Perhaps he was a second son, she reasoned. Not all young men could rely upon a good inheritance to set them up in society.

As they walked, she took shy glances at him when he spoke, enjoying the opportunity to study him at closer range than in the library. He had very short hair with no curls at all, but it was neatly combed back off his face, parted on one side. His nose was chiseled, sideburns well-trimmed, and his mouth, small. Overall, his features were pleasingly proportionate. She decided he was gentlemanlike and handsome, though not to the extent of Mr. St. John. And like her, he wore spectacles!

"Is this your first JASNA tour?" he asked with a brow raised politely as they waited in a short line at the front desk.

Margaret stared for a moment. "Um... *yes.*" Quickly she added, "And is it yours?"

"It is." He smiled. "We are both greenhorns, then." With a little grin he added, "To use Regency terminology." Claire had told her that their period in time was called 'the Regency' in modern times after the regent, of course, so this remark only brought a wan smile.

When their turn came, Margaret explained that she had left the "key card" in her room. Due to her costume, she received no trouble at all about proving her identity without having any upon her, and promptly received a substitute card. "I am so glad!" she breathed afterward to Stewart. "I left my bonnet, reticule and my card of credit in the room!"

He leaned in, brows furrowed. "Your card of credit?"

Oh, dear! What had Mr. St. John called it? Wasn't that it? she thought frantically. "You know, the little card that works like money?" She blushed, as it was poor manners to discuss money. He pulled away again, searching her face, and smiled a little.

"Well, let us retrieve them, by all means," he said.

About ten minutes later, after Margaret had dropped off her newspaper, got her things and felt much more comfortable in her spencer and bonnet, and with her reticule and the card of credit inside, they returned to the company. The conference attendees were conspicuous for their period clothing, though not all were in costume. As she and Mr. Russell joined them, an impossibly huge equipage pulled to the curb and stopped with a loud hiss. It was so enormous, and its hiss so loud that Margaret unconsciously reached for his arm. Startled, he looked at her.

"I beg your pardon." She blushed and hurriedly removed her hand. "I—I've never seen such a large coach as that—"

"The bus?" he asked with incredulity, looking from her to the bus and back. "Do they not have tour buses in Great Britain?" he asked with a little grin. "But wait, you have the double-deckers! Are they not so tall as this one?"

"I..." Her voice died off as she had no answer. As she continued to gawp at the sheer size of the enormous thing called a bus, like a huge hissing beast, he added, leaning in as if to tell a secret, "You've obviously led a sheltered life. I am quite intrigued. Either that, or I have a lot to learn about your country." He smiled affably.

Margaret needed to move the conversation on. "What is this bus here for?"

"It's not for us, not today, anyway. Some other tour group, I suppose. Our first event is a short walking tour while our guide expounds upon Jane and, oddly enough in New York, the city of Bath, isn't it? Then, we are to have lunch at a chic café. After that, we don't meet again until dinner."

"That sounds interesting," she said sincerely. *Jane and the city of Bath*. A strange pairing to her ears, an authoress and a popular watering spa; she was eager to learn of the connexion. A walk to lunch sounded lovely as well. The library could wait.

He glanced at her hands. "Did you not get the welcome bag? With the itinerary?"

"I did not. I, er, arrived late."

"Let's get back inside and get you one. C'mon, if we move fast we'll have time." To her surprise he grabbed her hand and hurried them back to the hotel lobby where he said something to the clerk behind the counter. It was a different clerk than before.

"What is the name, please?" the man asked.

Margaret balked. "Why do you need my name?" The cheek of the working class in this day! She glanced at Mr. Russell to share her indignation, but he seemed as surprised by her question as the clerk.

The clerk frowned. "I need your name," he said heavily, "to find your welcome packet."

"Are they not all identical? Just give me any welcome packet," she returned, reasonably, she thought.

"They are only for registered JASNA guests."

"Miss. Margaret. Andrews," she said imperiously. She and St. John had registered the previous day, hadn't they? Mr. Russell gave her a little reassuring smile when their eyes met, but he seemed somewhat abashed, though she had no idea why.

Soon the clerk's face puckered. "We don't have anyone by that name. There are two bags unclaimed, but neither belongs to a Margaret Andrews."

Mr. Russell cut in. "That's right, my apologies. We have two no-shows. Miss Andrews is a substitute for the lady who did not come."

The man blinked, as if considering this.

"Only look at her costume," Mr. Russell said patiently.

The clerk looked her over and then said rather sourly, "We'll have to print a new nametag. Will you wait?"

"I'm sure you'll manage quickly," Mr. Russell said with an ingratiating grin.

Margaret stood by with a torn heart. She ought to tell him outright that she was not a substitute for some lady that hadn't shown up. That she was not a JASNA member at all. But it was so fascinating, and she was with her mystery man. She held her tongue.

The tag was soon procured and handed to Mr. Russell. He reached toward her but Margaret jumped back, giving him a look of alarm. "What are you about, sir?"

He stopped in surprise, looking utterly flummoxed, then chuckled. "I'm sorry, I only meant to help." He handed her the tag.

Margaret examined it, glanced at his nametag, and deduced how it fastened. She pinned it to her spencer. The clerk, eyeing her disdainfully, gave her a pretty paper bag with handles. Large flowery letters on it said JASNA: Sex, Money, and Power in Jane Austen's Fiction. Margaret blushed crimson. *Sex! Money!* Taboo subjects in genteel society to be sure. She turned it around to hide the words but they were printed on both sides. How mortifying! She removed the schedule of events and handed the bag back to the clerk. "May I retrieve this later when we return?"

He looked reluctant to take it back, but Mr. Russell added a hearty, "Plenty of room here for it. No sense in making her carry it all day, eh?"

The clerk, somewhat abashed, accepted the bag.

"Much obliged," she said meekly, mostly to Stewart. One peek into the bag had revealed that it held nice things which she would examine later. But she was an impostor, stealing what was not rightfully hers! She would tell Sue to charge her card of credit for the cost. But was it not propitious? A happy coincidence that a JASNA group should be here just when she, Margaret, was?

She looked over the schedule curiously and, with growing awe, saw how marvelous it was. "We have both missed so much already," she remarked.

He nodded with an uneasy look. "Yes."

"But you were in costume at the library yesterday. What brought you there when you might have enjoyed these fascinating talks?"

He looked startled, but countered with, "You were in costume and at the library also. What brought *you* there?"

She smiled. "If you shan't tell, neither shall I."

"Deal," he said, with a smile.

As they returned to the pavement and hurried to join the throng of JASNA members just beginning their midtown walking tour, she reflected that it was no coincidence at all, but the working of the tallit! Claire had been put into St. John's path, and Great Aunt Ashworth had been matched with the marquess—Margaret blushed again with the realization that perhaps she and Mr. Russell were meant to—were meant to…what? End up in conjugal bliss?

That seemed a preposterous thought—she, married, when she was destined for spinsterhood? Not likely!

She recalled, however, that Claire had once said, "I was not prepared to believe in a match-making shawl," but eventually she did believe. And both she and Lady Ashworth had found their loves with its help. Margaret believed it—for *them*. But she knew *she* would never find such love. Unlike Claire and her great aunt, she was no beauty. And a good-looking, personable young gentleman like Mr. Russell surely had other prospects. Even if he was in trade.

At one time, Margaret had entertained romantic notions. Before Clarissa made it painfully clear that she was hopelessly plain and could never make a good match. If she entertained any hope of marriage, it must be to a gentleman poorer than she would be once Papa died, to whom £500 pounds a year would suffice and make up for the lack of a pretty face. Mr. Russell, surely, could not be that gentleman. Even so, here she was with him. She wondered if she could swallow her rational objections, just for one day, and *pretend* that today's business was the work of the match-making shawl? Even St. John had said there must be a reason the tallit had brought them to New York. She could *imagine* being that reason. She and Mr. Russell. *What a lark this could be!*

The group stopped to listen to the tour guide. Margaret peeked at Mr. Russell, who felt her eyes upon him and gave a small smile. Could she pretend well enough to suppose he fancied her? He was too good-looking; and if he turned out to be a younger son of the upper class, he would surely seek a wealthy bride—did not all young men with good pedigree do so? But for now, she gave her attention to the guide.

I think perhaps love thrives on unlikely circumstance and chance.
Brandon Boyd

Chapter 9

Lunch for the group was held at a bustling café with crowded outdoor tables. She and Mr. Russell followed the group, winding their way past couples lingering at the door to a quieter, reserved section inside. Sue, the woman who had spoken to her earlier, stood at the front of the room, apparently waiting to give a speech. When she was satisfied that her group was all seated, she clapped her hands together and began.

She was *thrilled* at how wonderful the speakers had been thus far, and that this day had arrived, that the weather was lovely, that everyone but two had been able to come. She was sure they would all continue to have a *wonderful* time and make many *precious* memories. She said that, though there was not a great deal of emphasis on food in Jane Austen's books, Jane was nevertheless fond of "housekeeping," and wrote to her sister often about "receipts" (recipes, she explained) and menus.

Margaret felt alarmed for Miss Austen. Surely letters to her sister were not intended for public consumption? She wondered if the authoress anticipated this—doubtless not. If only the tallit could take her home prior to Miss Austen's death, (which, sadly, she'd learned, was two years ago in her time), she could try to warn her. She could write to the publisher and ask them to forward her letter to the authoress. She'd tell her about her astounding future popularity but also say—wait, what would she say? That she'd visited the future? That would hardly be credited.

During their meal, which Margaret survived by ordering exactly what Mr. Russell did, she determined to find out as much as possible about him. She looked sharply at him when he called her by her first name, however. She put her glass down hurriedly, swallowed, and said, trying to be gentle, "I daresay, we are not yet on such terms."

"Excuse me?"

"To use one another's Christian names," she explained, and then fell silent, grasping that she'd made an error. Awkwardly, she said, "Oh, unless it is customary here."

He gave a slow smile. "It is. Are you slow about that in Britain?"

She nodded. "I'm afraid so."

"So I would call you Miss Andrews?"

"That's right. I was formerly Miss Margaret but now that my elder sister is gone—" she swallowed— "that is, now she's married, I am considered the eldest female in the family."

Mr. Russell cried, "Oh! Just like in Jane's books!" He shook his head. "I knew the English are class-conscious, but I had no idea such social quibbles extended to this day."

The waiter stopped at their table to refill their glasses. She covered hers with her left hand, and Mr. Russel waved him away. But first he'd glanced with interest at her hand, she noticed. *Was he looking for a wedding ring? Could he possibly care whether she was married or not?* She was smarting at his calling modes of address "social quibbles," but determined she must forgive him, as he was, after all, from this tasteless century.

"What of your family?" she asked nonchalantly but hoping he was of good stock.

"I have very little family, actually." He cleared his throat. "An aunt in California, a cousin in Washington—neither of whom I'm in touch with—and my foster parents in Ohio."

"Foster parents?" she asked, sighing inwardly. Poor Mr. Russell—not only in trade, but an orphan!

"My father died when I was nine, and my mother put me into foster care six months later. I bounced around from one place to another for a few years, and finally grew out of it."

"Grew out of what?"

"The system. You can only stay in foster care until you're eighteen." He grinned. "Thank God for that."

Margaret took a deep breath, looking sadly at him. Claire got St. John, and Great Aunt Ashworth got the marquess. She, Margaret, *would* get paired with a penniless orphan!

Seeing her expression, he said, "Don't feel sorry for me. It isn't the worst thing in the world not to have family to answer to. And I have friends. In fact, one friend I know only considers his church his family."

Here Margaret looked shocked. "His church? Goodness, I've never heard of such a thing. Is he a curate or a rector?"

"No, just a Christian."

"People of any class, he considers family," she mused, rather appalled.

He nodded. "We don't think in terms of class." He looked at her blankly.

"That is extraordinary." Margaret simply could not relate. She'd always gone to church, of course, and her family were polite to people whatever their class. So long as they knew their place. Neighbors appeared for Harvest Home and other festivities. But no one of the working class would dare consider themselves part of the family, no, not even Denny, their butler for 27 years, since before she was born. Nor would she wish them to.

"You Brits are more old-fashioned," he said, amiably.

"I daresay we are. I definitely am…" On an impulse borne of her distaste for dishonesty, she added with large eyes, "I'm nineteenth-century, if you must know." She wanted him to know the truth about her and had spoken, she thought, bravely.

He chuckled and lifted his glass to her. "You're in the right group."

Margaret wished he'd believed her.

"With a little smile he said, "To be honest, when I read 19th-century works, I often wish I'd been born in that day."

She smiled. "Do you? Think of the conveniences you have, the cold box, and electric lights, and horseless carriages, elevators—"

Grinning, he said, "The cold box?"

She blushed. *What had Mr. St. John called it?* "You know—it keeps food and water cold?"

He laughed. "The refrigerator. That was great, really! You're making this conference much more fun than I expected."

She sniffed and concentrated on her plate. She ought to keep her mouth shut as much as possible. "What is it about the past that enthralls you?" she asked, perking up. If she got him talking about himself, she would be less liable to make faux pas' in her speech.

He put his glass down. "I love it all, the language of the day, the costume, the manners, at least as portrayed in books such as Jane's." His blue eyes, meeting hers evenly, were earnest and lovely.

"You mean Miss Austen?"

He swept his hands out. "Look at us. At a JASNA luncheon. Yes, Miss Austen." He grinned. "You're very good at it, this keeping to the time period. I'm afraid I'm pitiful." He chewed a bite of food and then added, "And really I should be better at it, for it's what I study, you know, 19th-century British literature."

"You study it?" she asked, smiling. "Now here is something we might talk about—that is, if you limit your discussion to the earlier part of the century."

"Do you dislike Victorian literature?"

"Vic—Victorian?"

He stared at her as if she hadn't heard him. "Victorian, yes. Dickens. The Brontes. Hardy."

At a loss, she said, "I like Miss Burney, and Fielding, Richardson, Samuel Johnson, and Walter Scott."

"You like the Georgian writers."

She smiled, nodding as well. "Georgian writers, yes..., after our kings."

He laughed. "You're a natural! Anyone would believe you were Jane's contemporary."

"It does come naturally, I'm afraid," she said, dryly, and then leveled a challenging stare at him. "You may as well know it now, I am a bluestocking. And I make no apologies for it."

His mouth opened a little in surprise. "That's wonderful!" he exclaimed. "You get better and better." He looked around and back at her. In a lowered tone he asked, "By any chance, were you hired to remain in character during our conference?"

She bit her lip, trying to decide how to reply. If he thought her strange, this would answer; it would explain her oddities in a manner he could understand. It would be lowering, of course, admitting to being in trade. And a lie. She was not comfortable with either thought. Finally, with a mischievous little smile she said, "I'm afraid you shall have to fathom that out for yourself. As you get to know me better." And then she blushed crimson. What a thing to say! He had no idea of the match-making tallit! He might have no wish to get to know her better.

But his eyes sparkled, and he nodded. "I think I'd like that." He smiled at her. "Don't worry, I won't tell your secret."

She only smiled wanly. "So, you are a student at university?"

"A graduate student. One more semester and I'll have a doctorate in 19th-century Literature." He chewed a bite of food and added, "I concentrate on female writers, including some 18th century authors. I love that you're familiar with Fielding and Richardson, but I can speak more intelligently upon women authors."

Margaret swallowed with widened eyes. "Astonishing. Women authors have finally been granted their due, their share of fame, like Jane?"

He smiled again. "I wish I knew how you do that so easily. You're phenomenal. We should have you address the group."

"Oh, dear me, no," she said, with a laugh. Then, to return to the former and safer subject she added, "I suppose you've read Anne Radcliffe and Maria Edgeworth?"

"Yes, I have! Have you?"

He seemed delighted at her merely naming the popular authoresses. "I have. And Walter Scott? I adored *Waverley*! Do you like him?"

"Sir Walter has his place," acknowledged Stewart.

"*Sir* Walter?" Margaret smiled. "Why do you call him sir?"

"Why? He's—he was a baronet. George IV created him one. Did you forget that?"

Margaret was struck. "George IV? Oh, yes, of course," she said, trying to hide her dismay. The regent would become George IV when the king died—only she didn't like to think about their beloved King George dying. She, like most of Britain, loved George III dearly.

"What year was that, do you know?" she asked.

He thought for a moment. "Around 1820, I believe."

Margaret gasped, but the waiter came just then to inquire if they wanted dessert, and Stewart missed her reaction. Her head and heart were reeling. 1820 would be next year in her time, which meant the king was shortly to die! They had lost good Queen Charlotte only a year earlier. She blinked back tears.

They declined dessert, but Stewart ordered coffee "to go," so Margaret did also. He continued discussing authoresses, Hannah More, Felicia Hemans, the Countess of Blessington, and more, while they waited for their drinks. It distracted her from her grief, and she was able to master her emotions. It pleased her, moreover, that her familiarity with the writers he named seemed to excite him. How unlike the many young men of her day, who appeared affronted by Margaret's literary prowess!

He leaned in secretively, his eyes alight. "Do you have any idea how rare it is to meet someone who knows and has read Radcliffe? Edgeworth? Hemans? No one! No one except my professor and classmates. What school are you in?"

Without giving it a thought, she answered, dryly, "The Blue Stocking School." There was a very real Blue Stockings Society for literary stars of the day, but Margaret had no illusions of being welcomed into its hallowed circle. But before he could ask further questions, she cut him at the chase. "And what university do you attend?"

"It's right here; New York University. I live on a grant, actually."

"Whose grant? You mean a benefactor, I suppose." She was surprised because most people would proudly disclose the name of their wealthy patron without being asked for it. But his look made her realize she'd goofed again. He sputtered a laugh. "You don't miss a trick! Good for you, *Miss* Andrews."

When the meal was over, Sue gave another little speech. She reminded everyone where and when they were to meet for dinner, adjured them not to be late, and gave ideas on how to spend the ensuing hours between meetups. Margaret and Mr. Russell strolled to the pavement.

"Do you have plans?" he asked.

"I *long* to explore the library more."

"The Morgan? Did you take the tour there with the group?"

"I'm afraid I did not."

"Well, I've just been there," he said, "but if you'd like to go…"

"No, The New York Public Library," she said.

His eyes lit up again. "Perfect! I need to go there! I go often, you know." With bright eyes, he said, "It's where we saw each other first, isn't it? Shall we go together?"

"Yes, please." She suddenly felt breathless. Wouldn't Papa be displeased if he knew she was accompanying a young man without a chaperone! Even Claire and Mr. St. John would give her a combing for it. But this was her tallit-inspired adventure, wasn't it? She had every reason to see it through.

"It's a bit of a walk," he said. "We could split cab fare, if you like."

"A hansom?"

He smiled. "A hansom cab, of course. You don't even have to think about it, do you? You just spill off these old words and phrases like you were born to speak that way!"

Margaret looked away but only smiled. If only he knew. "I am happy to walk if you are," she said. "I've seen 5th Avenue, so may we go along Madison until we turn off for the library?"

He smirked. "Indeed, we may," he said answering her in kind. "But I suggest we walk briskly." He turned to her as they set off. "Have you been to New York before? Because the library, wonderful as it is, would not be the first choice for most tourists."

"Oh, I assure you," Margaret replied swiftly, "I have no other ambition except to see more of it. My great Aunt Ashworth, Lady Ashworth, you know, allows me to use her library, which is vast.

But the one here—Lud! More than I could have imagined!" (She hoped that he did not find her exclamation unbecoming for a lady as her father did. Alas, at times it just slipped out.)

He smiled, and then looked up at her over his spectacles. He didn't seem to care in the least. "If you wish to study Miss Austen's letters and manuscripts, we should go to the Morgan. It has an impressive collection of rare materials. The rare books room is magnificent, architecturally and artistically."

"It sounds fascinating," Margaret agreed, "but why aren't her letters and manuscripts in Britain?"

"Many are, I believe. We have mostly facsimiles, and only a few originals, letters by Cassandra, I think."

"Does the Morgan have a public reading room like the New York library?" she asked, turning large eyes to him.

"Of course, though not so large."

"Does it have a Pforzheimer collection?"

He grinned. "No."

She continued, "I saw you go into the Pfzorheimer Collection. Seeing you were dressed properly, my curiosity about you and that room was piqued. I should really like to see more of it."

He chuckled. "I'm glad I was dressed *properly,* then. Lately that room is my home away from home." He paused. "But you must have libraries to equal it in Britain, or surpass it, considering the literary history of your country!"

She countered, "Perhaps. But yours is stunning, with many millions of books." Looking up at him, she asked, changing the subject, "Do you stay in costume for the entire weekend event? I must say, it was quite the surprise to see you dressed so!"

He turned to her with veiled eyes. "I, uh, have been dressing like this for the past week. I, um, enjoy it and I like to think it enhances my study of the period." He cleared his throat. "In New York, you know, anything goes. But that reminds me, when I saw you, you weren't alone. Where is your friend, the man you were with?"

She hesitated. St. John had no doubt stayed in the past because of Claire's impending lying in. But speaking about a woman with child was vulgar. How should she frame it? "His wife needed him," she said simply.

He gave her a wide-eyed look. "So he's *married.*"

"Yes, and it's their first child—" Oops. That was a slip, and she blushed.

"And is he—a good friend?"

She met his eyes. Something in them told her that he was forming a very wrong idea about her and St. John. "Not so very good as all that!' she cried, laughing. "I am a relation of his wife's, Claire. We are r*elations,*" she repeated, emphasizing the word.

He nodded. "A relative. I'm glad to hear it."

As they walked on, traffic seemed to increase, both on the street and the pavement. She gave him a perturbed look.

"Is something wrong?" he asked, speaking loud enough to be heard.

In a reproving tone she said, "You have not offered me your arm." Looking around at the sudden flow of people she added, "This crush is abominable."

All due remiss showed on his face and he quickly held out his arm. "Like this? Is this right?"

She smiled and took it. "Very good." They walked on in silence, partly because the crowd hurried them and speech was difficult, and partly because Margaret, enjoying being upon his arm, felt no conversation was necessary. They turned at 42nd Street. As they approached the library, suddenly Mr. Russell brought them to a stop. He was staring with a look of alarm ahead of them. Margaret looked to see what might be causing his concern but saw only pedestrians and people either sitting about on the steps of the library or waiting at the curb. It seemed like the usual coming and going.

"Is something wrong, sir?" It was now her turn to ask.

He glanced at her and then looked back toward the library. "Let's go this way," he said, taking her west instead of crossing the street, to the next corner. They fell into the crowd waiting for the light. "There's another entrance to the library, which I prefer," he said. "We'll use that one." But his eyes darted back toward the library and along the street as if something there haunted him. "I should have worn my hat," he said.

Margaret was no simpleton. "Are you endeavouring to hide from someone, Mr. Russell?" she asked with a small grin. No doubt there was a tiresome bore in the vicinity, or someone else he was loath to speak to.

He stared at her in consternation and swallowed. "Am I that obvious?"

She nodded.

"I'm sorry," he said. "I didn't want to mention it and possibly worry you."

"Worry me?"

He looked pensive. "There are some, er, bad men who are looking for me." He turned his clear blue eyes to hers. There was pain and hurt in them. "I've told them I don't have what they want, but they keep turning up. They are decidedly...menacing."

"Which men?" she asked curiously, scanning the sidewalk by the library.

"The two black suits, over there." He pointed.

She saw them then. One of them stopped a woman who had just come from the library. He held his little camera out—just like the one the tourist had used to take photographs of her and St. John— for the woman to look at. The lady shook her head, and the man in the suit went on to someone else.

"Do they have your photo-graph in their camera?" she asked.

He paused, digesting her question. "Their cell phone, you mean. I guess they do." He paused. "I haven't done anything wrong, but they're after me. And they must *not* find me."

Chapter 10

Lady Ashworth blinked, taking in her surroundings, but could scarcely credit her eyes. She was in the future, but not at her old home, Dove Cottage in Maine. No, a bustling city. She realized that like St. John and Margaret, she must have come to New York! Cars, buses, flashing streetlights, overhead wires and skyscrapers assured her of that.

Her sudden appearance in the recess of a doorway had gone unnoticed. Beeping horns, pedestrians passing, and the hum of further-off sounds—all continued unchanged. Hastily checking her attire, she saw she still wore her green French silk walking dress with bands of white lutestring—that was a mercy! For had the tallit meant her to stay in the future, she would have found herself dressed for it. Instead, she now had her reticule, a spencer, and, feeling the weight of it upon her head, a walking hat—all accoutrements she had not had in St. John's library. She hadn't meant to visit the future, hadn't meant to use the tallit at all. But she adjusted it now to hang over one arm and paused to plan her next move.

St. John had left Margaret here and now that she, Lady Ashworth, had arrived, she may as well try to discover how to get that young woman home. That meant procuring a second divinely empowered shawl, which, in turn, required finding that very same stall and shopkeeper. But that was in Israel. She hadn't been brought to Israel, had she? Looking for a street sign, she saw on the corner store in very large writing, "47th Street Diamond Exchange".

Then she noticed that many passersby were of the *Hasidim,* the sect of Jews that wore the traditional garb including curled, untrimmed beards, and high, black hats. Her heart fluttered for a moment, but she knew this wasn't Israel. Scanning more buildings on either side of the street, she saw *Finest Jewelry Exchange, KLM Jewels,* and other similar stores. This was New York's Diamond District, one of the great diamond markets of the world! She remembered it was notoriously Jewish–and that meant tallits might be available as well as diamonds! Her heart lifted.

She crossed at a light with a swarm of pedestrians, reading the names of the stores and examining every window she passed, peering in at the merchandise. Her clothing drew amused and admiring looks. To the admirers, Lady Ashworth gave a condescending, regal nod. She was, after all, a marchioness.

She stopped at a double-glassed storefront with a metal gate overhead. The sign said, "Israeli Rose Jewelry and Gifts," and, in smaller print, "Jewelry, Antiques, Watches." The window showcased gleaming specimens, sturdy gold rings with diamond, ruby, or sapphire stones, as well as bracelets and earrings. They looked to be of the best quality, sparkling in the light. And then she saw it. Beside the tiers of jewelry, hanging unfolded right in front of her nose: a tallit! It was a pretty specimen, with a multi-colored, embroidered border. A little card before the display revealed it was made of raw, hand-painted silk, "not to be used for rituals," which required wool, if her memory served. The background was off-white with a design of an ancient town like Jerusalem or Bethlehem in light shades of blue, green, yellow and pink.

Never before had Lady Ashworth searched for another magical tallit that could transport people through time. Never before had she considered others might exist. Her shawl had offered quite enough excitement and adventure, thank you. But now another was needed, and here she was, outside of a shop that sold them. The divinely mystical tallit was at work again, for

Lady Ashworth knew this was no coincidence. She went inside, her heart alight with hope.

As she slowly traversed an aisle, she remembered clearly how she'd obtained hers, the first tallit. She'd no idea it was magical or would land her in the Regency, or that, years later, Claire would be transported by it as well. She'd been on a pilgrimage to the Holy Land with her church. It wasn't her first pilgrimage, but it was the first time she'd explored a crooked little side road of street vendors selling wares beneath fabric tent tops. She was with an Israeli friend, Miriam, a Messianic Jew whom she'd met on a previous trip. Like Lady Ashworth (Mrs. Grandison, then), Miriam was a widow.

She'd stopped at a table of pretty, hand-crafted shawls. "These are Jewish prayer shawls," said Miriam, trying to pull her along. "They're not for everyday wear."

"But they're beautiful," purred Mrs. Grandison, looking longingly at a pale ivory shawl with multi-colored, embroidered birds around the edges, love birds, they looked like. She held it up.

Miriam whispered fiercely, "If you want a tallit, we'll get one elsewhere. This woman is crazy! I've heard she says her merchandise is divinely mystical."

"How so?" Mrs. Grandison asked, smiling.

Miriam shrugged. "Who knows? But I don't trust it. She's too weird."

The stall-keeper, smiling, approached them. She nodded toward the merchandise. "Each one is unique."

"Is that so?" Mrs. Grandison asked politely.

"I make them myself," she added. "Each for a special person."

Mrs. Grandison smiled indulgently. "Yes, we are all special in our way, aren't we?"

The lady said, "Of course. But each tallit is made *only* for one special person. The one who must own it."

Mrs. Grandison wasn't certain how to answer that. Miriam nudged her with an elbow, as if to say, "Didn't I tell you? Crazy."

The woman smiled at Mrs. Grandison with penetrating, glowing eyes. "Why don't you choose one? Let's see what you choose. I'll let you know if you choose right."

Mrs. Grandison looked down at a row of very pretty tallits, all folded so their tasseled edges and embroidered designs faced out. Miriam grabbed one with a design reminiscent of Egyptian hieroglyphics in tan and purple thread.

"Here," she said. "See what she says to this one."

Mrs. Grandison took it, but the stall keeper shook her head. "Not that one. *You* choose."

Mrs. Grandison tried not to look at the shawl with the embroidered birds that she'd admired earlier, casting her eyes instead over others. Somehow, it still beckoned to her, but she refused to give in. Finally, she shook her head. "I can't decide."

The lady smiled but shook her head too. She went directly to it, the one with birds, drew it out, and held it toward her. "This one. It's special, just for you. I could sell it to no one else." She took the other shawl.

Miriam hissed in her ear. "She probably says that to everyone!"

But the woman, as if having heard her, smiled at Miriam. Looking down fondly at the Egyptian-looking tallit, she said, "This one is for a certain gentleman who hasn't come yet. I expect him soon." She turned and smiled gently at both women. "Mrs. Grandison must take this one." Again, she held it out.

Miriam whispered, "Don't!"

The woman said, "Oh, she must. She must." Turning to Mrs. Grandison she said, "It is meant for you." She told her the price, making Miriam exclaim in her ear, "Highway robbery!"

Since vendors were accustomed to negotiating, Mrs. Grandison repeated, without even thinking about whether she agreed or not, "Highway robbery!"

The woman sputtered a laugh. "If you knew the value—no, no! It is a bargain price. I tell you, it is meant for you and only you; and you *must* buy it!" Her look became so serious that suddenly Mrs. Grandison agreed with Miriam; the woman was too weird. And it *was* probably overpriced. But really it was beautiful, and she felt deep inside that she *ought* to buy it. Was she gullible to a sales gimmick? If so, she couldn't help it. She turned to Miriam as she opened her purse. "Never mind. I like it."

The seller was strange. So what? The world was large and endlessly surprising. Why couldn't there be a shawl sitting in an Israeli vendor's stall, waiting only for a woman from rural Maine in America, to buy it? She paid, and afterward, with the shawl in her hands, felt a surprising and deep delight. It was beautifully crafted. Despite her love for travel, with only a small cottage, she did not collect many mementos. This one she would showcase. She'd hang it behind glass on a wall.

Afterward, as they continued along the line of stalls, Mrs. Grandison looked over trays of rugelach, trying to decide which to buy and eat immediately and whether to take some home. Suddenly her head popped up, and she looked at Miriam in wonder. "The woman who sold me the tallit. How did she know my name?"

That night, her last in Israel, Mrs. Grandison joined Miriam and the other pilgrims for dinner but the two women had their own table. She'd been tempted to wear the tallit—it was so lovely—but it was, after all, a prayer shawl. It would seem sacrilegious.

"It was a good visit," Miriam said.

"It was," Mrs. Grandison agreed. "Especially seeing the empty tomb."

"Jesus' empty tomb."

"Yes."

"I have to admit," Miriam said, surveying Mrs. Grandison across the table, "the shawl looks perfect on you."

Mrs. Grandison looked down at the tallit, draped artfully across her shoulders, and gasped. "But I didn't put it on!"

Miriam chuckled. "You forgot! I think age is catching up with you, *chooki*."

"I distinctly chose *not* to wear it! This is downright disturbing."

Miriam's eyes twinkled. "Don't worry. Maybe that's part of its 'divine mysticism.'"

Mrs. Grandison eyed her with alarm. "Do you really think...?"

"No, I think you forgot you put it on! Now, don't worry about it, and let's enjoy our last evening. I'm going to miss you."

"And I'll miss you."

Two days later, she was back at Dove Cottage. How good it felt to be home. As she unpacked her things, she lingered over the tallit, wondering again how she could have accidentally worn it. Impossible! But what other explanation could there be?

She didn't believe it was really *meant* for her. Or that the saleswoman would not have sold it to someone else. But as she ran her hand along the fabric, she felt again that deep satisfaction of ownership. It did feel special. Not just unique or hand-crafted, but as if it was in fact tied to her in some mystical fashion beyond her understanding. Wait—she was letting her imagination run wild! In any case, she'd not wear it again. She'd have it framed in glass, as planned. One side of the long shawl would be enough to display the exquisite design and it would be kept safe.

A week later Mrs. Grandison was cleaning house and saw the tallit folded neatly upon a side table, just as she'd left it. She hadn't found time to make the run to Portland to get it framed. Outdoors, the wind whistled through the eaves and shutters. Her tiny home was usually snug with its wood stove, especially since she enjoyed baking and used the oven a great deal. Even now, a new and glossy challah bread sat on the counter, still warm. But tonight, it felt as if the wind was snaking through every crack of the old place. On a whim, she took the tallit, looked it over with appreciation, and unfolded it carefully. She'd only use it this once. She placed it gingerly around her shoulders, and crossed it over her bosom.

And then the wind that had been blowing and whistling around the corners of the house changed into a roar, and all was dark. Goodness, was it a tornado? Maine wasn't prone to tornadoes! And then the roaring died away, and Mrs. Grandison stood blinking, looking about her in astonishment. She was no longer in her home at Dove Cottage. She seemed to be in a movie set of some kind, for she was on a bustling street of old-fashioned shops, like a scene out of Dickens. And everyone was dressed in costume. She'd seen gowns like these in the movies, in adaptations of Jane Austen's novels. But how had she got there? And where was she?

As she wondered, she looked down and noticed that she, too, was in costume! Almost faint with surprise, and with the thought that she must be losing her mind or getting senile, she lost her footing. She was saved from falling only by a strong hand who took her arm and steadied her.

"Pardon me," said her rescuer, a grey-haired, kindly looking gentleman. "It looked as though you were like to fall, ma'am," he said, in a strongly English accent.

"I fear I was!" she agreed, looking at him curiously. "Much obliged, sir." She clapped a hand over her mouth. Why on earth was she speaking so oddly? She sounded English herself!

His eyes creased in concern. "Are you unwell, ma'am?"

"I believe I am. Unwell, that is," she said faintly. She tried to take a step and nearly fell again. He quickly circled an arm about her and called something out. As everything went black, she felt herself being lifted…and that was all.

Our greatest glory is not in never falling,
but in rising every time we fall.
Confucius

Chapter 11

At the green light, Margaret and Mr. Russell surged forward with the crowd on 5th Avenue. He continued to dart worried glances toward the library. Margaret was forced to believe her mystery man was trying to avoid the duns. His being in debt was not so very surprising. Well-heeled young gentlemen routinely ran up debts with their tailors or haberdashers. But if he had not the means to pay, or worse, the desire, that would be infinitely deflating. She sighed. *The poor you will have always with you, indeed!*

Once they gained the safety of a side street, he relaxed and seemed more his usual self. She decided she might need to confront him about his condition at some point, but supposed it must be done delicately, if at all. She only needed to ascertain that he was honorable and would not leave a string of debts in his trail as some young men in town were known to do before disappearing after the season.

Passing a bronze plaque on 41st Street, she stopped to read it. "Library Walk. A Celebration of the World's Great Literature." To her delight, she saw a series of similar plaques continuing along the street.

"They each contain a quote by a famous author or poet," Stewart said.

"Oh, let's read them all!" she cried. "There are sure to be Englishmen quoted."

"Or English *ladies*," said Stewart with a sideways smile.

"Yes, of course," she agreed, happily.

But he said, "Let's read them on the way back to the hotel if there's time. If we stop now, we won't have time for the library."

So she only admired the workmanship as they passed, seeing that each was inscribed with its own unique design to accompany the chosen quotation.

"Does Jane Austen have a plaque?" she asked.

Stewart thought for a moment. "Not that I recall." He flashed a lovely smile. "She ought to, though!"

They turned a corner and were now on Park Avenue, a wide, pretty, tree-lined street, replete with occupied outdoor tables and seating. It held a pleasanter atmosphere than on Fifth Avenue. It was so pleasant it seemed a shame to enter the library, but Margaret could not forget the huge reading room lined with innumerable volumes, many of which, in her day, had likely not been written yet!

As they neared the entrance, Mr. Russell came to an abrupt halt. Margaret searched his face to see why and saw him staring with the same dread that he had displayed earlier. He spun about to face her with a look of deep alarm. And then he snatched her into his arms and landed his mouth on hers. Margaret, utterly frozen in shock, did nothing to stop him. She *could* do nothing, so completely suspended in numbed disbelief she was. It could not be true, no, not for the world, that this man was kissing her. *Kissing* her! Not only that remarkable impertinence, but right there in full sight of anyone!

He turned them about slowly so that he no longer faced the entrance, and then withdrew his lips. Desperate eyes met hers.

"Forgive me!" he cried, in a low, haunted tone. "Forgive me! I—I needed to gather my thoughts."

She rubbed her lips together, registering the surprising feeling of his mouth upon hers. Should she give him a combing for his outrageous effrontery? She could give a scold worthy of Clarissa. But instead, a giggle bubbled up. What a lark! She'd been kissed! Wallflower Margaret. Kissed! No matter that Mr. Russell had behaved outrageously, or that to be kissed in such a manner would have sent Papa, had he seen it, to the magistrate demanding justice. No, she'd heard enough of this century to know it was not unusual, and therefore felt as if she'd engaged in a foreign custom to be polite. '*When in Rome,*' you know.

But she did not credit his claim that he needed to gather his thoughts. And she must not let him think he could behave so to her again. "I comprehend these men are after you, but I beg you to remember yourself, sir. I have not ever been subject to kissing before, and—"

"Not ever?" he asked. His eyes widened. "How young are you?"

"I am full eighteen," she said, taking a deep breath, as if that would enhance her age.

"Oh! I'm sorry. I took you for at least twenty-two or three. I really didn't think—my aim was to hide."

"And what is your age, since you have learned mine?"

"Twenty-four."

She motioned lightly with her head toward the black suits who were standing with seeming nonchalance at either side of the door. "These two are searching for you?"

He nodded. "I can't be sure, but I think so."

She made a little smirk. "How much is your debt?"

He blinked. "What's that?"

"How much is it? Your debt. They are your creditors, no doubt?"

He stared at her. "Are you...acting your part?"

She stared back. *Uh-oh. She'd said something wrong.* "What do they want from you?"

He frowned and led her by the arm to a bench facing the street.

She looked expectantly at him. He sighed and ran a hand through his hair. "I did nothing wrong," he said, indignantly. "But they wait for me outside school and my apartment and are asking about my habits—my next-door neighbor told me. They're trying to catch me in places I frequent." He turned troubled eyes to her. "That's why I didn't attend the conference workshops yesterday. I stayed at the library in case they were going to look for me there. I feel safe participating today as they've no doubt discovered as of last night that I hadn't shown up."

"If you did nothing wrong, why not face them and be done with it?" she asked. "You can explain your innocence in the matter—whatever it is—and bring an end to this hide-and-go-seek game."

He grimaced. "It's not that simple." He turned to her, moving sideways in his seat to face her, his eyes earnest. "And it's no game. Here's the thing. I overheard something I shouldn't have. I wish I hadn't. It wasn't on purpose. I wasn't trying to eavesdrop or anything."

"Yes?"

He continued, "I thought I was alone. I went all the way to Queens' Botanical Gardens.

"Do you have a queen, now?" she asked with a smile. Imagine if the 'States had returned to a monarchy!

He stopped, looking at her with troubled eyes. Margaret realized she'd erred again and let out an exaggerated laugh. "A bad joke, sorry," she said.

"Oh." He paused, and then resumed. "Er, in Queens County." Sheepishly he added, "I like gardens." He took a deep breath and continued. "My quarters here in the city are cramped and there's always a racket of noise from the street. I wanted to be alone where I could hear myself, so I found an empty bench and I had printed out my thesis to read it aloud—what I've finished of it, anyway. My plan was to record myself and listen afterward to catch errors the eye can miss. My professor encouraged us to do that."

Margaret's brows furrowed again, but faintly she recalled Claire mentioning how such a thing as the preservation of sounds was possible in the future. How wondrous!

He continued, "I never got to practice. When I was about to start, I heard voices. There was another bench behind some tall bushes that separated us, which I hadn't seen earlier. It was this lawyer and a client. I thought I'd just wait for them to be done. I was tired. I didn't want to find a new spot. I wasn't trying to overhear anything." Again he sighed deeply. He looked away, thinking.

"What did you hear?"

He turned his gaze back to hers. "I heard one man telling another he could not get him any more than half a million for 'taking care of' someone named D'Angelo."

Margaret's eyes widened. "Half a *million* for tending to someone? That sounds utterly fantastical."

He stared a moment, puzzled, and then his brows cleared. "No, not taking care as in tending, not in that way. He meant, *kill* him."

Her hand rushed to her breast. An assassination! She remembered the terrible incident of how poor Mr. Percival had been assassinated—shot—right in the halls of Parliament. She'd only been ten and four at the time, but the gravity of the event had left its mark on her mind.

Stewart continued, "He must have given him something, and then he said, 'After it's done you can collect the rest.' He said it would be delivered in a package inside a mailbox, and he would get the details of where and when at that time. He gave him a phone—I believe he did anyway, from what he said about it, that it was not to be used to call his law firm; he reminded him he should *never* be contacted *there*, and that it was to be used strictly for this business only and then disposed of."

They sat in silence for a minute while the weight of this burden of knowledge impressed itself upon their young shoulders. Margaret said, "But how do they know you heard?"

He shook his head, his lips compressed. "I dropped my phone. They must have heard it fall, and I'm afraid they saw me shutting if off as I picked it up. It was recording and I hadn't even realized it. And then they were around the bush and coming at me before I knew it. I pocketed my phone and ran! I saw one reaching in his pocket and I don't doubt he would have shot me right then and there if not for a group of people who came between us.

"But you got away! How is it they know to look for you?"

He frowned. "I ran so fast I dropped a few pages of my thesis. My name was on every page." He paused and added, "The next day they were outside my building when I left for school. I managed to dodge them—"

Margaret cried, "They want the preserved conversation! If you give them this evidence, they will have no reason to hound you further."

He gave her a sideways look of appreciation. "'Preserved conversation.' I like that. I don't know how you do it. You think very fast." He slumped in his seat and crossed his arms, looking troubled. "In my panic after it happened, I threw the phone away. When they confronted me the next day, I told them what I'd done but I could see they didn't believe me." With a bitter laugh he said, "Why would they? Who would believe I could be so stupid?"

She turned large sympathetic eyes to him. "But you were all a-muddle, in a flummox. We all do things we regret when we are not in our right minds."

The bitterness left his eyes and he took her hand. "Thank you, Miss Margaret." A sparkle returned to his gaze when he added, "I can't tell if it's just because you're British, but I could swear you speak effortlessly like a character in one of Jane's novels."

She gave a shy smile. And then a thought occurred to her. "Can you not search the place where you threw it away?"

He shook his head. "It was a public trash receptacle near my building. When I brought the men there to do exactly that, it had already been emptied."

"Then you must find who emptied it."

"I don't think that's possible." He sighed again. "Even if we found where they dumped it, there would be tons, literally tons, of garbage to wade through. This is New York City."

Another silence fell. Margaret was very moved by Mr. Russell's plight. If only Mr. St. John were here! He would know what to do, surely. She would check at the hotel to see if he'd returned as soon as they got back. He'd reserved the rooms for two nights, she recalled. She asked, "If you threw it away, the evidence is gone. What do they hope to gain from you now?"

He shuddered. "They don't want anything *from* me. They want me to disappear."

She frowned. "They want you to move away?"

He surveyed her a moment. "I can't tell if you're sincere and incredibly naïve, or just—"

"Just what?"

He never finished the thought. Instead, he said, with pained eyes. "They want me dead."

Margaret sat back in shocked silence. "Perhaps we can see the library another time. If they truly want you dead, 'tis far too risky today."

Large blue eyes surveyed hers. "No. I refuse to let them run my life. I'll get us in." Staring at the street he said, "They don't know I'm in costume, or with a woman. We should be able to get past them."

"What blackguards they are!" she cried.

He gave a breath of a laugh. "Blackguards. Right." Admiringly he said, "You ought to do a one-woman show, ad-lib, in some off-off-off Broadway venue. You'd make a ton of money."

"Earn money? Me?" She giggled at the thought. But she wanted to help him with his problem and asked, "Can you not go to a magistrate or judge? Surely some authority must help you in this!"

He gazed at her, the corners of his mouth curved; he lowered his head. "A 'magistrate.' Only you could make me smile about such a situation. But no, I sealed my fate when I threw that phone away. I went to the police, but they said I had nothing but hearsay; I don't even know the name of the man whose voice I recorded. The only name I heard was D'Angelo, and there are hundreds of them in New York City alone." He gave her a little, bitter smile. "Neither side believes me. The good side will do nothing, and the bad side wants me dead." A silence fell while they both reflected on this.

Margaret said, "In that case, I suppose your safest course is indeed to disappear."

He raised his head. "I'm within inches of earning my doctorate! How could I leave now? I have an extended grant for nine months after I'm done with school to search for a job in my field."

Search for a job. A reminder that he was of the working class, though he seemed so gentlemanlike. No one in Margaret's circle would approve of Mr. Russell as a possible love interest for her, no, not even Claire, though she was from this century. Margaret was no heiress and could not afford to marry a man without means, it was simply a fact of life. But the tallit had thrown them together…and this was her adventure…and she liked Mr. Russell.

And that settled it. Though he was not a suitable match for her in the 19th century, she would stand by him and try to help him as best she could here in his. Their futures might not be shared, but nevertheless his life and future mattered.

"Concerning the doctorate," she said gently, "if you lose your life to obtain it, you gain nothing."

He sighed deeply. "I know it."

"Is that why you joined the conference? To disguise yourself in our fashions, er, the fashions of the period?" she asked.

He said, "No, I'm an Austen fan." He looked at her sideways and grinned. "It gave me the idea to dress in costume, though. I've been staying in Queens with a friend, dressed like this all week to disguise myself. You see these?" He took off his spectacles and held them up. "There's no magnification. I don't need them." He put them back on. "And these?" He pointed to his neatly trimmed sideburns. "They're fake." He took two fingers and gave one just the gentlest lift at one corner. Margaret gasped lightly, then giggled. "'Tis a shame. They suit you exceedingly well."

"Thank you," he said, bowing his head with mock solemnity. "I would have added a moustache, but I understand there were precious few of them in the upper class in Jane's day."

"They are dreadfully gauche," she agreed. But she could not forget his dilemma and had a new idea. "Have you considered purchasing a commission? 'Tis doubtful these low characters could reach you within your regiment or on board ship."

He blinked, studying her, and seemed at a loss for words. Finally he said, "If I were already in the military it might have helped, but to enlist now—no, I've no heart for it. It wouldn't do."

"Well, then. Since they expect you not in these clothes, why do we not enter the library and find out what we can to help your case? We'll use an analytical engine!" she added, as if with a momentous idea.

He blinked. "A what?"

She stood up. "An-er-analytical...oh, a lapdog!"

He stood also. "A *what*?"

Margaret's eyes were desperate. "A lap—, no, a com, a com...:

He put his hands on his hips. "A *computer*? A laptop?

"Yes, of course, that's it." She smiled.

With an odd look he said, "Are you playing with me? Is this a game to you?"

Her brow furrowed. "Sir?"

"*That*! Like that. Why are you calling me 'sir'? I get that you enjoy the JASNA thing, being in costume and pretending and all that, but you're going too far."

She swallowed and looked away. "I beg your pardon."

"And like *that*! Really, uh, Margaret. I've been telling you the worst thing that has ever happened to me. My life is in danger. I've been serious. And you can't stop playing games. Shall we just end it here and part ways?"

She looked stricken. The anger in his eyes faltered.

"I am very sorry," she said, carefully. "I am not playing, I assure you!" She looked ready to cry.

His mouth was compressed in a line, but he said, slowly nodding, "I'm going to catch you out of character soon enough, I'm sure of it, and then I hope you'll drop the charade, so I know I'm being taken seriously."

She said, "Mr. Russell—"

"Stewart!" he cried.

She stopped and compressed her lips. It was highly irregular, but so be it. "Stewart, then." But suddenly her eyes blazed at him and she cried, "May I remind you, sir—er, Stewart—at fear of seeming impertinent, that I allowed you to—to—well, your lips touched mine, for an *extended* time! Had I not been serious would I have allowed that?"

He looked amazed, but at these words, looking around quickly to see if anyone was listening, he said, "All right. I'm sorry. You are *different*. I didn't mean to doubt you." He straightened his jacket. "We still have two hours before dinner. Let's get in the library. I'll show you the Pforzheimer Collection."

"And an analyt—er, a com-puter?" she asked, eagerly.

"Are you sure you're eighteen? You look all woman, but at times I feel like I'm with a child."

Margaret blushed with pleasure as much as pique. She looked 'all woman?' She, skinny Margaret? "As I said earlier, I am fully ten and eight, as of February 12th!"

He shook his head. "There's something not right about you."

"I comprehend that well enough." Her eyes sobered. "I've known that all my life." She spoke with such sobriety that he said, "I'm sorry, I shouldn't have said that. Right, let's go." He took her hand, making her look up at him with a return of her usual mischievous sparkle. But as they neared the door, he said, "Wait." He put her hand upon his arm, the way they'd walked earlier. "Don't look away from me until we get inside," he whispered. And in that manner, arms hooked and looking into each other's eyes, they strolled past the black suits and entered the library.

We do not have to become heroes overnight. Just a step at a time,
meeting each thing that comes up, seeing it is not as dreadful as it appeared,
discovering we have the strength to stare it down.
Eleanor Roosevelt

Chapter 12

When Mrs. Grandison came to, she was in a posh
bedchamber. She was to discover that it was one of many guest
chambers that belonged to the huge estate of the man who had
prevented her from falling. He, it turned out, was the Marquess
of Ashworth. The marquess was a widower, and despite the
evident misgivings of his housekeeper (and, unknown to him the
murmurings of disapproving servants), insisted upon allowing
Mrs. Grandison to convalesce in his home. The doctor had been
summoned at once, and a distant female cousin, Miss Latimer,
who arrived the next day to serve as a chaperon. Mrs. Grandison
was installed.

When asked about her relations and where she lived, the
marquess was flummoxed, but not put off, by her answers. That
there was no family of the name Grandison in the society book
mattered little to him. That the direction she gave to her home did
not exist in London, was also overlooked. Mrs. Grandison had
natural dignity, bearing, and was still attractive in her fifties. The
marquess was a lonely soul. This lady had a manner of
conversation that was delightful to him. She spoke with
directness and a disregard of etiquette that was wholly refreshing.
After suffering years of obsequious flattery from women hoping
to catch a marquess for matrimony, her honesty, though
disconcerting at times, was soothing. Providence, he felt, had
dropped this lady into his lap, and he was not one to question God.

For two weeks they dined together in the large dining hall, but
afterward, more intimately, in a parlour. When it turned out that
she was from the future, the marquess, for some reason, had little

difficulty believing it. Little became none after he witnessed her vanish with the tallit right before his eyes. Mrs. Grandison continued coming to the past, always to find herself gowned and coifed to perfection, and in the path of His Lordship.

Once they were married, the tallit disappeared.

Lady Ashworth suspected her new husband had disposed of it for fear lest she disappear to the future one day and leave him bereft. She could accept that. She adored the marquess and had no misgivings about living out the rest of her days in the past with him. Over the course of the ensuing year, despite her dubious heritage, a marchioness cannot long be ignored by society, and Lady Ashworth fit so naturally into the upper class—growing up American gave her an air of assurance and entitlement that society could only recognize as aristocratic—they enjoyed her rather than dismissed her. The marquess, meanwhile, had arranged to leave her his London mansion and a good fortune due to having a wizard of a barrister. The crown received a goodly share, but Lady Ashworth, a fortune; she was not left penniless or homeless, as was the sad fate of many a widow.

Her only regret about having been transposed in time was that she had lost friends such as Miriam. She had one daughter but had effectually lost her simply by telling her honestly about time traveling. After that, her daughter refused to visit, rarely called, and would not let her see her granddaughter. The daughter was Claire's mother.

Claire, of course, had discovered the tallit in her grandmother's abandoned cottage—Lady Ashworth did not know how it got there, but it had brought Claire to St. John and to her. No, she had no wish to leave her life in the past. She hoped, as she searched the offerings at Israeli Rose Jewelry and Gifts, that her stay would be short. She would find another time-travelling shawl so Margaret could return to the past, and all would be well.

She tried not to contemplate the thought that *only* the mysterious tallit maker from Israel could supply what was needed. Nothing about the working of the tallit was rational or sensible, so why couldn't there be another mystical craftsman or seamstress right there in New York? The odds were not in favour of this, as most prayer shawls, she knew, were perfectly normal garments meant for spiritual or traditional rituals. But this wasn't about the odds; it was about the *stakes*. Too much was at stake for there *not* to be another!

Margaret and Stewart headed directly to the Pforzheimer Collection on the third floor, stopping to look cautiously around before entering. No one was in sight, and, to their relief, the room was empty.

Stewart said, "The books I had out yesterday are still here on the table."

He went to one and held it up. Margaret exclaimed happily, "*Evelina* by Mrs. Burney! From memory she recited, "The History of a Young Lady's Entrance into the World." Smiling she added, "I've read it more than once. Have you enjoyed it?"

"I did! How phenomenal that you have! Do you read a lot of early English authors?" He looked delighted as he spoke.

Margaret almost giggled. She'd never thought of her time as 'early.' "I suppose I do," she said.

"I love that!" he cried. Looking at the book he said, "This isn't the novel, though. It's literary criticism about it."

Margaret's face lit with curiosity and she held out a hand for the book. "This I must see. What do later generations make of Mrs. Burney?"

He regarded her with a mystified look but was silent. He took another book from the day before and went to a sofa where he sat and opened it.

She thumbed through the opening pages of hers but said, "The first section of this book is about the authoress. How delicious."

Stewart looked patiently at her. "You can safely speak out of character now... Whether it's a man or a woman, we say 'author.'" He smiled.

Margaret's brow went up. "Do you mean, if I write a book in your time, er, today, I'd be called an author, not an authoress?"

He frowned. "You know you would. You're over-doing it."

Margaret averted her eyes and swallowed. Why had she questioned him? He'd told her the custom—why couldn't she simply take his word for it? To change the subject she asked, "Do you read the novel first, or the critical literature?"

Stewart said, "I like to read the book first and form my own opinions. I come here to read what critics have written to compare notes, so to speak. There is much I could look up online, of course, but not nearly as much as what's here. Besides, I love the solitude of this room."

Margaret raised her eyes from the book. "On what line?"

He stared at her with perplexity. "Excuse me?"

"You said you could look up information on a line."

He frowned severely. "On the internet, of course," he said strongly, his face darkening. Margaret returned hastily to the page before her while she racked her brain for the meaning of 'on line,' or 'internet.' Had St. John ever explained these terms? Suddenly it hit her and she cried, "Oh, the world-wide-web! Of course."

Stewart scowled. "You're overdoing it again. I'm about ready to leave."

Margaret swallowed. "Forgive me. I'm coming it too strong; I see that."

Stewart scowled again. "No, you're not 'coming it too strong,' you're overdoing it! Say it. *I'm overdoing it.*" He stared at her forbiddingly.

Margaret looked stricken. "I-I beg your pardon."

Stewart let out a sigh. "You're hopeless, aren't you?"

Margaret's eyes narrowed and she raised her chin. "Yes, I've always been, I'm afraid."

He shook his head, looking away, and then back at her. "You couldn't have been born speaking like you're from Jane Austen's

England," he said reasonably. "How long have you been doing it? You've made it a habit, that's all, and I, for one, am determined to break you of it."

She looked at him soberly, perhaps sadly. She was silent a long minute and then said only, in a small voice, "Why?"

He put his book down and fell back in his seat, took a deep breath and blew it out. "Why? Well…" He paused, thinking. "Because it's dishonest. You're acting, and that makes me feel like nothing between us is real."

Margaret's brows furrowed. Slowly she went and sat a foot away from him. How she wished she could explain! But if he thought her muddle-headed already, how much more would he think her out of her senses if she tried to explain? It wasn't as if she had the tallit with her and could prove she had come from the past.

Finally, seeing the hopelessness of her predicament, she said, "May we talk, please, about the authors you enjoy most from my century? Er—the 19th century?"

He turned and stared at her, his brows raised. With set lips, he said coldly, "Of course. We'll only talk about that. I can see you aren't going to be transparent with me."

Transparent? Margaret looked at him in alarm. What on earth did that mean? Surely he didn't want her to pretend to be a ghost one could see through? But the meaning dawned on her.

"I assure you, I have been completely honest—" but she stopped, unable to continue. Because she hadn't been completely honest. To be completely honest, she'd have to tell him her history, where she was from, or rather, *when* she was from.

"I have *tried* to be completely honest," she amended.

"And I have tried not to mind your little game," he said. "But frankly, I'm tired of it."

She felt very sorry and lowered her eyes. "You are tired of me, you mean."

He regarded her for long seconds, then frowned. "No, no, I'm not tired of *you*; just the way you keep carrying on, as if you're from another world."

He was clearly out of patience. Again, Margaret racked her brain to change the subject. Going up to a wall of books, she asked, not turning to face him, "Why are Miss Austen's letters and documents not in this library?"

Stewart said, "Perhaps there are facsimiles here…If I get another grant, I hope to go to your country and have a look at the real things." He turned his gaze to the room.

Margaret said flatly, "A grant. From a benefactor."

He looked back at her, frowning. "You never quit." He shook his head. "A grant is money put aside for the express purpose of enabling certain pursuits or endeavors which people apply for to fund those endeavors." *Why was he bothering to explain it to her? She must understand and was only playing dumb for some unknown reason.* But he continued, "You have to qualify to earn a grant. It's not from a simple 'benefactor.'"

When she continued to merely stare at him with large eyes, he picked up his book and began reading. They fell into an uncomfortable silence while each paged through their chosen volume. Margaret was hardly able to take in anything of what she read. Her mind was heavy with the thought that she must convince him she was from the past, for elsewise he thought her ingenuous; but this made her despondent because if she tried to convince him, he would not believe her, and it would no doubt end their already floundering friendship.

Suddenly Stewart said, "Shall we keep reading or go elsewhere?"

She shut her book. "Yes, we have forgot to find help for your cause. There must be some authority who will take it up. Shall we search—on the com-puter?"

He gave her a look of mild disdain, but said, in a practical tone, "I can't see any point in trying. I've done that. Without proof, no one will give me the time of day."

"May I—take a look—at a com-puter, nevertheless?"

In an annoyed tone he said, "It's one word, Margaret. Computer. Not com.puter. One word. How can you be so well read and not able to say a simple word?"

"I beg—"

"And DON'T say, 'I beg your pardon!'" To her stricken look, his face softened. "What do you need to look up? We can do it quickly in the reading room or return another time." He paused, studying her. "That is, if you're staying in New York beyond the conference?"

Margaret gazed at him, her eyes clouding with troubled thoughts. "I am not certain how long I may stay. When I hear from St. John, I'll know better."

He looked at his cellphone, which made Margaret lean to look at it also.

"If we hurry," he said, "We can make it to a breakout session."

Margaret withdrew the folded schedule from her reticule, and they looked over the workshops together. He said, "I'm registered for 'Coded Sexual Indiscretion in Austen's Fiction.' What about you?"

"I'm not registered for anything," she murmured, inwardly scandalized at the title of the session he'd chosen.

"Good! Come with me. I'm sure you'll be allowed to stay." He smirked. "I've not met a lecturer yet who doesn't want as many people as possible to hear their brilliance."

"Afterward, there is a musical performance, 'Jane Austen and Her Music,'" continued Margaret. "We are to procure dinner on our own, apparently, and are encouraged to browse the book tables and other merchandise."

"Sounds great," he said. He came to his feet, and Margaret picked up their stack of books. "We had best return these to their proper shelves."

"Leave it for the librarians."

"Very well. A bibliothecary will replace them correctly," she agreed. But even these benign words seemed to irritate her companion.

"Normally, I'd love that word, 'bibliothecary,'" he said, "but are you never going to quit? Is this something you really can't help doing? I find that hard to believe."

"I am putting you out of countenance," she said, sadly.

"You're quite the Watson," he shot back.

"Excuse me, I am what?"

They were at the door but he paused. "A Watson. You know, Watson and Holmes. You're British and well-read, surely you know them."

"Of course," she said, turning away. Stewart continued to watch her and said, in a carefully nonchalant tone, "Is Holmes still considered the best prime minister you've had?"

She continued looking away, trying to hide the streak of alarm in her breast. "Oh, er, I never pay attention to such things, I'm afraid."

Stewart's voice hardened. "Where ARE you from? Holmes wasn't a prime minister."

She turned with a gasp. "But I am from England!"

"You have some sort of—issue—or problem, then—I don't know what it is, exactly. Is it memory? Do you forget things? How could you not know Sherlock Holmes and Watson?"

Margaret frowned and put a hand to her hip. "I am sure there are a great many things *you* are not cognizant of, but it would hardly cause me to accuse you of amnesia!"

"But *everybody* knows Holmes and Watson, Margaret. Everyone over the age of...five, I suppose."

He had his hand on the knob of the door but waited. Margaret had turned back to the books on the shelf. She ran a hand along the spines, savoring the feel of books. In a bright tone, she said, "Let us discuss things we both enjoy and agree on. We may only have a few more hours in one another's company. And if Mr. St. John has returned for me, I may not even have that long."

"He would make you miss the rest of the conference? Does *he* determine when you come and go? Is he your father?"

"As I said, a relation by marriage, but we travelled here together and must leave that way."

"What about his wife? You said his wife needed him. Does she live here?"

"No. I—I can't explain it right now. All you need understand is that—" her tone grew lower. "That we can enjoy one another's acquaintance for not much longer. Let us be friends, please."

Stewart turned to her and surveyed her thoughtfully. His look softened and he took her hand. "If you can't beat them, join them," he said in a soft tone, more to himself than her. He bowed and took her hand. Louder he said, "Allow me, then, to apologize. I'm sorry I distressed you."

"Spoken like a gentleman," Margaret said approvingly with glowing eyes.

"Thank you, indeed," he returned with an echoing smile. But the smile vanished and his eyes became serious. He drew her gently toward him. With a start, Margaret realized he meant to kiss her again!

"Sir, you forget yourself!" she cried, putting a hand against him to stop him.

Smiling, Stewart said, "You continue to amaze me, the way you play the part of a nineteenth-century virgin, but—"

"But I AM a nineteenth-century virgin!"

Stewart froze, searching her eyes. Did she really believe in her charade? If so, it all made sense now, her continued acting this part. It ought to repel him, and yet it did not. There was something highly appealing about having a nineteenth-century virgin in one's arms. Not that he believed it, but *she* did. She was brilliant, in fact. She'd even forgotten Sherlock Holmes to keep it up. This was admirable, in a way. And a challenge.

He continued to draw her up to him, his eyes locked onto hers. "But you must acknowledge, my sweet 19th-century girl, that it is now the 21st century, and not at all unusual for a man to kiss a girl he likes."

Margaret swallowed. He'd accepted her explanation? Just like that? Or was he humoring her? "But-but-we have only just met."

Taken aback, he said, "In this century, men and women who like each other kiss, even if they've recently met."

"A respectable woman surely would not allow it!"

"His head lowered yet more, his lips hovering near her mouth. "Only if she doesn't like the one who wants to kiss her. Are you so respectable that you can't allow it, or do you not like me?" He leaned away to survey her.

"You are impertinent to ask," she said, but her voice was weaker than before. In truth, she was rather fascinated at his nearness, and the memory of that surprising kiss earlier outdoors was not unpleasant. Besides, if she returned home, what chance that she'd ever be kissed again? She said, beginning to soften to the idea, "If I allow it, you will not think me a lightskirt?"

Stewart thought quickly. Lightskirt meant a loose woman or even a prostitute. He almost lost his composure at this but determined to play along with her delusion and said only, "Never!" His lips came nearer hers.

Margaret's mischievous nature took over. "If I do allow it, you must give your word that you will not construe it as permission for any further impertinences."

Her tone and demeanor assured him she was serious, so he nodded gravely. "I give you my word as a gentleman."

Margaret smiled. Her lips parted and Stewart kissed her, gently, gently, like a curator cradling a Ming vase. Then he drew apart and gazed at her.

Margaret smiled shyly. "I am no genius at the art of kissing," she said, "but I must say I think that was very well done on your part." He chuckled, drew her in again, and this time kissed her with more passion.

Afterward, Margaret immediately stepped away and made for the door.

Stewart, smiling, said only, "Thank you, my dear Margaret."

She found herself overwhelmed suddenly, shocked at her own behavior and such intimacies between them! During the kiss, warmth had diffused through her like butter melting into toast. With cheeks reddened, she could say nothing.

Stewart looked at his watch. "Unless we get a cab, I'm afraid we may miss the workshop. But we can eat and make it to the concert this evening. Let's go!"

Margaret turned to him in real distress with a sudden realization. "I do not have evening dress!"

He seemed confused. "But...what you're wearing is fine."

"This is day dress," she said, as if everyone should know it.

He looked her up and down. "Does anyone know the difference? I love it. C'mon."

But when they exited the room and reached the turn in the corridor to the stairs, Stewart stopped cold, taking her arm. "Quick! Back to the room! It's them—the black suits."

Courage doesn't always roar. Sometimes courage is the quiet voice
at the end of the day saying 'I will try again tomorrow.'
Mary Anne Radmacher

Chapter 13

Stewart and Margaret hurried back to room 319, thankful for carpet runners that muffled their steps. Once inside, Stewart turned and put his back to the door. "What if they're on their way here? They must have figured out what I'm studying by now. Anyone could find out what this room holds."

Margaret looked around frantically, but there was only one tiny, mullioned window. "You are still in costume," she whispered. "They are looking for a man with no sideburns or spectacles."

He nodded gratefully, came to her and drew her by the arm to sit beside him on a reading nook loveseat. Sitting close by her, he said, "If they open the door, we must be…occupied." To her look of confusion, he said, "I'll have to kiss you again."

Margaret's heart jumped but she giggled. "I will endure it." It was very naughty of her, perhaps, but she knew she would more than endure it!

In another minute, they heard the handle of the door click. When it opened, they did not look to see who was there, but with both hearts pounding, were in one another's arms, kissing.

"Hey!" said a voice. They broke the kiss. Both heads turned, Stewart with a look of annoyance. The man peered with narrowed eyes, especially at Stewart. "What's your name?" he asked.

Stewart's head went back as if he were appalled at such poor manners. Margaret thought it a very convincing gesture. "What's it to you? Who are you looking for?" Stewart replied.

The black suit hesitated, glancing at his companion black suit, and then said, "Stewart Russell, a graduate student. Do you know him?"

"Never heard of him," Stewart said heavily. Then, turning back to Margaret, he added. "If you don't mind, we're busy."

Margaret blushed crimson, but it didn't matter. She was back in Stewart's arms and in truth quite liked it there.

"Why are you in *this* room?" the one man persisted.

Stewart broke the kiss again and answered pointedly, "Because we looked inside and saw we could be ALONE here."

The man hesitated. "Why are you dressed like that?"

Stewart sighed heavily as though taxed to the utmost. "We are actors. Do you have a problem with that?"

When the door closed after them, Margaret would have drawn back, but Stewart wrapped her closer in his arms than before and continued the kiss. Finally, their lips drew apart. Margaret gazed at him in a flutter of emotions.

She'd only just met this man. But now, surely, they must be married. That could be the only logical conclusion of sharing such intimacies. But he lived here in the future. And he was a poor orphan of lower class. Her heart and her head were instantly at war.

The rational part of her knew marriage was out of the question. Even were Stewart as rich as Croesus, he was a creature of the present, and she was not. He might not even *wish* to marry her. No, marriage was impossible. Which meant, her behaviour was that of a hoyden!

The thought burned in her heart but yet she could not wholly regret a minute of it.

As they made their way back to the JASNA conference, leisurely, for they were too late already for the session, Margaret tucked her arm within Stewart's. But she noticed he was frowning.

"I was wrong to involve you in my troubles," he said.

"Not at all," said Margaret sincerely. "While 'tis true we are new acquaintances, it does not follow that we cannot exchange a confidence, particularly when one is dealing with such dire a matter as you are."

He looked at her pensively. "You really can't help it, I see that."

Margaret sighed. He thought her addle-brained and insincere. If only she could mimic his manner of speech! Or, better yet, prove that she really was from the past, from the time when such literature as he enjoyed studying was still being written. A safer time, for that matter, when mysterious barristers weren't sending men to kill you for overhearing things. And then it struck her. Her day *was* safe; safer for Stewart than this time. If only she could get him there! An arrow of hope shot through her. If he came to the past, a future together for them might be possible after all! But then her heart sank, for she was unable to get even herself back. And St. John hadn't been able to. How could she hope to help him escape his present danger?

He led her around a woman with two Dobermans on leads, and another lady riding a bicycle with a large basket in the back. Margaret stared at the bicycle, even stopping to look back as the rider grew smaller in the distance and disappeared, swallowed by pedestrians.

"Lud!" she exclaimed. "What an improvement in design!" Belatedly she realized she should not have spoken her thought aloud, but it was too late. She gave Stewart a weak smile, hoping he'd paid no attention. Happily, he was so caught up in his thoughts he hadn't noticed.

"The problem, you see," he went on, still enveloped in his dark cloud of worry, "is that involving you puts you in danger too. I should have thought of that from the start."

"Do not fear on that head," she cried, scornfully. "Soon enough, St. John will be back and we'll both vanish from New York, I assure you!" She turned large eyes to him. "If only you were to come with me! You should be safe where I live."

He smiled wanly. "Thank you for the thought, but you underestimate these black suits and what lengths they'll go to, to silence me once and for all. Were I to go to Africa, they'd find me. Anywhere on this planet, they'll find me." He sounded dead sure.

"But they can't find you in the past," she said gently. His eyes swung to hers and stayed there, locked in uncertainty.

Stewart couldn't help worrying that Margaret was out of her mind. He'd found her speech and manners delightful at first, intriguing. Then, they became annoying because he knew they must be an act. Now he realized that she could not seem to help behaving and speaking as if she were from the early 19th century because, incredibly, she believed she was! *Just his luck.* Bad enough, he'd overheard something he shouldn't have. Then, equally disastrous, he'd panicked and been a fool and thrown away the evidence. Now, after all that, he had to meet a lovely and intelligent young woman who turned out to be severely deluded at best. Insane, at worst.

"I see it all plain, now," she said, breaking their gaze and continuing to walk. "St. John said the tallit—that's the prayer shawl that takes us through time, you see—he said it had a purpose in stranding us here." She proceeded to speak quickly, explaining the series of events that had brought her to New York, and even telling how it all started with her Great Aunt Ashworth, who was Mrs. Grandison from Maine before she'd come to the past. She explained how Claire had found the shawl in her grandmother's home, Dove Cottage, where she and St. John had *thought* they were to visit. She told how they had become stranded, that even St. John had left and so she was alone. Finally, she told him how, if they could manage to both get back to her time, he would be forever safe from the dastards who were after him.

As she spoke, his countenance only grew darker.

"Please. Stop." He looked at her grimly. "I've heard that people can invent the most extraordinary circumstances to support their delusions but this is—too much." Carefully, he continued, "I believe that *you believe* you are from the past, and so I won't try to dissuade you."

But Margaret had been thinking. She saw his eyes darken as she spoke and knew that only something significant could convince him. "My elder sister can prove it to you," she said, quietly. "My sister is the famous author, Clarissa Channing."

"The historical romance novelist?" he asked, his brows raised. "You know her?"

"She is my sister. I told St. John I wanted to see her, because she came here to the future three years ago, the same time Claire switched places with her and came to our time to marry St. John."

He shook his head. "This is more…invention." His eyes were filled with regret. "It's a delusion, dear Margaret."

"No! Upon my word! If you know of her, you must know she is famous for writing such details of our time period as no other author has. This is why she can do that—she is FROM the past, as I am. You must help find her, she has apartments here; overlooking a huge park, I believe?" She remembered hearing St. John mention that once.

He was still watching her warily. Doubtfully he said, "She's your sister and you don't know where she lives?"

"I have not been to the future before! And I haven't laid eyes on her since she left our time, 1816 it was then, to come here. But I distinctly recall that Mr. St. John said she has a lovely prospect of a large park."

Stewart looked doubtful but suggested, "Central Park?"

"No doubt that is it!" Margaret replied, vastly relieved. "If we can use an analytical—I mean a com-computer, we can find her and show up at her door and she will confirm everything I've told you."

He looked away. Of course, her story would be foolproof. There was no way they could locate a famous author and just show up at her door. She'd live in a locked building, first of all, and they'd be denied access by the security guard. But he had a thought: if they could locate the building, he could show Margaret her delusion when Ms. Channing denied knowing any Margaret Andrews. Only it would have to wait. He did not want to miss anything more of the conference, as he'd blown almost all of it already.

He assured her they would search for her sister as soon as their schedule permitted. He felt badly for humoring her, but what else could he do? Agree that she had come 200 years into the future by means of a—a *shawl*, of all things! Like Aladdin's magic carpet on steroids? No, he had no recourse but to appear to go along with her.

They ate at a sidewalk café and then joined the JASNA group in a large conference room of the hotel for "Jane Austen and Her Music." To Stewart, it was entertaining and enlightening. To Margaret, the music was thoroughly enjoyable, and the little talk about the authoress beforehand, fascinating. She still marveled at the evident adoration of an authoress of her day, astonished at the many little details they knew of her life. For some reason, the things they did *not* know for certain, such as what Miss Austen really looked like, or why she broke off her one engagement, she found just as intriguing. She was terribly saddened that the lady had died in 1817, two years earlier in her day, marveling that she did not recall any notice of the event.

She and Stewart had little chance to speak and parted ways shortly afterward. He was not headed to his apartment, he said, but to Long Island, adding that the trip by the "LIRR" would take some time and so he must be off. Seeing her questioning look, he added, "The Long Island Railroad. My friend lives right off the Massapequa stop."

They agreed to meet the following day in the morning, and agreed on the sessions they'd attend together. Afterward, it was a "free" day for shopping and sightseeing, or, if one wished, for period dance lessons to be ready for the highlight of the conference, a gala ball that evening. Before the ball, was a scheduled promenade, for which everyone was admonished to wear their period clothing.

He leaned in to kiss her, but Margaret swiftly interjected her hand at him, suddenly reverting to the mores of her day and too embarrassed to allow a kiss in public. Stewart froze momentarily, but then bowed and kissed her hand quite satisfactorily.

"Wait!" she exclaimed. "Would you mind accompanying me to my door?"

He raised a brow. "Not at all."

On the 15th floor, Margaret eagerly knocked at Mr. St. John's door, but there was no answer.

"He has a room here, even though he's not using it?" Stewart asked.

She turned to him. "Remember, he went back to 1819, rather unexpectedly. I think Claire must have had their child by now, or he would have returned for me." Her look became wistful. "I am terribly sorry to ask you this, but without my maid, getting undressed is incredibly difficult." She was removing her spencer as she spoke. Stewart looked hastily around.

"Shouldn't we go inside, first?"

"Oh, there's no need," she said, innocently. "I only require your assistance undoing the buttons on my bodice." She turned so he faced her back. "Do you see?" she asked.

Stewart was silent, putting his hand gingerly to the fabric of her dress.

"Your gown is truly lovely," he murmured. His hand wandered up to caress the curls at the back of her neck. "*You* are truly lovely."

"Sir—Stewart," she said reprovingly, though trying not to smile. "My buttons, if you please. If you will undo the top four, I should be able to manage the rest."

He said, "Of course." As he started the task, he said, "There's one that wasn't closed, you know."

"I could not reach it," she said.

When he'd done more than four, she turned, holding the dress up carefully. "Thank you. I don't know how women manage in this century without a maid."

He bit his lip. "I'll be your maid anytime." He leaned in toward her, making Margaret turn hurriedly to slip the card into the lock of her door and open it. "Thank you!" she said, and would have disappeared inside, but he said, "Wait."

Still facing the door, she turned only her head. He was looking intently into her eyes. He moved forward and leaned his head in, and Margaret was suddenly mesmerized, welcoming his nearness, his touch. The world was a lonely place but for Stewart. He kissed her gently, gently. She felt warmth go through her body, through her heart and soul, and almost turned around but would not. *Her gown was half undone. This must end.*

"Margaret," he said soberly. "Think for a moment. When did you first decide you were from the past?"

She took a breath. He still thought her muddle-headed. "I never did think of myself as being from the past. Not until I got here in the future."

"And when was that?"

"Yesterday. Shortly before we saw you in the library."

He frowned. "You came from the past to go to a library?"

She said patiently, still holding her gown in one hand, "We came to see Clarissa. My sister, as I told you earlier." She saw it was hopeless for the time being; he would never believe her without further proof. "If we find her tomorrow, you will believe me." She paused, surveying him sadly. "I am very tired, Stewart. Good night!" And with that, she went in and closed the door behind her.

To her closed door, Stewart said in a low, unsmiling voice, "Goodnight. Dear, deluded, Margaret."

Inside the room, Margaret was soon curled up in bed, stripped of all but her chemise. As she lay there, she realized her head ached. How exhausting a day in the 21st century was! The constant noise, maneuvering through foot traffic, the endless sights, signs, and equipages in the streets—the enormous coaches—all of it had taken its toll. Even Mr. Russell—Stewart—he'd kissed her! And more than once! And his life was in peril! Really, it had been an enormous day. Learning about Miss Austen, the new customs at lunch and elsewhere—she felt as though she'd lived there for a week already.

And suddenly it felt like a very long time since she'd seen Mr. St. John or been home. And then she remembered that King George would die soon. Poor, afflicted king! Perhaps it was a mercy, to end his misery. She thought of Papa, and even Denny and the other servants, and homesickness assailed her powerfully.

She tried to ward it off by focusing on Stewart. She must find Clarissa to help prove to him that she wasn't fit for a madhouse, that she really was from the past. Soon she was nodding off, however, and then she heard someone try to open her door. In horror, she stared at it. Had an unsavory person obtained a key card?

"Open up, it's me."

Mr. St. John! A flood of relief sent her running to open it, so overjoyed she thought not about wearing only her chemise. But when she saw St. John, all her earlier bravado vanished like a child braving a stormy night only to collapse into tears the moment Mother appeared in the doorway. "You left me here!" she cried.

"Not willingly. Deepest apologies, dear Margaret." He made his way in, saying, "We cannot determine why, but the tallit has weakened in that it only works when the halves are together now."

"We—you and Claire; or did you speak to my great aunt Ashworth?"

"Lady Ashworth is equally befuddled but came to the future to secure a new shawl for your sake, so you may return home."

Margaret's heart flooded with relief but then sank again nearly as quickly. Lady Ashworth would surely find a working shawl so that she, Margaret, could return home; this thought was a comfort.

But could she find two so that Stewart might escape to the past also? How could Margaret leave him behind when he was in such peril of his life? Also, if Lady Ashworth *and* St. John were here in the present—but wait. How could they be, if only one was able to travel now with the tallit? She stared at him disconsolately. "Do you mean my great aunt is here now?"

He nodded. "She is."

Margaret's lips pursed. "But if that is the case... how did *you* get here?"

He gave her an inscrutable look, and then, to her horror, the image of St. John began fading, fading, first becoming ghost-like, and then dissipating into nothingness. The last time he'd vanished on her, it had happened instantly, in a second. This gradual disappearing was frighteningly similar to a dream...

But he was gone. Again. "No-o-o-o!" Margaret screamed.

And woke herself. It *was* a dream.

Chapter 14

The law offices of Yeltsin, Yeltsin, and Brock, Madison Ave, NYC

The junior partner of the firm, young Mr. Mikhail Yeltsin, checked his cell phone the moment it buzzed. The caller was Mr. Black, and he answered.

The junior Mr. Yeltsin was in his early forties but was always referred to as young to differentiate him from the elder Mr. Yeltsin, his father and senior partner of the firm. He raked a hand through prematurely greying hair before taking the call.

"Well? Are we done?"

"No, sir. "

He gripped the phone involuntarily. "Why not?" He listened for a minute and then said, "Look, Black, you have his name. You have his picture. You have his University and his address. Have men at each location and wait for him. He'll have to show up sooner or later. And when he does, take care of him."

He listened again and then said, "Not another cent if you don't come through soon! I need this out of my life. Clean, the way we discussed. No messes left behind."

He ended the call but swiveled his chair to face the view of New York from his 39th floor office window. If his father ever caught wind of the gaffe he'd made in letting someone overhear his compromising conversation, he'd be furious. He might even oust him from the firm. He was already on rocky ground with dear old dad for mishandling a multi-million account that cost them big. And it wasn't the first time.

He couldn't afford to let an insignificant graduate student implicate him in another mess, something more dire than financial bungling. Discovery could mean prison.

If it meant cornering the boy himself, he wasn't about to let that happen.

The following day upon rising, Margaret hurried to dress, happy her short stays were laced in front and easily accessible. She was pleasantly shocked to discover new attire beside her own walking dress where it hung in the little wardrobe. There was a lovely, modish *jonquille* dress with a triple-ruffed hem, laced and edged. The long sleeves were topped with separate matching laced puffs that continued along an attached bodice, and the sleeves, she saw to her delight, were removable, meaning the gown would be suitable for evening wear to the ball!

She thanked heaven for the provisions, for there was also a very elegant cap with curling feathers for the ball, as well as a darling hat of white straw with gauze ribbons and white flowers for day wear. There were gloves, satin slippers, and, in place of her spencer, she now had a lined pelisse with braided trim and frog fastenings. How marvelous! Had she not recalled a similar thing happening to Claire and Clarissa, whose clothing often appeared to match the need when they traveled in time, Margaret would have suspected a fairy godmother had come during the night to place it there.

When she met up with Stewart near the coffee urns, she saw he too had changed clothes, at least his tailcoat, which was now a close-fitting style with cuffs and a fur collar. He complimented her prettily for her outfit, and Margaret fancied they made a respectable-looking pair who would bring no shame to the promenade along 5th Avenue that afternoon. The promenade was both to advertise the existence of the organization and for sheer fun, Stewart assured her. He told her, too, that JASNA members took great time and expense to have their glittering Regency attire crafted, and enjoyed displaying their gowns and bonnets, or waistcoats and breeches. Margaret had seen that some even curled their hair in modish styles, or included parasols, muffs, or scarves, as well as feathers and sundry other adornments to their attire.

Having just come from 1819, she found it amusing that the gowns were a startling array of fashions from different years. Some resembled what her mother might have worn in 1800! She was no dandyess, had never been overly concerned with modishness, but was surprised to recognize how old-fashioned some of the dresses were. In her day, to appear in anything less than the latest modes for an upper-class social event was to invite withering glances and scorn, not to mention gossip. The company here strutted confidently along in blitheful unconcern—and what was the "latest" fashion of her day to them, anyway? Only *she* considered 1819 the standard. She supposed, moreover, the concern now was for the general era of her day, not a particular fashion of a particular year.

The longest part of the day passed quickly between breakout sessions that she and Stewart attended together, lunch on their own, and a browse through the "Regency Emporium," of the conference. The tight schedule left Margaret little time to fret over being stuck in the present, or how she would convince Stewart she wasn't hare-brained, or how she could help him escape his danger for the past. She still hoped to find Clarissa and to finally get her hands upon a com-puter. She hadn't forgot her quest.

The company followed their promenade guides like spring chicks trailing a mother hen. Feathers bobbed, shawls flapped in sudden gusts of breezes that came bowling down the avenue, curls flew out of place, and men tipped their hats at female passersby with their heads against the wind, who smiled. Margaret was thankful for her pelisse, and Stewart his tailcoat.

As they conversed lightly, and with her worries cast aside for the time being, she was so engrossed in enjoying her companion's banter that she failed to notice when they passed a television news crew covering the event with cameras. Not that she would have recognized the activity or what they were doing. Stewart, however, did; he saw them at the last minute and hurriedly looked away lest they caught his face and aired it. Even with spectacles and fake sideburns, he shuddered to think he might be recognized. He said nothing to Margaret about the news crew.

She enjoyed being upon his arm and was ready to throw herself wholeheartedly into what might be her last evening with Stewart. The conference would end by the following afternoon. She trusted that St. John would return by then. She wished with all her heart that if he did, he would have found not only a way home for the two of them, but for Stewart also. He had to do something to stay safe. But as she was helpless to offer him a solution, she must try to focus only on the here and now.

Let the tallit, in its Divine way, do the worrying. Or, as the vicar of her church, Mr. Reynolds, would say, "Let God be God."

Back at the Israeli Rose Store, Lady Ashworth approached a sales clerk behind a counter. He took in her 19th century gown, shawl, and bonnet in a quick glance. Without a word about them, he said politely, "May I help you?"

Her ladyship explained that she was looking for hand-crafted tallits. He pursed his lips and said haughtily, "We sell prayer shawls that are manufactured to the strictest rabbinical standards, using only pure, unblemished wool. More New York rabbis choose us over any other distributor in the city, and we are the favorite source for our Hasidim brethren all over the country."

Lady Ashworth said diplomatically, "And very fine specimens you have, I'm sure; but you see, I'm looking for one like this." She drew the tallit from about her shoulders and held it out for him to examine— "which I purchased from a street market in Israel."

He took the shawl and frowned. "It's been torn. Is that why you want a new one?"

"Not exactly."

He examined it again and said, "We have none like this."

"I didn't expect you would," she said, hiding her disappointment. With sudden inspiration she continued, "But you may know of the woman who makes and sells them. She is highly particular regarding who she sells her shawls to. This shawl, she insisted, was only for me." As she spoke, the clerk's eyes had narrowed, but in such a way to give Lady Ashworth the impression that he knew of whom she spoke.

"Do you know her?" she asked bluntly.

He averted his eyes and began rearranging the rings in a glass box before him. "No."

"But you've heard of her, have you not?" Lady Ashworth demanded imperiously. As a marchioness, she had grown accustomed to demanding answers from the servant class and brooked no game-playing or subterfuges.

He looked at her quickly. "I don't know for sure. I may have."

On an impulse, her ladyship opened her reticule. It had appeared on her arm when she arrived, and, with little surprise, she saw it held coins. Looking sagely at the man, she drew forth a beautiful new gold sovereign, and placed it gently on the counter.

The man stared at it. Slowly he picked it up and examined it. He looked at her with new eyes and said, "I think I may be able to help you." He swallowed. "Let me make some inquiries. I'll be right back." But he stopped and turned back to say. "I'd be happy to give you what this is worth in gold weight, if you'll take it."

"Of course not," she replied huffily. "I know it's worth far more today than that."

"What year?" he asked, peering at the coin to see if it was inscribed.

"1819," she said with great satisfaction.

"The Regency," he said nodding, looking again at her spencer and bonnet, this time with more interest. But his eyes returned to the sovereign and stayed glued there as he asked, slowly, "If I find what you're looking for…is it worth this coin?"

She nodded, wishing she had produced only a newly minted silver crown, still of great value now, though less than the sovereign. But what did it matter? The important thing was to get Margaret back to the past. "It is."

With a perfunctory nod, he disappeared into a curtained doorway.

When he'd gone, Lady Ashworth noticed a TV high on the wall to her right. The sound was turned low, which is why she hadn't heard it sooner, but she could tell it was a news broadcast. To her amazement, the camera showed a parade of people in early 19th-century clothing! She leaned in to hear, struck by the odd happenstance of seeing this in 21st century New York. And then suddenly she gripped the countertop, gawping at the screen. There, right before her eyes, was Miss Margaret! The clerk came back through the curtain just then and started to say something, but she held out an imperious arm and shushed him immediately.

A bystander on camera was asked what they thought of the promenade. The young woman flipped her hair behind a shoulder. "Oh! There's no place like New York to see anything in the world!" The anchor turned to the camera. "That's for sure. The Jane Austen Society isn't the only place to see colorful costumes today in New York." The camera switched quickly to Shakespearean actors in Central Park, and then to Polish dancers in a club wearing traditional folk costume. Lady Ashworth turned to the sales clerk. "This Jane Austen Society gathering," she said. "Do you know where they're located?"

"I'm sorry, I don't," he said, "but you can find it on the internet." He gave a start, looking at her doubtfully as if remembering that this time-traveling Regencian might not comprehend what he meant. He started to say, "I mean—"

"I know the internet," she assured him. "Now, about the shawl…"

Since Lady Ashworth's disappearance with the tallit, St. John had done his best to ignore the rankling thought of having left Miss

Margaret in the future seeing that his only means of getting back to her was gone. He tried to push aside all worries about what the young woman might be up to or what difficulties she might encounter because the possibilities plagued him. He dared only entertain thoughts of Lady Ashworth and her doings. Yet with each passing hour, his annoyance at that lady grew. Unless she returned with a second shawl, he would comb her over for the delay she'd caused.

Claire was resting, and as yet there was no return of the early birth pangs. They'd breakfasted together against Mr. Wickford's orders, for he had told Claire that she was to partake of liquids only. But Claire remembered how the physicians of poor Princess Charlotte, the Regent's daughter, had starved her for days before her labor which only weakened her, contributing to her tragic death. She ate, therefore, but lightly, for too much food was probably as detrimental as too little.

St. John took care of a few small matters in his office, opened a lower drawer of his desk and came upon a small stack of newly minted crowns. He thought of Margaret, happy to know she had the credit card. He turned the shiny bright coins over in his hand and pocketed a few. Little chance he'd get back to Margaret with them, but if he did, they'd be worth a fortune in the future. And it might take that to discover their way back home.

After the promenade and a short rest period, it was time for the ball. Margaret had checked for Mr. St. John's return at every opportunity, but as she prepared for the evening, she could not be sorry at his absence for it meant she could go to the ball. She would stand up with Stewart!

Margaret had studied dancing as well as any other young lady in the upper class and knew the steps backward and forward. But she'd only just come of age and had never been asked to stand up with a gentleman upon a dance floor other than her dancing instructor.

As directions were given for the first dance, a minuet, Stewart admitted, "I was miserable at it during the dance workshop." He looked regretfully at Margaret. "And you weren't there at all. I'm afraid we'll have to sit out the dancing."

Margaret smiled impishly. "Speak only for yourself. I shall enjoy dancing, I assure you!"

"Do you know this dance?" he asked in surprise. Her quelling look startled him. He thought worriedly that she could not know the dance, that her illusion of knowing it was soon to render her ridiculous, and he only hoped she wouldn't make too much of a fool of herself.

For Margaret, though she was very disappointed not to dance with Stewart, finding a different partner proved to be a challenge. Most people were there in pairs. Finally, a middle-aged gentleman, seeing Margaret waiting expectantly at the outskirts of the floor, went and bowed before her and asked, with perfect charm, to have the honour of her hand for the dance. His companion, a lady friend, he explained, chose not to stand up.

The music began and Stewart watched anxiously. There were, of course, giggles and hasty corrections on the part of many a dancer. But not by Margaret. To his amazement, she knew every step perfectly. She danced, in fact, with elegance, even joy, meeting his eyes now and again with an impishly triumphant smile. By the second dance, people were noticing and making way for her and her partner, who, though not perfectly in step, was proficient enough to make them, as a pair, look graceful and practiced.

Stewart was relieved, and yet something nagged at him. It was beginning to give him a headache. How did she know the steps so well? He was tempted to believe her crazy claim to be from the past! But no, to believe that would make him crazy, too! But her dancing, her speech, her naivete...he sighed deeply and sank back in his chair.

Margaret was enjoying the ball more than she'd expected to. She was a success! The admiring looks from others, the way they made room for her and her partner, was the sort of experience she'd never dreamed of! Only beautiful, popular ladies garnered such attention in her day. Whether because she was famous as a bluestocking, or because she had always considered herself unattractive, the sudden admiration was intoxicating.

How glad she was now, that her father had engaged Mr. Santoni, an Italian dance master of the first water. How glad now, for his exaction, his correction, of the smallest deviation from the steps or anything considered less than graceful. Margaret deplored pianoforte lessons and had little talent at the easel. So, while members of the *ton* might not seek out her hand for the dance floor, still she was a proficient at the dance. She saw Stewart watching her and smiled with tremulous pride. Was he admiring her also? Heady thought! But how much more fun it would be if he had learned the steps. She determined, that if given sufficient time, she would teach him.

Chapter 15

Lady Ashworth wasn't the only interested party watching the news that night. Margaret's sister Clarissa, now going by Clarissa Channing, regency romance author, had also watched from her ritzy apartment on Central Park West. She'd been leisurely paging through "People Magazine," enjoying what she felt was a much-deserved break. Adam, her husband, was up at the lodge in Maine, and having submitted her most recent book to her publisher, she had her feet up, ready to enjoy a relaxing evening. She'd sent her cook home and had just taken a sip of wine when the coverage of the JASNA promenade began.

At sight of her sister, Clarissa sat up suddenly, sputtering wine as she exclaimed, "Margaret?!"

Back at the Israeli Rose, when the clerk returned from a back room, Lady Ashworth was elated to find that he not only had written down the whereabouts of the mysterious tallit-maker but that she operated a shop right there in New York! *Freida* was her name, he said, spelling it carefully, and handed her ladyship a slip of paper with the shop's street address.

"She keeps uncertain hours, but there's a phone number if you care to call or text first." He glanced at the paper. "No website, though."

Lady Ashworth had no way of knowing whether this young man was reliable or if he was trying to bamboozle her to gain the sovereign. She thanked him, but said, "If your information is not accurate, rest assured I'll be back for my sovereign."

He stared at her disdainfully. "I can't guarantee that Freida will have what you need, but we're certain she is the lady you're looking for. Our information is correct."

"I hope it 'tis," she said, "for I should hate to have need to bring you to 1819 to see you thrown into Newgate as a swindler!" This was an utterly empty threat, of course, as at present she had no way of bringing anyone to the past save herself. But Lady Ashworth felt her time and trouble were valuable and was loathe to have either wasted. Especially under the current distressing situation with Margaret.

The clerk's eyes widened. "There'll be no need for that. As I said, this is the lady you're seeking, though whether she can help you or not, we cannot guarantee." An older man came out from the back through the curtain at that point, and sized up Lady Ashworth curiously, taking in her spencer, bonnet, and the shawl.

"Trust us," he said simply. "Freida is one-of-a-kind. As soon as I heard what you were looking for, I knew it had to be her." He paused. "I've never believed the rumors about her shawls," he added, 'but we've all heard them."

Lady Ashworth nodded regally. "Well, sir. Believe what you will." She smiled coyly at him. "Much obliged."

"No, madam," said he, holding up the sovereign and admiring it as it glinted in the light, "We, I can assure you, are much obliged."

Lady Ashworth read the address on the slip of paper. "But how do I find this place?"

"It's not far from here, a few blocks," he said. "But to be safe, you could take a taxi."

She nodded and turned to go but remembered she had only British money. Turning back, she said, "I suppose you can give me taxi fare from what that sovereign is worth to you?"

In minutes, Lady Ashworth left the shop with a wad of reassuring American bills in her reticule. She was feeling much encouraged, for if Freida was indeed the strange woman who had furnished her with the original shawl, her business, she felt, could be short. Though she would have liked to sit and rest with perhaps a cup of tea, she decided there was no time to lose. She must find Freida, obtain another shawl, and then return to St. John and let him find Margaret and bring her home. If St. John could not come on account of Claire's lying-in, thanks to the news broadcast, Lady Ashworth had a good clue as to that young woman's whereabouts.

But her first order of business was getting the shawl. What a blessing it was to find that her mysterious tallit-maker was right there in New York City! Now it made sense that they'd arrived there instead of Maine. It would have been easier all around if the shawl had simply worked as it always had in the past, but at least they had found the means to procure another. All she had to do was hire a hansom, er, a taxi, and find the lady's shop.

After the ball that evening, and after Stewart sheepishly complimented Margaret's dancing, they agreed to meet the next morning, the final day of the conference. He reminded her that he was off to his friends' house on Long Island to avoid the black suits, and her eyes clouded.

"If I had Mr. St. John's key card, you could use his room, but I fear he took it with him."

Stewart rubbed his chin. "It would save me a great deal of commuting to borrow the room—if you don't think he'd mind?"

"Why should he?" She gave an impish grin. "I am the one with the card of credit that is paying for it."

He stared at her a moment and then said, "The credit card is *yours?*" He asked this rather sharply, for to his mind, if Margaret had a credit card, she would of course have an income, a job no doubt, and above all a very 21st Century residence.

"It belongs to Clarissa, my elder sister."

His eyes widened. "May I see it?"

Margaret drew the card from her reticule and handed it over. To his astonishment, the name on the card was Clarissa Channing! He looked back up at her with surprise and returned the card. There had to be an explanation. Perhaps she really was Miss Channing's sister, only the crazy story of coming from the past was an invention. Or maybe the card was part of the hoax or delusion.

"If the card's good, we should be able to get another key for the room."

"Of course, it's good," Margaret said, smiling. "My sister is enormously wealthy in this day and age, which is why she chose to stay here, no doubt. At home, you must know, we have no inheritance, as my father's fortune must pass to the nearest male heir." She made a grimace. "My cousin, Charles Hartley, a virtual stranger to us all."

He nodded sagely, remembering that 19th century English law favored male primogeniture to the detriment of many a woman. He was torn between admiration and distress; admiration, because most people (saving Austen fans) were not aware of the workings of primogeniture, and distress because it was, sadly, part of her delusion.

"Let us see if we can get you a key-card," she said, brightly.

Stewart followed her and they made their way to the front desk, where Margaret, more confident now, explained that Mr. St. John had misplaced his "room card" and a new one was needed.

"You lost your key, earlier, didn't you?"

"I am afraid so," she acknowledged.

He asked for identification, which Margaret took great umbrage at, reminding the man that the room was in her name (though it was in Clarissa's name, really) and that ought to suffice him. She delivered this message while handing him the credit card.

"May I see your driver's license?" he asked.

Margaret hesitated for only a moment. Without revealing that she had no idea what he was asking for, she replied smoothly, "I have nothing with me, saving what I needed for dinner."

Stewart, tempted to jump in a dozen times already, saw she was holding her own and decided that staying out of it was best. When the clerk still looked doubtful, Margaret exclaimed, "Surely, you can see we are part of the JASNA conference!" He accepted defeat at that, for he *could* see. Who else would wear such costumes? A new card was produced and handed over.

When they reached their rooms, Margaret stopped in consternation at her door. Music was emanating from inside. "What is that?" she asked. "A-a-sound recording?"

Stewart grimaced but made no answer. He was weary of this. How he wished he could make her stop pretending!

But Margaret's expression lightened into a smile. "Mr. St. John must have returned!" She opened the door with her card and pushed it open, stopping to take Stewart's arm to pull him along with her. "Come and let me present you!"

Stewart's frown deepened, but he allowed himself to be pulled inside the room. But they'd only gone a few steps when Margaret, so eager a moment earlier, froze.

There, lounging elegantly atop the bed, was a smiling Clarissa. "Hello, dear sister," she said. She held out a device and pressed it, making the noise from a large screen (the source of the sounds) stop immediately.

"So glad I've found you." Clarissa smiled again.

Margaret at first had stared at her dumb in shock, but now moved into the room. She and Clarissa had never been affectionate, but to see her after three years brought a surprising smile to her heart. This, despite her looking markedly changed from the Clarissa of her memory, for her fine pale complexion was now ruddy, even tanned like a farmhand's! And she had lost her British manner of speech. For a moment Margaret felt unsettled, it was so surprising, like seeing an opposite double of her sister. But as she drew closer she saw it was, indeed, her attractive, dark-haired sibling.

"Clarissa!" she cried, more effusively than she meant to. "How good to see you!" Then, self-consciously, she motioned Stewart forward. "May I present my new acquaintance"—she began, only to have Clarissa giggle.

"We don't 'present' people, we only introduce them," she explained, though it does my heart good to hear you speak in the old way!

Stewart cringed, feeling these words would only encourage Margaret's delusion.

Clarissa turned to him. "Hello, friend. I am Margaret's sister, Clarissa."

Stewart resisted the urge to swallow. "Stewart Russell. Pleased to meet you. I've read one of your books. It was quite good."

Margaret felt a twinge of jealousy. She'd imagined the idea of writing books here in the future too, after learning how successful her sister was. She could write with just as many authentic details as Clarissa, and probably devise better plots to boot! But she'd sooner take on a hungry lion than draw the teeth of Clarissa. And teeth would be sharpened, she knew, if she dared to compete in her sister's book market. Besides which, Maragret had to return home for Papa.

"You've read only one of them?" Clarissa inquired of Stewart with a smile that belied her miffed tone.

"I'm afraid so."

"Which one did you read?"

"No, no, no, you can talk of your books later!" Margaret cried. "I must know—how did you find me, and where is Mr. St. John?"

Clarissa said, "Yes, where is St. John? I haven't seen him in months."

And suddenly Margaret could hardly talk fast enough. Clarissa was the only person in the 21st century—literally, in the world just then—who could completely understand her plight, who might even be of help. The relief she felt was surprisingly deep.

She reached the point where St. John vanished with the tallit. "He went back without me—when he disappeared, I saw the shawl can work only for one person, now. I've been stuck here waiting for him to come back." She paused, remembering she'd quite enjoyed the wait. "I've been able to explore the library with Stewart's help, and at the hotel they—they mistook me as part of a conference for one of our authoresses!" She grinned. "Miss Jane Austen. Do you believe it?"

"Oh, it's wonderful," Clarissa said dismissively. She hoped that one day there would be conferences for her and her books.

"Tell me again why you came to New York?" she asked. And Margaret went through the story all over again, this time with more detail, while Stewart, listening, went and sat down. His legs were going a little weak, actually. If this was a hoax, it was incredibly intricate, and Clarissa Channing was in on it. And it had to be a hoax. *It had to be!*

"Now tell me, how did you find me?" asked Margaret, going to sit gingerly upon the edge of the bed after she'd finished her story.

Clarissa smiled. "I knew St. John must use my credit card and therefore my name. After I saw you in the promenade on TV—"

"You saw me?" Margaret asked, mystified and yet delighted.

"Pictures of you," Clarissa said simply, making a mental note to explain the workings of the television to her younger sister later. "And then, since you booked rooms in my name, I had only to call around until I found the hotel where I'm staying." She laughed gaily. "Which is why I've made myself at home, as you can see."

Margaret noticed the wide, glittering wedding band on her sister's finger, studded with diamonds, and remembered that she had married Adam Winthrop, the owner of the ski lodge that bought out Dove Cottage. "I wish you joy for your wedding," she said.

"Thank you," said Clarissa smartly. When there was no barb to follow, no scathing remark, nothing aimed even at her husband, Margaret had to admit that marriage agreed with Clarissa. She'd changed for the better. She even looked more relaxed and yes, happier, than she'd been back home, though her appallingly dark complexion suggested she was not as hale. But Margaret had been in her presence for many minutes now without having received one set-down or stinging remark. Clarissa had softened.

"The future agrees with you," Margaret said with a little smile. "Or perhaps 'tis marriage."

"They both do," she replied, sincerely. Her look changed to concern. "How is my father? St. John tells me he has recovered from my loss. Is that true?"

Margaret reflected on her parent for a moment. "Aside from telling me often that he wishes I were you, Papa is fair recovered." She frowned. "He still longs for you to come home with your husband. It is well that you send letters via Mr. St. John as though you are only gone to America."

Clarissa smirked. "But I have gone to America."

Margaret pursed her lips. "Of course. But he thinks you are in 1819." She shook her head. "To my father, your living in America is little different than losing you to the heart of Africa. To him, the distance between you *is* as 200 years!" She raised her chin. "In any case, there is no question of my staying here for it would be the death of him."

Clarissa nodded. "Quite." She looked up sharply. "You had no thought of staying, did you?"

Margaret's lips hardened. "You certainly would not wish me to, I see."

"I didn't mean it that way," Clarissa said gently, surprising Margaret a great deal. Had she ever heard her sister speak in so gentle a tone? She thought not.

Glancing at Stewart Clarissa said, "But we neglect your friend. I take it he understands you?"

Margaret looked over at him sitting with arms folded with a look of bewilderment. "I suspect he believes I should be in Bedlam," she said.

Stewart knew what Bedlam was and didn't deny it but looked appealingly at Clarissa.

"Please. Tell her it's a delusion. I gather that you encourage her in it. I don't want to hurt her feelings, but this delusion is growing stronger the longer I know her and you are no help—"

Clarissa rose from the bed, straightened her blouse and shook out her hair. She looked up frankly at Stewart. "I know it's a lot to handle," she said, "but it's not a delusion." She picked up her purse from the bedside table. "I was born in 1796 on Red Lion Square in Mayfair, England, delivered at home of my mother. I came here— to what was the future to me, then—three years ago. I'm sure Margaret has explained it. Everything she told you is true."

Clarissa picked her sweater off the back of a chair and said, "Come. Let's go to my apartment. It's more comfortable there."

Margaret wanted to go, but she had two thoughts that gave her pause. "Do you have an analytical—er, computer there?" It seemed suddenly ridiculous to her that she had as yet to research an invention. Stewart had been a powerful distraction from her quest. Perhaps it was due to the conference ending the next day, but she felt a growing conviction that she was running out of time. Or maybe it was on account of that disturbing dream when Mr. St. John said Lady Ashworth was there in the city to ensure her return.

Clarissa smiled. "Of course."

Stewart came to his feet, still frowning mightily.

"But if we leave, how will Mr. St. John find us?" Margaret asked. "I presume he hasn't abandoned me to this place and must return."

"We'll leave him a note," Clarissa said.

"I saw a set of smallish paper here somewhere," Margaret began, but Clarissa had already pulled out a minuscule notebook with a pink print on the cover from her purse. "A notepad," she said. "You saw a hotel notepad. I prefer to use this."

Stewart got a glimpse and saw her notebook had a letterhead with her name on it. This was the real author, Clarissa Channing, telling him to believe that she—and Margaret—were from the past, from 200 years past! He couldn't wrap his head around it. There was no good reason why they should want to pull an elaborate trick on him. But how on earth could he believe such nonsense?

Clarissa stopped before him, hands on her hips. "Well?" she asked. "What is so difficult for you to believe?" She glanced over his clothing and stifled a snarky remark, for it was evidently not well tailored. But what could one expect from this century of mass production and an appalling lack of tailors?

Stewart sighed. "Who in their right mind would believe the two of you are really from 200 years ago?"

"We do, for a start," said Clarissa. "As does my husband, Claire and Mr. St. John, and Lady Ashworth." To his still frowning look, she shook her head. "I suppose it will have to wait until St. John returns with the shawl. Then you'll see." She motioned to Margaret. "Come on. I'll take you home with me."

"May Stewart come?" she asked.

"I can stay in the next room," he offered quickly, not wanting to be a burden to anyone.

"Oh, do come," Clarissa said. "I have two spare bedrooms. And with Adam away for the week, I can always do with male company."

Margaret, thinking her sister had not changed her flirtatious ways, cried, "Clarissa! Please."

But she only laughed. "I'm joking, Margaret, dear! But why shouldn't he come? He can tell me which of my books he's read and why he hasn't read more of them."

But Stewart held back. "We have to tell her first," he said to Margaret. "She must know that associating with me may be dangerous."

Margaret nodded. She gazed soberly at Clarissa while she thought about how to tell her. Finally, she said, "Stewart overheard something he should not have and is wanted by blackguards who wish to kill him." She thought she'd given a fine summary of their dilemma.

Clarissa's eyes widened. "Blackguards? Who are they?" She looked to Stewart for the answer.

He said, "That's just the trouble. I don't know who they are. All I know is, I overhead a lawyer giving an order to do away with someone, and now they want to do away with me too." Clarissa said. "Oh, dear. Quite the mystery." She surveyed Stewart. "But come with us. You are safer with us, I'm sure, than here alone."

She called the lobby to order a taxi, and they left.

What the three did not see as they exited the hotel at night were two men in dark suits across the street watching carefully. One began snapping photos.

The other said, "That's gotta be the guy. We should have snagged him in the library."

The first man pocketed his phone. "They're taking a cab. C'mon, we gotta follow them!" As they rushed to cross the busy street to flag one down, the taxi with Clarissa, Margaret and Stewart started off. Stewart, turning to take a wary look behind them as was his new habit, saw the dark suits scurrying to cross the street, trying to hail down a cab.

There were probably thousands of dark-suited men in Manhattan that night, but he knew, he just knew, these were after him.

"They've found us," he said quietly to Margaret. But the car was already half a block away and Margaret could not make them out in the gloom, even despite the city lights. Her hand crept into his and they fell silent.

The men managed to flag down another cab but by the time they were inside, it was impossible to tell where the three had got to. Yellow and black taxis dotted the street, and in the distance, all was a blur at night.

"Send your photos to Yeltsin. He'll get people on it. That other woman looked familiar; I'm sure I've seen her before—if we can identify her, we can find where they went."

They told the driver to keep driving and each checked the passengers of every cab they drew abreast of, but after traversing blocks and blocks of slow-moving city traffic, Stewart Russell and his lady friends were nowhere to be seen.

Chapter 16

Between the tall buildings and above the traffic, the sun had turned a downy pink and yellow, a slice of color hovering over the city as Lady Ashworth left the "Israeli Rose" to find Freida the tallit maker. A plump dove grey pigeon pecked at her feet, picking up miniscule crumbs on the ground. Looking ahead, the pavement was crowded. "A few blocks," the clerk had said, but city blocks were long and her feet not as swift as in younger days She wished to lose no time and so hired a taxi as the clerk had suggested.

The cab was forced to stop often due to thick, heavy traffic. Car horns beeped and blared, and crowds surged over the crosswalks at every stop. To her chagrin, her ladyship realized pedestrians were moving along at a brisker pace than the cab.

But they arrived at last. Lady Ashworth peered out at a single-windowed storefront with a sign that said, "Curiosities." Her heart gave a flutter—the shawl she wanted was certainly a curiosity. She paid the driver, allowing him to keep the change, and hurried across the pavement.

Inside the window she noticed all manner of articles, many that looked antique. But not a single shawl. Still, she was determined to find this Freida woman and see if she was indeed the mysterious lady from Israel that had sold her the tallit.

As she reached to open the door, a woman was just turning a sign facing out that said CLOSED in large letters. Lady Ashworth rapped the window of the door. The woman turned but pointed to the sign, shaking her head.

With all the authority a marchioness was accustomed to, her ladyship cried, "I insist you allow me to enter!"

The woman frowned but came and peered out at her ladyship. With a relieved gasp, Lady Ashworth saw that it was the same lady that had sold her the shawl! Freida, she now knew her name was. Her curly dark hair had greyed but was otherwise very much the same, and she could never forget the large, percipient eyes that met hers now. With alacrity, Lady Ashworth drew off her shawl and held it up for the woman to see. "This is your handiwork, I believe?" she asked imperiously.

The woman's face became curious, and she unlocked and opened the door.

"Come in," she said, with a genuine smile. "It's not often I get to see people who have bought one of my shawls."

"Obliged," said her ladyship as she stepped inside, feeling as victorious as if she'd just delivered a rousing speech to Parliament.

"What is the trouble?" Freida asked.

Lady Ashworth put a hand to her bonnet. "We are in desperate need of another of your shawls."

"Ah," she said, though with little surprise. "Come, we'll talk as I tidy up." Her ladyship followed her to the far end of the store where a table of folded tallits, each arranged to show their beautiful tassels and borders, was a welcome sight.

"Now," she said, glancing at her curiously. "You can tell me your predicament if you like, but I doubt I can help you. I only have one special shawl per customer."

"No, no," Lady Ashworth hastened to explain. "'tisn't for me. Miss Margaret needs it, for she is stuck here in your century." She went on to explain, as best she could in a truncated version, how the tallit had been sadly torn in twain, but that led to the discovery that two travelers could come through time if each had one half. It had been working just fine, she told her, for the past three years. But now suddenly, after arriving in the present century, it had sprung back to one piece and only worked for one person. Miss Margaret, she explained, was here, but must needs return to her home. 'Twould be the death of her father were she to stay," she added for good measure.

As she spoke, Freida nodded from time to time, listening while she straightened up the shawls that customers had jostled. Lady Ashworth gazed with hungry eyes at the assortment of lovely tallits. One of them was no doubt the special one that would solve their dilemma! But Freida now turned, arms folded, and leaned against the table to face her ladyship.

"Most of my shawls are not special." She motioned at the table of folded specimens behind her. "But I believe I have the shawl you seek," she said, standing and moving to a locked glass cabinet against the wall, while Lady Ashworth followed, her heart growing lighter with each step. Freida pointed to an ivory tallit with dark green embroidered edges, its tassels dangling over the shelf. "This is the one."

Her ladyship stared at it as if it were the crown jewels. "How propitious!"

"But I'm afraid I cannot sell it to you," Freida added.

Lady Ashworth, not often rendered speechless, blinked at her. "I will meet any price," she began haughtily, but Freida smiled gently and waved a hand.

"Price is not the problem," she said. Her eyes fell upon her ladyship's shawl. "Let me see this one." Her experienced eye immediately noticed the scar from the tear, which she examined closely. "You say this was torn in two?" she asked.

"Yes; it was two pieces. My granddaughter sewed the torn edges with seams of their own, but as you see, it has gone back together, no seams at all. It can be forced apart, but simply won't work anymore that way."

Freida wore a little smile. "I have never heard of one being torn in two, or of this capacity to transport two people at once," she admitted. "I am considerably surprised."

She handed it back to Lady Ashworth and said, "Well. I am certain I have the shawl you want, but unfortunately I can only sell it to the right person, and it is not you."

"Oh!" exclaimed her ladyship, putting a hand to her chin. "I suppose it must be Margaret!"

"No, it waits for a certain gentleman."

Lady Ashworth's head went back. "A gentleman?" And then it hit her. "St. John! Of course. But if you sell it to me, I can give it to him."

"I'm sorry but that is not possible," she said kindly with large, serene eyes upon her ladyship. "I can only sell the shawl to the right person, just as I could only sell yours to you."

"But other people have used my shawl. Why should I not bring this to the gentleman it was fashioned for?"

Freida took a breath and shrugged. "I cannot tell if he is the right man. He must come himself."

Her ladyship pursed her lips and accepted defeat. "Very well. I'll return to my time, er, the Regency, and fetch him." She gave Freida a pained look. "Oh, but poor Margaret! Stuck here, friendless, for another night."

Freida smiled again. "There is always a divine purpose where the shawl is concerned. The timing is never wrong. Don't worry about your young lady."

The marchioness took a deep breath and sighed it out. "In that case, I'm obliged." She took her shawl from Freida but folded and tucked it in her reticule. "Thank you for selling me this many years ago. As you can see," and she motioned at her Empire gown and spencer, "it was certainly meant for me. I am a marchioness, now. My granddaughter came across it a decade later and she is now happily married in 1819."

Freida nodded as if she wasn't in the least surprised.

Lady Ashworth said, "But do you never think on what might be changed in the time continuum, that is, how the present may be changed because of our transposition, if you will, to the past?"

Freida shook her head confidently. "I do not concern myself with things I cannot understand. I simply make the shawls as I am led to do so and sell them to the one the Spirit chooses."

"Are you…Hebrew?" asked her ladyship.

Freida smiled. "A Jew, yes, a complete and fulfilled Jew, for I follow our Messiah."

"I see," said Lady Ashworth, her mind roiling with the thought that the shawl's divine guide was God Himself. Did he really care so much for her to send her back in time to find her soul mate and destiny? *And* do the same for Claire? She felt utterly undeserving.

It was still a mystery, an utter mystery, but its divine inspiration was no longer in question.

Freida continued, "We all like to put God in a box and assume He can only work in such-and-such a way, or through this or that means. But He is the Master of time. He lives outside it, He created it, He is beyond understanding and works in mysterious ways. The only way to judge whether something is of God or not is His Word, the Bible, not our preconceived ideas."

The marchioness thanked her again while making a mental note to spend more time in the prayer book and devotions when she returned home. She said, "I'd best return and fetch Julian. But first—" she looked curiously at Freida. "Where can I get a good bagel and lox? We don't have them in my day, you know."

Freida smiled and directed her to a kosher deli only a block away. "Have a knish too," she advised. "With mustard. They're wonderful from there."

Lady Ashworth giggled like a schoolgirl. "Oh, my! Too many carbohydrates, I think, after a bagel." She shook her head. "How good it felt to use that word, carbohydrates! Do you know, it never even crosses my mind to use it when I'm home in the past? It's as though I no longer know it."

Freida smiled.

The wise adapt themselves to circumstances,
as water moulds itself to the pitcher.
Chinese Proverb

Chapter 17

St. John and Claire were just finishing dinner when their butler, Mr. Grey, cleared his throat and entered the room. Looking very troubled, he bowed and said, "Her ladyship," but had barely spoken the words when Lady Ashworth bustled in after him. She had returned from the future to the library, exactly where she had left.

The butler had come upon her in the corridor, unable to understand how she had got into the house without his knowledge, and stared at her now in perplexity, still trying to work it out. The mistress had asked for her not forty minutes since, and he had sent footmen scurrying about to find her, to no avail. Clearly, she had abandoned the premises. The master himself, when told that his wife wanted her grandmother, had confirmed her absence.

Then, suddenly, the marchioness was outside the library, though he hadn't seen nor heard from another servant that she'd entered the house. It reminded him of that former unsettling occasion when the mistress—she was Miss Channing, then, before marrying the master—had appeared in the house without a single servant's seeing *her* enter. It was enough to bamboozle any diligent butler. Grey did not like this appearing and disappearing of guests when he was supposed to be abreast of the comings and goings of the house. He feared he'd been lax in his duties, or worse, was growing beetle-headed.

Her ladyship joined Claire and St. John at the table.

"Grey, a plate for the marchioness," Claire said.

But Lady Ashworth said, "No, I thank you," having just refreshed herself at the Jewish deli. "Thank goodness you're here!" she cried to Julian.

"I should say the same of you, I think," he replied politely, choosing not to comb her over for leaving him high and dry for an extended absence. Noticing the butler was still in attendance with a curiously troubled countenance, he said, "Very good, Grey," to dismiss him. He had no idea why the man seemed flummoxed.

Grey bowed and left, flummoxed indeed.

"Still no new pains, my dear?" her ladyship asked Claire.

Claire shook her head. "It seems our little man or woman," she said, smiling and patting her protruding middle, "has no wish to come early."

"'Tis just as well," Lady Ashworth returned, seated across from Claire. She leveled a serious gaze upon her and St. John. "I am afraid that Julian must return for Margaret." She shook her head to the servant who came with a glass and a decanter.

"I have every intention of doing so," he interjected. "Unless she had accompanied you upon your return to us."

Lady Ashworth shook her head. "I only saw her on TV." Quickly she brought them up to snuff on what had transpired, from finding the Israeli Rose jewelry store to locating Freida's "Curiosities" shop. She told how only St. John could purchase the tallit, but added, "I was very much in mind of locating Margaret to check on her before returning to you, but Freida (who seems to know a great deal more than she allows) assured me not to fret on her account."

Claire turned to her husband. "You ought to go at once, then," she said. "The sooner you procure the tallit and come home with Margaret, the better. We don't know how much longer this little one can wait."

He nodded in agreement.

Lady Ashworth said, "Do it first thing; but no sense in leaving now, for the shop is closed until 10 o'clock tomorrow."

They spoke fondly then of Margaret, her endless appetite for books, how she'd wished to explore the New York Public

Library and study all manner of subjects on a computer. Her spunk and mischievous streak, too, more marked in earlier years, but still part of her character. And even how she'd changed physically of late, blossoming into young womanhood and beginning to resemble Clarissa.

Her ladyship sighed. "Since she wished to read and explore, let us hope she is having a diverting time doing so, and managing to keep from mischief—or trouble."

Miss Margaret and Stewart were having a late bite with Clarissa in a posh New York Club where she pointed out celebrities and a billionaire or two. It would have been great fun at any other time, but Margaret noticed Stewart was unable to relax. He was often looking around worriedly—for the black suits, she knew.

Clarissa noticed also. "Let's talk more at the apartment," she said with a nod at Stewart as though she understood his anxiety.

She paid for the food and ordered a taxi but when they went outside, it hadn't yet arrived. Stewart said, "May we wait inside?" Margaret's heart went out to him. How dismal to be plagued with such fear!

The cab arrived and they were shortly at Clarissa's building. They took an elevator to the 28th floor and were soon inside her expensive, roomy, home. While Margaret went smilingly from room to room, for Clarissa had decorated it just like home, which meant traditional Georgian style but without its restraint. She'd added exotic additions like lacquered and gilt furniture, and intricate roundels of plasterwork adorned even the ceiling. There was an ornate pedestal cupboard topped with an equally ornate urn, and fitted carpet. It all felt familiar and cozy. Stewart accepted a drink and then was shown to his guest room.

"I have nothing with me," he said, "and will be off in the morning. But a hot shower would be wonderful, if you don't mind."

Clarissa sized him up. "You look about the same height as my husband, though rather thinner. Come, I'm sure something will fit you; you can pick an outfit for tomorrow, and bedclothes for tonight."

"Bedclothes," he repeated with almost a grin. "You remind me of Margaret—" but he stopped, realizing the implication, that they were both from the past. He still refused to believe something so fantastic.

Margaret, done with her home inspection, joined them just as Clarissa said, "After your shower we'll talk more. You'll hear all about our travels through time."

"Using a shawl," he said flatly.

"A tallit," Margaret amended.

"A special shawl," Clarissa said, but then she giggled. "It does sound utterly absurd, does it not?"

"My word, you're speaking more and more like your old self!" Margaret said.

Clarissa covered her mouth with one hand. "How odd! I pray it means nothing."

"You *pray* it means nothing?" Stewart said.

Clarissa gasped. "Did I say that?"

"You did," Margaret said. "I wonder…"

Clarissa raised her chin and went toward the master bedroom, motioning for them to follow. "'Tis only on account of your being here, Margaret, I'm certain."

Stewart said, *"'tis* only?"

Clarissa turned to give them a look of alarm, but then swirled about and entered the luxurious room. Pointing to a door she said, "There is Adam's wardrobe. Choose an outfit," she said airily. "I shall fetch the bedclothes. I mean, pajamas!" She drew in a breath and shut her mouth tightly. Then, blinking, she turned on Margaret. "Your presence is to blame for this! I am dearly glad to see you, my sister, but what made you come? Surely it was not only to see me?"

"I am truly sorry, Clarissa," Margaret said sincerely. "But I didn't come only to see you."

"Then why?" she demanded.

"I came to find a proper invention to bring home with me."

Clarissa looked scandalized. "An invention? You can't be serious! You'd merely be stealing someone else's idea."

"Mr. St. John introduced safety straps to carriages. I daresay he has saved countless lives already! Would you wish him to undo that?"

"He only did it," Clarissa replied calmly, "because he nearly lost Claire after a hairpin turn on a London road."

Margaret sniffed. "That is neither here nor there. The fact is, he did it," she pointed out, "using a modern idea. Why should not I be useful to society in a like manner?"

Clarissa stared. "You wish to be useful to society? Since when?"

"I do." Margaret's face fell. "I *must!* I must be an inventress, or I have no secure future, otherwise. You told me yourself, over and over, that I am too plain to expect marriage, and am doomed to be a spinster. And with my father's estate going to that horrid cousin of ours, I have no security other than the kindness of Lady Ashworth to depend upon."

Clarissa seemed moved. "Surely papa will direct that you be given a yearly income."

Margaret scoffed. "Oh, to be sure! A full four or five hundred pounds, I have no doubt! I will not only be a poor spinster but a pathetic creature scorned by society even more than I am now!" Her voice was filled with more conviction than she'd intended to reveal, and hot tears, to Margaret's horror, brimmed in her eyes. She hadn't realized how deep was her longing to escape this sad vision of her future which had long shadowed her existence.

Clarissa folded her hands together and apart. "Margaret," she said quietly. "The truth is, you've grown quite remarkably pretty. I daresay what I told you in the past is no longer true."

Margaret looked up at her wonderingly. "Do you mean it? You think me pretty?" For some reason, Clarissa's opinion meant the world to her.

"Of course, I do." She paused, studying her. Margaret's previously skinny limbs had filled out, as had her bust. Her skin was smooth, her eyes, even behind spectacles, were large, pretty, and glowed with intelligence. Her lips were full, her hair had darkened to match Clarissa's ebony locks, and shone softly. "You look like my sister, now. You never used to."

Margaret's heart swelled. The two women had forgotten about Stewart, but he came slowly into the room from the wardrobe, one of Adam's shirts hanging loosely in one hand. His face had a look of deep concern. The ladies realized his presence with a start. He stopped and looked from Clarissa to Margaret.

"What's this about your never getting married? Being a spinster? Plain?" He looked accusingly at Clarissa. "You told her that?"

Clarissa was momentarily rendered speechless with a look of guilt on her face.

Stewart went up to Margaret and took one of her hands in his free one. "You," he said, in a low, sweet tone, "are lovely. Lovely now, and dare I say it? You will always be lovely, *forever* lovely." He looked up to give Clarissa a reproving gaze and then back at Margaret. "Even if you had not grown in loveliness, you are uncommonly smart, and caring, and delightful. I would have found you stealing my heart, whatever the case."

Margaret blinked back tears. Why was she feeling so maudlin? These were the sweetest words directed at her that she had ever heard. "Thank you," she managed to whisper. He bent and kissed her on the lips, right there in front of Clarissa! Margaret, with admirable courage, allowed him.

When he straightened again to his full height, he swung his gaze to Clarissa and then back at Margaret. "You know, I think you've convinced me. Nothing else you said made me believe your story, but now I think I do!" He kissed Margaret's hand. "I heard it in your voice, how earnest you are. Suddenly I believed."

Margaret smiled with relief and gladness. But then she remembered that the problem of getting back was still a problem, and that removing Stewart from his danger was not possible.

"If only we could both get back to my time," she said wistfully. "Do you have a suggestion as to an invention for me to borrow?"

"That would change history, though, wouldn't it?" Stewart asked.

Margaret sighed. "Just a small improvement, nothing too dramatic or world changing."

He gazed down at her. "You don't need an invention." She looked questioningly up at him, her eyes pools of dark silk, questioning but trusting. *Lovely,* he thought. "What you need is a husband. I know it sounds incredibly chauvinistic, but, in your day, it would solve everything." While Margaret blinked and joy rose in her heart, for she thought he meant to make an offer, he added, "A man with a good income can solve your difficulties. Your sister was wrong about you. There isn't a reason on earth why you shouldn't attract a good husband."

Her heart did a flip from joy to pain as she realized he was not speaking of himself. He had no intention of making an offer.

She turned her head away to hide her disappointment.

Clarissa, watching, said sagely, "I think you have already attracted a husband."

Margaret turned again to see Stewart's reaction, but he dropped her hand and said, hurriedly, "No, I—that is, my life is in danger! I can't offer her any security, and my income is practically nonexistent. Margaret deserves someone better!"

But Clarissa was not to be dissuaded. With a hand on her hip she continued, "You, my dear sir, are what my sister needs—and what she *wants*, I daresay?" she added astutely, turning to Margaret, for Clarissa was no dull-wit. Allowing Stewart to kiss her on the lips clearly portrayed her heart in the matter.

Margaret blushed crimson but did not deny it.

Stewart looked at Margaret and squeezed her hand. But his face was fallen. "I wish—I have nothing!" he protested. "My life is in jeopardy—even to associate with me may be dangerous for you—and, as if that were not enough," he turned to Clarissa. "How could I ask her to stay so far from her own time?"

Clarissa went and drew a pair of unopened pajamas from a dresser drawer. "You have it all wrong. Margaret cannot stay here. My father would have apoplexy. You must return with her to the past," she said calmly, returning to give him the clothing.

Stewart was silent but the edges of his lips were turning decidedly upwards. "Me—go to the past? I—I can't imagine it." But he frowned again and turned to Margaret. "I would love to go back with you but think! I would have no identity in your time. Here, I have precious little, but at least I have a name! Think of what you're suggesting. I'd be a man without family, occupation, income, a fairly worthless education—"

"No! Not worthless," Margaret chided. "You would find yourself right at home in literary circles and enjoy excellent conversation with other learned men." A little bitterly she said, "That is a thing I am denied simply for being a woman, but you would be welcome!" Brightening, she added, "All our literary hostesses will long to have you attend their dinners or routs."

He smiled gently at this, but said, "I don't think I'd be welcome for long. I'd be an alien and a stranger and my conversation a disappointment to anyone who is learned in your day. I've read enough contemporary literature to know that we have lost the art of intelligent discourse that men in your day are proficient at. I could never hold my own among them."

"You can and you will! You have merely to learn the art of it," Margaret said loyally, and with such utter faith that he smiled. He raised her hand to his lips and kissed it. Shaking his head he said, "I wish it could be so easy." His brows furrowed. "But what are we saying? Aren't you stuck here yourself?"

Clarissa said, "St. John is no doubt working on that. When he returns, we'll see what's what. In the meantime, I suggest you take that shower, while I find something modish for my sister to wear."

Not a word was said regarding her using the term 'modish' instead of pretty or modern. No need to invite remorse on Clarissa's part, Margaret thought!

For her part, Margaret was walking on air. Stewart had called her lovely, *forever* lovely! He'd kissed her on the mouth right in front of her sister and said he'd love to go back with her if he could! And the fact that he hadn't followed it with an offer of marriage was only because he felt unsuitable and didn't think it possible, not because he didn't want her. It was astonishing, and heady, and made her heart race, this feeling of being admired and wanted!

Her sudden happiness made her feel almost ashamed of the mean thoughts she'd had of others in the past. She had used to watch from the back of the room at a ball and see who she could insult—secretly, of course—using all manner of derogatory terms to describe the ladies in attendance. Florid or ghostly in complexion, a pudding face; ghastly in dress; insipid; exceedingly plain; exceedingly fat; and on and on. Having been made to feel pretty and wanted for the first time in her life, she now cringed at her former meanness. She would change her ways. She would, if she was given the chance.

Which meant, St. John must return with the means of going back home. But not only for the two of them, but for Stewart too.

There had to be a way. There just had to be!

Chapter 18

The following day, St. John, to his annoyance, arrived right back at the public library where he and Margaret had first arrived. He wondered whether to search the library or hurry back to the hotel. Where would Margaret most likely be, was the question. Finally, since the tallit had brought him there, he headed up the stone steps to search the library first. Remembering Margaret's curiosity about room 319, he went there directly. Empty.

He continued on that floor, doing a complete tour of what was open to the public, but to no avail. He did the same on the 2nd and ground floors. Astor Hall was crowded but he saw no sign of Margaret and eventually made his way back to the revolving door and went outside. Just as he did, he met eyes with a young woman in contemporary clothing going in—Margaret! She had seen him too but was already inside the revolving door and had to go with it. He stepped out of the way of others and waited at the side. In a minute, Margaret came back out, along with a dark-haired, bearded young man.

Clarissa had found a black wig and cut it short to fit Stewart. She'd also ordered an overnight delivery (such a convenience, marveled Margaret!) of a synthetic dark beard. With such a different disguise, Stewart was able to abandon the spectacles and was yet a transformed man.

"Sir!" Margaret cried joyfully upon joining St. John outside. "I am prodigiously relieved to see you!"

"I expect you are," he said apologetically. "And I, to see you." He had half-thought to find Margaret sunk in despair at being left alone in a strange century, but her lively eyes reassured him at once that all was well. Smiling, he took a pointed look at her modern appearance.

Margaret smiled self-consciously at his perusal—rather anxiously, too. Clarissa had lent her skinny jeans and a blouse and had used a hair straightener to undo Regency curls so that her hair was down, shiny but straight. She'd borrowed a pair of low-heeled black pumps and had exchanged her reticule for a light crossbody bag. Would Mr. St. John disapprove? Her anxiety vanished when he said, "You look comfortable—and quite pretty." She swallowed a burst of pride.

Stewart had called her lovely and now Mr. St. John had called her pretty! How glad, how very glad she was to be there in New York, to have found Stewart, and in truth, a part of herself. When Stewart had found her perusing the history of inventions using Clarissa's laptop (wonderful device!) and asked why, she explained again why it might be vital to her future.

Firmly, he said, "You don't need an invention; in fact, you already have one, for you've reinvented yourself. Even if your cousin inherits the lion's share of your father's estate, you are not the plain Margaret you thought, but the *lovely* Margaret any man would wish to have as a wife."

She blushed with pleasure, but returned, "That is hardly an invention, as I have not actually done anything but changed the poor opinion of myself that I was accustomed to keep."

"That is no small thing," he said quietly. "Many people never manage it."

Margaret's heart had swelled at his words, and she felt close to such happiness as she'd never known before. Now, with Mr. St. John's return, if they could only manage to get Stewart back to the past, her happiness would be complete!

St. John motioned them away from the busy entrance area. When they reached a quieter spot, Margaret introduced the men, mentioning Stewart's interest in writers of their day, particularly women writers. But she could hardly contain herself. "I dreamt of you being here! And in the dream, you told me Lady Ashworth was here also!"

He said, "I am, and she was."

"Did she find another shawl?" she asked eagerly.

St. John looked at Stewart, wondering how much he knew. As if reading his thoughts, Margaret said, "Stewart understands! Speak plainly, sir."

St. John nodded at Stewart approvingly. "Lady Ashworth found the woman who makes the shawls right here in the city, but *I* must go and purchase it."

"Right here in New York!" cried Margaret rapturously. "How propitious! But why did she not procure a new tallit for us?"

"She tells me the woman is particular about whom she will sell the shawls to, and that I must go myself. I suppose, because I am the one in need."

Margaret's face lit. "Since you have yet to go, please purchase an extra one for Stewart!" She proceeded to quickly explain, as she had to Clarissa, about Stewart's predicament and the villains who were after him." Shyly, she put her arm through Stewart's as she spoke, and St. John saw at once that there was more than practicality at stake in her wish to remove him to the past.

But he was none too sure that he wanted the man to go back with them. To begin with, he knew nothing about him except that he was embroiled in something dangerous. Danger might be appealing to young, adventurous Margaret, but he decided instantly that he would need to interview Stewart and learn more about him. Or must he? For all he knew, it would be impossible to bring him back even if they wished to. He had yet to see the tallit-maker where he might find out.

All he said was, "I am having a deuced time trying to get us both home; I cannot guarantee passage for us, much less your friend." He thought for a moment. "Let us repair to the hotel where we can better speak on this. From there, I'll go and fetch the shawl to take us home."

But Margaret and Stewart exchanged worried glances. "We cannot go to the hotel," she said. "The black suits—the men after Stewart, you see—are aware of our staying there. 'Tis not safe."

"We had to miss the last day of the JASNA conference today," Stewart added. With an appreciative look at Margaret, he added,

"Margaret could have gone, but she was willing to forgo it for my sake." He gave her a grateful look.

"Men in black suits, you say?" St. John asked.

"They are watching this place too, most like," Margaret said. "We dared to come only so I could see a traveling exhibit called 'Fortune and Folly in 1720'—which I discovered on Clarissa's laptop and thought would be quite the lark." She paused. "And because my sister gave us wonderful new disguises." Leaning in confidentially she added, "Stewart looks nothing like himself."

Not knowing that Stewart was blond-haired, for he did not associate him with the young man they'd seen upon their first visit, St. John looked curiously at him now. He wondered how he was not looking like himself but said only, "How is your sister?"

"Quite well," said Margaret confidently. "The future agrees with her."

"In that case," he motioned at the library, "stay inside until I return."

"After the exhibit, we thought we had best return to Clarissa's apartments," Margaret said. "It seems the safest place." She was happy to have this chance to see more of the library and the exhibit, but no diversion was worth incurring further risk to Stewart. It was he who had insisted they come when he saw how much the subject of the exhibit intrigued Margaret. They would be sure to go nowhere near the Pforzheimer Collection.

As they parted, Margaret looked up at St. John wistfully. "Pray, sir, do not forget! Stewart must needs obtain a tallit!"

Out on the street, St. John looked with a longing eye at the many taxis but searched his pockets and found only the coins he'd put there at home. He'd forgotten to get the credit card from Margaret, his ticket for withdrawing cash. And he didn't relish the thought of having to explain the value of Regency legal tender to a modern New York cabbie who might not believe him or accept silver in lieu of cash if he did.

He set off on foot for the long walk, for Lady Ashworth had given him the location. He ignored curious glances directed his way for his dark blue superfine tailcoat and spotless buff-colored breeches. He'd eaten only a hasty breakfast, hoping to make quick work of the business to be back home before the birth of his child, but now realized he was hungry. He searched for a coin changer's shop but saw none; and had to walk past tantalizing food carts, restaurants that exuded wonderful aromas, and a bakery that set his mouth watering.

He lingered outside a bank, wondering if they'd accept the silver for ready cash, but worried they might put in a call to the police. They might find it odd, this strangely dressed person with valuable antique coins. If that happened, it would delay him for who knew how long? He kept walking, now and again stopping to ascertain whether he was on the right path. Fortunately, the city had mostly numbered streets, making it much easier to navigate unknown territory than it was in London.

When he finally found the shop called "Curiosities," the window was dark, and the CLOSED sign hung ominously on the door. Closed? He was certain it was not yet five o'clock. But there it hung, and no one came to his knock.

His disappointment was acute. He turned back, deciding to stop for refreshment. Then he remembered that Margaret had the credit card! Would this day's vexations never cease? He was tempted to use the tallit and go right back home, but then Margaret and the others would wonder what became of him. Suddenly he remembered that Lady Ashworth had traded an 1819 coin for modern cash at the "Israeli Rose" shop. Why should they not do the same for him? And why had he not thought of it sooner?

He was forced to ask for occasional assistance, but at last found the store. A clerk greeted him with profuse politeness—her ladyship had left a good impression for people of their day, he saw—and, upon his showing a single silver crown, was treated royally. They wished to know if he had more where it came from. He asked what they would give for it. When he heard the amount, he decided to sell two. Who knew how long they might continue to be stuck there? Or what another tallit might cost?

He would join the others at Clarissa's apartment and then return home until the morrow when he hoped the Curiosities shop would be open. If not, he would return home and try again the following day until he found it so. He'd have to keep trying until he was able to procure the new tallit. In the meantime, he had cash to spare for any of his or Margaret's needs. With luck, her ordeal of being stranded would soon be at an end.

He had yet to discover that luck had nothing to do with it.

After stopping for pizza, which he found much to his liking, he took a cab to Clarissa's building, "The Majestic." He was curious to see if it lived up to its name. As the cab pulled to the curb at the entrance on Central Park West, St. John spied Margaret and Stewart coming toward the building. He disembarked from the cab, paid the driver, and then stood waiting for the young couple to notice him. They were engaged in lively conversation, and he thought he had never seen Margaret looking so contented. They were evidently unconcerned about possible pursuers and confident their changed appearances secured their safety. With that thought, he suddenly realized he ought not to allow Margaret to walk abroad with Stewart Russell. His danger could be hers also.

Earlier, before leaving the museum, Stewart brought them to the gift shop where he bought her a set of notecards showing two cats with the saying, "You are purrfect."

"They may vanish forever when we leave for my time," she warned him.

"If they go with you, but I do not, you can write letters to me for posterity, and direct them to me, and I'll read them when they reach me," he said, his lovely eyes probing hers with grave earnestness.

"Will they reach you from two hundred years ago? I think not. If so, you would have had them already."

"I'm giving them to you anyway," he said with a smile. "And since I've had no such cards from you, it means that either they did not survive through time, or I am to go back with you!" But he shook his head. "I don't think I am. You need a rich man."

For his benefit she said, "Perhaps not for my sake, then, but for your own. I am certain you will come back. You *must*! But recall, the tallit follows a divine directive, and surely did not have us meet to no purpose."

Leaving the library, they searched warily for the black suits but were relieved not to see the two men. There were men in suits, but their purposeful strides coming or going, without looking around, assured the two they were not a threat.

They noticed St. John and quickened their pace. Margaret's heart quickened, too—her hopes were soon to be realized or dashed! As they came abreast of St. John, Stewart was just saying that he and Margaret should both get cell phones.

"We won't need them if we're going home!" Margaret cried, looking at Mr. St. John hopefully. "Were you able to procure the tallits, sir?"

"The shop was closed," he said flatly.

Margaret's face fell.

"Do not alarm yourself," he interposed. "I'll go again to the shop tomorrow, for it must be open some time."

As they headed for the elevator, he inquired, by the by, how Margaret had found her sister. She explained that it was the other way 'round, that Clarissa had seen her on "tel-e-vision" and then found their hotel due to their using her card of credit.

"Your great aunt, when she was here, saw you also," he said, which astounded Margaret. She began to think that everyone in this century must neglect their lives to watch the tele-e-vision constantly. Clarissa had hers on quite a lot.

"Will you stop here with us?" Margaret asked as they exited the elevator on the 29ᵗʰ floor. "My sister has guest rooms. Her apartments are quite grand."

Stewart touched her arm. "We say apartment, singular, no matter how large it is."

"Oh!" Margaret laughed. "How strange."

St. John said, "I'll give my regards to your sister and her husband, but, as Claire is so close to her lying in, I will return to her for the night."

"I have yet to meet her husband, Adam. He is in Maine," Margaret told him.

St. John nodded but said nothing. He wasn't unhappy to miss seeing the man, as he had mixed feelings about Adam. On one occasion, the man had knocked him unconscious with such force that it affected his memory for a time. Claire had gone through quite an ordeal until his mind was restored and he remembered her. That was in the early days of his time traveling before he and Claire had wed. Thank goodness he'd found her. Thank goodness for the tallit! Now, if he could only get another so that he and Margaret could return home. As for Stewart, he had no assurance that he too could get to the past. With any luck, the shop would be open tomorrow and they would know.

When the cab drew up to the curb in front of Clarissa's building with two doormen out front, both Stewart and Margaret drew in their breath. "The black suits!" Margaret cried.

The two men were positioned at either side of the covered entrance foyer that extended halfway onto the pavement.

"We need to move on," Stewart said urgently to the cabbie. "Just a little further down the block." As the cab began to move, St. John turned to look back at the two men.

"If I mistake me not," he said, still watching them, "they are, I believe, a sad modern version of butlers employed by the building's owner."

"We don't have butlers in your sense at such buildings today," Stewart said.

"Stewart," Margaret whispered urgently. "If you correct an upper-class elder, you must do it politely. Call him sir."

"I'm sorry, we don't have butlers, *sir,*" he said again, eying Margaret for her approval.

St. John watched as one of the men nodded at a woman entering the building. "They are hired hands, whatever you call them."

"Doormen," said Stewart. All three heads were turned now, straining to watch the men. One went to the curb to help a lady from a cab. Margaret said, "If they are the black suits, they are playing at being doormen."

"I doubt they could get away with that. Someone who lives there would know the usual men," Stewart pointed out. "So they're probably safe."

Margaret said, "Very well, I suppose we must trust them. And even if they are looking for you, they won't know it's you due to your disguise. And if they're looking for both of us, they won't know it's us, because we have Mr. St. John with us."

Stewart pulled out his cell. "Let me tell your sister we're here. She can buzz us right in and we won't have to wait."

After about a minute, he said, "She's not replying."

Margaret had been watching eagerly. "May I call her?" she asked. "I've not had the chance to use one of these tel-e-phone devices, and the thought quite enthralls me!"

Stewart smiled, hit the call icon, and then handed Margaret the phone. He leaned over to put it on the speakerphone and then sat back. Margaret said, "I hear a strange sound! But 'tisn't my sister."

Stewart smiled gently. "She hasn't picked up yet."

When it went to voicemail, Margaret cried, "I hear someone!"

"No, no," Stewart said, taking the phone. "It's a recording. He waited and began, "It's Margaret and me, Stewart, and Mr. St. John—"

Clarissa got on. "Hello! I didn't recognize your number. Where are you?"

"We're in a cab at the curb."

"Come on up," she said, "I'll buzz you in."

"Wait!" Stewart cried. "Are there normally two men in dark suits at the doorway on the street?"

"At the entrance, you mean?" she asked.

"Right."

"I'm sure they must be our doormen," Clarissa said.

With that, Stewart paid the cabbie and in minutes they were strolling past the men. One stopped them, saying, "I'm sorry, but are you new to the building?"

"We're visiting someone," said St. John, affronted.

"Sorry, but may I ask who?" The man took a pointed look at St. John's Regency garb.

"Clarissa Channing," he replied coldly. "She is expecting us."

"Oh, Ms. Channing!" he said, as though he'd been greatly enlightened. "Ah. Are you the cover model for her next book?" he asked, smiling.

St. John was so aghast that he could hardly answer. The steel that filled his face and eyes spoke for itself, however.

The man's smile vanished, and he said hurriedly, "Go on, please. My apologies." With a final glare that could wither the staunchest soul, St. John strode past, while Margaret and Stewart followed. The doorman watched as they went to the wall with its list of occupants and door numbers. When Stewart pressed Clarissa's door number with no hesitation, the man finally looked away. Clarissa's voice came through crisply. "Come up, come up!" A loud buzz opened the heavy door to the elevators and nearby stairs, and they went through.

Clarissa was at her doorway awaiting their arrival, all smiles. She wore a flowery blouse and black skirt (with a great deal of leg showing, Margaret thought) and dangling earrings and a heavy black necklace. She was especially happy to see St. John, she said, as now that the cottage was unavailable for most of the year, she would see him and Claire less often.

She led them into the perfect replica of a Regency townhouse parlor that Margaret found so comforting. St. John nodded his approval, while Margaret, smiling, settled upon a settee, boldly patting the spot beside her for Stewart.

"Shall we have dinner together?" asked Clarissa. "I take it that you've not been able to find another tallit?"

"Not yet," St. John told her. He went on to explain how Lady Ashworth found the craftswoman who had made theirs, but that it seemed he alone could purchase it from her. He told how he'd found the shop closed and must return on the morrow.

Clarissa smiled. "Well, it seems your problem is on its way to being solved."

"Not necessarily," Margaret chimed in. "We do not know if there is a way for Stewart to come with us. He needs a tallit as much as we do, but who knows if this woman will accommodate him?"

Clarissa surveyed the two of them sitting comfortably side-by-side. "I am sure she will. But there's no sense fretting over it now."

Margaret stared at her. She was so…so equable! So unruffled! Quite unlike her old self. She marveled again at how well this century agreed with Clarissa, making her altogether more pleasant. This change, coupled with her success as an author, might have encouraged Margaret to stay in the present too, perhaps, but did not. Her conviction that Stewart *must* go back had only strengthened, and she, of course, wanted to be there with him. Not to mention her father's need of her.

Clarissa served sherry, even to Margaret, encouraging them to relax. Margaret was so pleased that her sister had included her that she even took a few sips. Afterward, a cab was called, and the four of them took the elevator to the ground floor. As the doors drew apart, Margaret's heart sank to her shoes. They were face to face with the black suits, and these men were not the doormen! Both had a wire hanging from one ear, and a deadly serious look on their face.

St. John gave Margaret a little nudge to move forward, for he had no idea that these were the men after Stewart. Stewart grasped Margaret's hand and squeezed it hard. The men seemed to study them, then moved aside so the four could exit the elevator. Stewart and Margaret, still holding hands, went first. St. John and Clarissa were fast behind them, but suddenly one of the men cried, "Stop! Stewart Russell? We have business with you!" He moved to grab Stewart's arm, but he and Margaret ran quickly through the entrance vestibule and out to the street. They continued on, expecting any moment to be overtaken, but finally, after maneuvering around people and traversing a full city block at top speed, they stopped to catch their breath. No one was in pursuit.

"I don't understand it," Stewart said, shaking his head. "How did they know me in this disguise? And how did they associate me with your sister?"

Margaret added, "And how is it they are not on our heels?"

"I don't know," Stewart said, "but let's not wait and give them time."

"Where shall we go?" Margaret asked.

Stewart looked around them. "Let's try that store," he said, pointing to a clothing shop. We can watch from inside. Once they pass, we can find the others." He took another look around to be certain the men weren't in sight, then nodded at Margaret, and they crossed the street with other pedestrians.

"I think I know how we got away," Margaret said, when they entered the store. They went only as far as a corner rack where they could see the street. "Mr. St. John must have stopped them."

"I hope it didn't get ugly," Stewart said, worriedly. "God forbid something should happen to him for my sake."

"He is quite capable of watching out for himself, I assure you," she returned.

"But these men are armed," Stewart said despairingly. "How could he be ready for that?"

"They're not after him," she reminded him. She did not add, "They only want you," because they both knew it only too well.

Stewart gave a deep sigh. "It's no use," he said. "I may as well give myself up."

Margaret's heart took a dive. "Lud, no!" she cried.

He turned to look her full in the face. "If they could find me with this new disguise and with your sister, they'll find me anywhere."

Margaret frowned. "I cannot fathom how that happened. No one in this century knows Clarissa has a sister, and even if they did, they could not know that I am she."

Stewart looked thoughtful. "You've been using her credit card. They must have found whose name your reservation was in—your sister's name, right?"

"Yes, but why should they wish to track her?"

"Not her. You. Because you're with me. Perhaps they saw us on TV, too. I used my real name to register as a JASNA attendee." Both faces became despondent.

"But how did they know it was me in this disguise? Dark hair, a beard! The whole thing was a waste of time and energy." He shook his head and tore off the beard, peering outside.

Margaret smiled. "I must say, you look much better without that nasty thing."

He looked at her appreciatively but was too much on edge to give a real smile. Minutes passed while they watched for the men. A clerk approached and asked if there was anything special they wished to see? Stewart said no with an air of finality, and that was all he said.

The clerk moved away unhappily, as if reluctant to allow these two to loiter in the store without even bothering to browse the racks. The nerve of some people.

"What shall we do?" asked Margaret. "I do not believe they have followed us."

Stewart pulled out his cell. "I'll call your sister."

When Clarissa answered she said, "I'm glad you called. Is everything all right?"

"I'm still breathing, if that's what you mean. Are you two all right?"

"Yes, we're fine," she said. "St. John scuffled with the men; he's had lessons in pugilism, you know," she said proudly, "and knocked them both out cold. We've called the police, but we're back upstairs now. Where are you?" she asked.

Stewart looked outside to see the cross street but couldn't see a sign. "Not very far."

"Good, come on back, then. I imagine those scoundrels are in custody by now, but the police will want you for questioning." She paused. Then, laughing, she added, "My sister and St. John will have to make themselves scarce, as they shan't be able to prove they exist!"

Margaret noticed her use of "scoundrels" and "shan't" but said nothing. Clarissa was being wonderfully helpful, and she did not wish to ruin her high spirits by pointing out another Regency lingo slip.

Stewart said, "Give us a few minutes."

He and Margaret had only reached the first corner when he stopped and rubbed his chin. "You know, it seems odd your sister and St. John would be back in the apartment without having spoken to the police yet."

"Does it?" asked Margaret, who knew nothing of modern police protocol.

"If they called the police, they would have waited for their arrival, especially if St. John knocked the men out cold and they were no longer a threat."

Margaret digested this but didn't know what to make of it. "What does this mean to you?" she asked finally.

"That something's fishy." He stopped walking. "Let's wait a bit and see if they call us."

The right word may be effective, but no word was ever as effective
as a rightly timed pause.
Mark Twain

Chapter 20

Stewart noticed they were standing in front of a small art
gallery. Motioning at the place he said, "Let's admire some art."
Just then his phone buzzed, and Margaret watched with great
interest as he thumbed it open.

"If only I could invent such a thing for my day!" she sighed to
herself.

In seconds, they heard Clarissa's voice. "Where are you?" she
asked. "I thought you were close by." Her voice sounded irritated.
Just like the old Clarissa, Margaret thought.

"We are," Stewart said. "Did the police arrive yet?"

"Er, no. I don't think so."

"Why didn't you wait downstairs near the men?" he asked.
"What if they woke up? And won't the police want to speak to
you?"

They heard the sound of a car door slamming shut. "Stewart,
where are you? St. John and I will come to you and then we'll have
dinner."

Stewart gave Margaret an alarmed look. Holding his hand over
the phone, he hissed, "I don't think those men got knocked out. I
think they're holding your sister hostage!"

"I heard that!" Clarissa said. "Don't be ridiculous! Just tell us
where you are."

"Mr. St. John?" asked Margaret. "Are you all right?" When
there was no answer she asked, "Is he there, Clarissa?"

At that moment a cab in the street suddenly veered toward the
curb in their direction, and, narrowly missing other cars, came
screeching to a stop. A man in black hopped out before Stewart
and Margaret could react.

"Get in," he said. "Or you can say goodbye forever to Miss Channing."

They saw Clarissa, her eyes a torment of sorrow, in the back seat with the other thug with his gun pointed at her head. Stewart turned veiled eyes to Margaret. "Run into the gallery. I'll do my best to save your sister!"

"No! I won't leave you!" she cried.

The first man grabbed Stewart's arm to force him inside the car. "Get in!" he said again.

"Let her out, and I'll get in. I won't if you don't."

"Get in first," he said heavily. "Then we'll let her out."

"I don't believe you," Stewart said.

"Get in, or I'll shoot her now and then your other lady friend as well!" the man holding a gun at Clarissa growled.

Stewart said, "You would have to kill all of us, as well as the cabbie, and you'd never get away. Let her out." The man in the back seat called out something to the other. As the second man leaned down to confer with him, Stewart wrenched his arm free, grabbed Margaret's hand and tore into the art gallery.

As soon as they did, a man inside with a phone to his ear shut and locked the door behind them. "This way, hurry!" he cried. "I saw he had a gun on you. He scurried them toward the back of the store. "I've got the police on the line now." Behind them, they heard banging on the door.

"No, they're still out there," he said into the phone. "I have the couple in here, but I think those men are going to break in." He shook his head. "No, I will not go to the window to see." As he spoke, they heard a loud crash as the window shattered. "They're coming in!" the man cried. He motioned to Margaret and Stewart to follow him and took off running down a corridor, shoving his phone into a pocket. Margaret and Stewart ran close on his heels. He turned down another short hallway, quickly unlocked a door, and the three of them burst out into a side alley. He shut the door after them and cried, "Hurry! This way!"

They were running along what to Margaret looked like an impasse with no way of escape. But the man stopped at a door on the opposite side and shoved against it with his shoulder. It opened reluctantly, creaking as if little used, and led into a shadowed, carpeted hallway.

"I'm Daniel, by the way," he said, holding out his hand to Stewart.

"Stewart, and this is Margaret," Stewart replied, as he ushered Margaret in ahead of him. On a hunch, she took a last glimpse back the way they'd come and saw the men in pursuit.

"They're coming!" she cried.

Stewart slammed the door shut, even as distant sounds and music reached their ears from elsewhere in the building. "That sounds like a movie," he said.

"It is. We're in a multi-plex," Daniel said. He turned the manual lock on the door behind them.

"A what?" whispered Margaret to Stewart.

"A theater with lots of movies—um, giant televisions," he whispered back. They continued down the dim corridor. Daniel said, "Look, the police should have arrived at the gallery by now, they said they were close. Perhaps you should hide in one of the theaters. I plan on going back to my store before it's looted."

"I can't thank you enough," Stewart said, fast on his heels. "I think you've saved our lives! And I'm terribly sorry if anything happens to any of your paintings."

"I hope they're not damaged or missing, but no worries, I'm insured." He shook Stewart's hand.

"I am much obliged to you also, sir," offered Margaret with shining eyes.

Daniel smiled. "You're British".

"I am," she said, with a smile.

"I didn't realize you still said that sort of thing. Well, we're almost at the front," he said. "You should duck into a theater." But voices ahead stopped them in their tracks.

"Wait! You didn't buy tickets! Stop! You're not the police!"

"Quick! Into a theater!" Daniel hissed.

But Stewart turned back the way they'd come and was hurrying past the various theater entrances that opened onto their corridor. All three ran as quietly as they could but had to wait when they reached the door they'd entered only minutes earlier while Daniel fumbled to undo the lock. Margaret kept a worried eye on the corridor behind them but saw no one. Once outside, they took a collective sigh of relief.

"Let's find the police," Daniel said, when suddenly a tall figure turned into the alley from the street.

Margaret gasped with relief. "Mr. St. John!"

He strode purposefully toward them. "The police are questioning Clarissa. Stewart, I suggest you join her while Margaret and I move on." He glanced at the art gallery owner, who was giving St. John a once-over due to his impeccable Regency garb. St. John always dressed to the nines, so that in his boots and tailored breeches, shirt, waistcoat, cravat and tailcoat, he looked impressive.

You're British also," Daniel said, stating the obvious. "Love the costume!"

St. John raised a brow but turned to Margaret. "Let us be off."

"The police will want statements," Daniel said.

Stewart said, "He's right. Let me speak to them. Maybe they'll believe me now! Maybe they'll help protect me." Just then, the alley door burst open. The grim-faced men in suits rushed out. Seeing Stewart, their eyes bulged. "Stay right there! You run and I'll shoot!" one cried.

"The police are out front!" Daniel cried. "If you shoot him, they'll shoot you."

"Not if they don't hear it," he returned, cracking a humorless smile. He brandished his gun, replete with a silencer.

"They'll hear me scream!" Margaret warned.

"The second man drew out his gun. "I advise against it," he said.

"But 'tis all a mistake!" she pleaded. "He doesn't know who he heard speaking; he cannot cause trouble for anyone!"

The first man took Stewart's arm. "Let's go."

Margaret looked at St. John. Surely he must have a plan. She'd never known him to be helpless against ruffians. Why, he'd disarmed two cutthroats right on South Audley Street one dark night when they might have killed him. Another time, on

Hounslow Heath, he'd shot a would-be highwayman from the window of his coach and averted a robbery or worse, for him and his company. Many travelers didn't survive a meeting with highwaymen. Looking at him now, she hoped he was formulating a plan, but he hadn't moved. Then she saw that, peeking from his waistcoat pocket, was the tallit! The tallit that could send Stewart away from the awful fate these men had in mind for him.

"Sir!" she cried, in such a heart-stricken voice that all four men looked her way. She lowered her eyes to his waistcoat pocket and back up. He remembered what was there, of course; one did not forget when one carried a time-traveling tallit, but he shook his head in the negative.

"Please, sir!" she cried, desperately. "Give it to him! We must!"

"You ask for my only means to return to Claire. She may be at childbirth as we speak." He was immovable.

"C'mon!" one gunman cried, beginning to walk Stewart off by the arm.

Staring at St. John tragically Margaret cried, "But it may mean his death!"

One of the men asked, "What is this about?" He looked curiously at St. John. "Do you have the phone? With the recording?" He held out a hand. "Give it here. No one needs to get hurt." When St. John didn't answer, the man glared at him and put his gun to Stewart's head.

"Sir!" Margaret screamed. "Give it to him! Now!"

The gunmen hesitated. If this man had the recording, he'd rather take it than kill a man.

"Claire would want you to!" Margaret cried, tears pooling in her eyes. "You know she would!"

St. John's mouth firmed into a determined line. Margaret's heart sank. But then, in one swift movement, he grasped the cloth from his pocket and shoved it toward Stewart. "Hold onto it!" he ordered through gritted teeth.

To prevent it from falling, Stewart automatically caught it against his chest. At that moment, a shot rang out.

Stewart was gone.

"I've often heard Old Granny say:
'He longest lives who runs away.'
Thornton W. Burgess

Chapter 21

The gunmen turned, circling frantically to find Stewart. "Where is he? Where'd he go?" Daniel, too, was searching for him, his face full of perplexity. Soon, all three turned to St. John and Margaret, the black suits with murderous expressions, Daniel with dawning admiration.

"What'd you do with him?" asked the first black suit, now pointing his gun at St. John. "What was that, some kind of magic trick?" He waved his weapon at St. John's clothing. "Is that why you're dressed like that? Are you a magician?"

"Do not be absurd," St. John replied. He took Margaret's hand. "Come."

"No, you don't," the man said, hurrying to block their way.

The second man joined his partner. "Take us to him and no one will get hurt."

"I am afraid that is impossible," St. John said. "I do not know where he went. Come, Margaret." He tucked her hand upon his arm. He began to escort her down the alley just as if they were taking a promenade in Hyde Park in 1819, and as though there wasn't the least possibility that they could be shot from behind. Margaret did not share his nonchalance, but as she looked back to assess what those horrid men were doing, two policemen hurried into the alley ahead of them.

The two black suits, without a word, turned tail and ran. They veered back to the theater door, opened it and ran inside. Seeing them run, the police instantly gave chase.

"Those men had pocket pistols!" cried Margaret, as they passed.

One glanced at her curiously, but called, "Wait here for questioning!"

"I'm the gallery owner!" Daniel called to their retreating figures. "I'll be in my shop!" He studied her and then St. John. "Where *did* Stewart go?"

When neither replied, looking steadily at St. John he persisted, "How did you do it?"

Margaret swallowed, wondering what her companion would say. Would he hazard the truth about the tallit? It seemed sacred, to be guarded at all costs from most people. But what then? Would he invent something outlandish?

St. John turned to Daniel with a sigh. "That, my good man, is a mystery, even to me."

Margaret looked ahead with a smile. St. John had revealed nothing and yet had told the truth. But her countenance faltered, for suddenly she remembered that a shot had rung out just before Stewart vanished—or had he gone first? It happened so quickly, she couldn't be sure. And, though he was safely in the past, was it not to him a foreign time and land? She trusted that the tallit had taken him to *her* past, to 1819. But what if he'd ended up elsewhere? Or, if he'd been shot, would their medical men be able to save him? Her heart trembled.

In the future, Stewart was a wanted man and in danger of death. In her day, if he was injured, he was also in that danger! Had she been wrong to urge Mr. St. John to give him the tallit? But no, for those men had such murderous looks! She was sure that for Stewart to go with them would have meant his certain demise. At least in the past, (for surely that is where the tallit took him) if he was not injured, there was hope.

As much as Stewart had come to believe that his new friends were in fact time travelers, still he stood gasping in complete and utter shock at what had just happened. One moment he'd been in that alley. He caught the cloth from Mr. St. John, the tallit, they called it—and then everything had gone black. Flashes of light, a dizzying sense of spinning in space, a roaring in his ears, and then here he was, in a completely different location! And "different" was hardly a strong enough word for it. He was on a neat, tree-lined street of townhouses—British, if he knew anything—with a horse and carriage just coming around the bend. *A horse and carriage!*

His pulse quickened and he steadied himself against a polished black iron fence that graced the townhome behind him. In doing so, he saw that his clothing was completely changed! He was wearing Regency fashions, but unlike the costume he'd worn for the JASNA event, this clothing was finer quality, the jacket weightier, and fit him to a tee. Fascinating! He would have studied his outfit more, but the carriage was coming abreast of him, and he turned his attention to it.

A coachman was at the reins and a passenger, a well-dressed woman with a handsome period bonnet, looked out at him. She was probably in her thirties and returned Stewart's stare with undisguised curiosity. On some impulse, he bowed his head in a polite nod and only then realized he was wearing a hat. He removed it and saw that it, too, was fine, dark brown/black and probably beaver, as he remembered reading how fashionable it was for men at this time.

His heart hadn't yet settled down. Further inspection of his surroundings revealed no telephone wires, and the streetlights were clearly old-fashioned, though whether gaslit or candle, he did not know.

Still steadying himself with one hand on the railing, he took a deep breath. The shock began to subside, replaced with a sense of relief. The men in black were gone, the gun at his head, too. But the strangeness, no, the *impossibility* of what had happened to him was still sinking in. He was in another time! Another *time*! As he digested that thought, a stab of fear shot through him. Margaret was still with the gunmen! Not to mention St. John and Daniel. What would become of them if the men, full of rage at his disappearance, took out their wrath upon them? Morbid possibilities ran through his brain in quick succession like the cars of an express train. His shoulders slumped at the deflating thoughts. They could be shot, or tortured, or kidnapped. His heart twisted as he pictured sweet Margaret's face, surely in torment—

Suddenly the door of the townhome behind him opened to reveal a man with a dark jacket, cravat and trousers, a butler, no doubt, peering at him with a perfectly emotionless face. Stewart's attention snapped back to the moment.

"I beg your pardon, sir, do you have business here?" the servant asked, in a bored tone.

Stewart searched his brain for an apt response, but his hesitation was enough to make the man add disapprovingly, "Pray, move on, then, sir. This is no street for loiterers."

Still trying to formulate a reply, Stewart remembered he was a man without an identity in this era. With a sudden newfound empathy for Margaret, for she had been in such a spot since he'd met her, he thought quickly. Nothing reasonable came to mind. With the smallest hope of success, he asked the only thing he could. "Do you happen to know where I may find the residence of Mr. St. John?"

The servant's face remained impassive, but one brow twitched. "Do you have business with Mr. St. John?"

Hope rose in Stewart's breast. "Do you know him?" He looked again at the townhome before him. "Is this his home?"

The butler nodded. "Yes, sir. But Mr. St. John is not here. May I take your card?"

"I—er—that is, I need to see Mrs. St. John." He walked up to face the man. Inside, he was reeling with the thought that he had arrived exactly where he must have inevitably ended up, at St. John's home, for where else could he go?

"The mistress is indisposed at present, sir, and not accepting callers."

Stewart sucked in a breath. Had St. John's wife had his child? If so, he felt awful, for the man should be there with his family, not Stewart. "Is—has—that is, is there a child?"

The staid butler now looked at him squarely, as if sizing him up. "Not yet, sir."

"In that case, I'm afraid I must see her. It's very urgent, you see, and concerns Mr. St. John."

The butler hesitated. "Your card, sir, if you please." But even as he spoke, he moved aside and gestured for Stewart to enter. Once inside the entrance foyer, the servant held out his hand. "I will bring it to the mistress."

Stewart eyed the outstretched hand. "Unfortunately, I, uh, I have no card at the moment."

The butler's eyes narrowed.

"But tell Mrs. St. John, please, that I am come from...her husband and Miss Margaret, who *sent* me here." Suddenly he realized he was holding the tallit in one hand. "Show her this."

The butler's face was still impassive, but a flicker of feeling had crossed his eyes at mention of St. John and Miss Margaret. He took the shawl. "Whom shall I say is awaiting her pleasure?" He didn't meet Stewart's eyes as he asked.

"Stewart Russell. Thank you."

The butler nodded in what was almost, but not quite, a light bow. "Please to wait here, sir." He went toward a staircase and ascended. Stewart watched him until he had reached the top and then disappeared from sight. He looked around then at the well-furnished hall but almost jumped, startled to find a liveried footman at the door to an adjoining room silently beholding him. The servant looked away hurriedly as soon as Stewart saw him.

After a minute passed, he had to force himself not to question the footman, curious as he was to hear his manner of speech, or the little details of this era he might innocently divulge if Stewart got him talking. He could imagine writing an article that would be accepted as fiction, "A Conversation with a 19th-Century Footman." It would look good for his academic record. But what was he thinking? Could he even return to his own time and life safely?

The butler reappeared and came unhurriedly down the stairs. Turning to the footman he said, "Escort this man to the mistress. In the drawing room."

He turned with an outstretched hand toward Stewart who stopped, puzzled, wondering what the man wanted from him. A tip? He began searching his pockets. Who knew if they might hold money?

"Your hat, sir, if you please," the butler intoned.

"Oh. Yes, of course." Stewart hurriedly removed it and handed it over. The butler bowed.

As he followed the footman, Stewart's heart rose again. This was amazing! He'd only just arrived and yet he felt he was doing exactly the right thing. He knew from Margaret that Mrs. St. John had time-travelled herself. Surely she would know how to advise him. He was also curious to meet the woman an imposing man like Mr. St. John would fall in love with.

Remorse twanged through him when he thought of the trouble he may have caused for his friends. But how far would those men go when he, the one they wanted, was still at large? God willing, those men were not given 'carte blanche' to go and kill whoever they wanted to in this matter. But now he would have to apprise Mrs. St. John of the danger to her husband and Margaret. Danger that existed because of him. What if she threw him out afterward without giving him back the tallit? He could be trapped here without a friend in the world.

As they turned from the stairs onto a corridor lined with gilt-framed portraits and rich carpets, he swallowed and searched his mind for the best way to present his predicament to her. Seconds later, he was shown into a handsomely furnished drawing room. Mrs. St. John—for it must be her, welcomed him with a slight nod, and motioned to a settee facing her armchair.

The footman bowed and left while Stewart took his seat, but he had to check himself from staring.

If he didn't know better, he'd say he was looking at Clarissa Channing! A very pregnant Clarissa, that is, although she had a softness in her eyes that Margaret's sister lacked. With a start, he realized he'd forgotten to give her a polite bow—that was the custom, wasn't it?

"I beg your pardon, I forgot the bow," he said apologetically as he rose quickly to redress his error. He was rewarded with a charming smile.

"I daresay you would, being from the future." She smiled conspiratorially.

Stewart suddenly felt a great deal more hopeful.

Our brightest blazes of gladness are commonly kindled
by unexpected sparks.
Samuel Johnson

Chapter 22

No Regency woman worth her salt would be seen in society when she was huge with child, and only close relations and friends would normally be allowed to call upon her. Although Claire found this unwritten code of behavior stifling, she followed it for her husband's sake, and for her own, too, because she'd be the talk of drawing rooms if she did not. Women were also expected to remain abed for the last few weeks of pregnancy, but this, Claire absolutely refused. The isolation was taxing, however, so she was almost glad to receive this Mr. Russell, though her mind buzzed with concern as to why Julian had sent him. Even more concerning was why her husband had not returned himself, considering her condition.

Stewart cleared his throat, wondering where to begin.

"You look remarkably like Miss Channing," he said. "Margaret mentioned that you and she, er, switched places in time?"

Claire nodded. "Something very close to that." She paused. "How is Clarissa?"

"Oh, well, very well," he said, though remembering guiltily that she'd just been through an ordeal because of him.

"And my husband and Miss Margaret?" she prodded, hoping he'd get to the point.

"Oh, also quite well, I believe." He swallowed uncomfortably.

"You believe?"

"Well, they were perfectly fine, but you see, I, er, ran into some trouble, and they were helping me when suddenly I found myself here." He looked wretched, and added, "I may have left them in some danger."

Claire's expression changed to stern alarm. "Did you steal the tallit from my husband?"

"Steal—no!"

"How did you get it, then? And what kind of danger did you leave them in?"

"Margaret begged him to give it to me—your husband. And then he did, he threw it and cried, 'Hold onto it!' I caught it against me and suddenly I was here, right in front of your townhome."

Her brows wrinkled. "Did he mean for you to use it?"

"Yes, because I was being threatened."

Claire bit her lip, thinking. If Julian had done that, he must have agreed it was necessary. She said, "What was the danger?" She rose and rang a bellpull near a curtain. "Pardon my bulk," she said, self-conscious despite herself. "Julian would have me using a handbell to summon the servants, but, as you are no doubt aware, movement is better for me and the baby."

Stewart nodded, thinking that Claire's 'bulk' as she called it, did her appearance no disservice. Some women absolutely glowed during pregnancy, and she seemed to be of their number. She was certainly near "her lying in," as they would say in this period. Her gown was fronted by a pretty lace apron or layers of them, he couldn't be sure. This would be to hide any opening from the undergown due to her growing size, he knew from his studies of the period.

It hit him again with force that this was no historical reenactment—he was in the past!!

A scratching at the door opened to reveal a footman. Claire said, "Bring Mr. Russell a glass of sherry."

"Thank you. I may need two," he added miserably.

She nodded at the footman and resumed her seat. "The danger?" she prodded.

"Yes, er, to be brief, there are men after me who mistakenly believe I overheard some incriminating information and believe I recorded it on my cellphone." He searched her face. 'You are familiar with…?"

"Cellphones? Yes, of course."

"How long have you lived here?" he asked.

"Finish your explanation first, please," she said.

"Yes, quite! I'm sorry. Where was I?"

"Men are after you."

"Right. I did not overhear any details, certainly not enough for a court of law, but they are convinced I am holding the phone with incriminating evidence— "

"Are you? And evidence against whom?"

"I'm not! I panicked and threw the phone away, but it can't be found or I'd give it to them. And I don't know who I overheard talking! But the crazy thing is they feel I'm a threat and they've been shadowing me for a week. They've always been armed, as far as I can tell, and today I think they wanted to—to, well, to do away with me."

Claire nodded, putting the pieces together. "And so my husband somehow knew this and sent you here, out of harm's way."

Stewart nodded unhappily. "I'm sorry." He paused, thinking back. "It was Margaret, really, who urged him to it."

At that moment the servant returned with a silver salvo holding two small glasses of sherry. He held it out before Stewart who took one, immediately taking a good draught. The footman put the other on a side table beside him. Stewart bit back the thanks on his tongue. It felt awfully rude not to thank the man, but he knew it was Regency etiquette not to speak to servants unless necessary, and certainly not to thank them for small services.

Before he retreated, Claire said, "Charlie, tell Grey to send word to Lady Ashworth that I must see her at once. Tell her…it's not the child, but it's urgent. About the *shawl*."

The footman bowed. "Yes, ma'am."

When he'd closed the door behind him, Claire turned worried eyes to Stewart. "So you escaped your danger but now you think the men after you may harm my husband and Margaret?"

Stewart sighed and nodded unhappily. "That is a possibility. They will be angry that I vanished."

Claire looked stricken.

Stewart's expression rose. "Don't be alarmed! There were police coming, now I think about it. I'm sure they've been able to keep our friends safe."

"Your friends, perhaps, but my *husband* and my dear *relation,"* she returned. She looked at him truculently. "The police might take a long time to arrive."

"No, they were at the street. We were in an alley, not far from them at all."

This seemed to reassure Claire who sat back, nodding. "How is Margaret?" she asked. "We've been so worried about her, all alone in the future."

"She's not alone," he assured her. "She's been with me and with your sister, er, I mean, Clarissa."

Claire was tempted to use the tallit and go search for her husband and Margaret. How else could she be certain of their safety? But even as she thought it, she thought, too, of her little unborn infant inside her. Who knew what the commotion of time travel might do to a child? And what if the baby's birth took place in the future? Already Julian and Margaret were stranded there. How could all four of them hope to get passage home?

"What do you suggest I do at this point?" Mr. Russell broke into her thoughts. "If you want me to return at once, I will." He glanced at the tallit, which Claire had hung beside her on the sofa. "Assuming it will work for me."

Claire studied him. "I want to hear your story in its entirety, and particularly everything since you met my husband and Miss Margaret. Then I shall advise you."

Stewart nodded, took a sip of sherry, and then a deep breath. "My name is Stewart Russell and I'm working on a doctorate in 19th century women's literature…"

Margaret and St. John turned out of the alley to find that three police cars had arrived at the scene with their flashing, rotating lights. Clarissa was still speaking with an officer but when she spied them from the corner of her eye, her face lit up. "Officer, I've told you all I know. You have my contact number. I see friends of mine and I'm leaving."

"We'll need you to come to the station, Miss Channing," he replied apologetically. "Just to sign a statement. It's a formality and shouldn't take long."

Annoyance flitted across her face. "Julian!" she cried. "Here, take my keys. This one is for the apartment. I'm afraid I have to go to the police station, but I'll be back as soon as I can."

St. John took the keys. "I'm pleased to see you came through the ordeal unscathed," he said.

Clarissa made a scoffing sound. "My dear sir, you must know that after the sort of travel we've been subject to, very little flummoxes me." She turned her gaze to Margaret. "My biggest concern was for Margaret and Stewart."

Margaret's heart swelled at this further proof of Clarissa's softened heart. She had no intention of pointing out that "my dear sir," and "flummoxes me" were typical speech for 1819 and ruin the moment. But Clarissa suddenly looked startled and put a hand over her mouth. She leaned in and whispered, "I really don't speak that way anymore. I think your presence, the both of you, must bring it out in me."

Julian bowed his head with a wry grin. "Happy to restore proper English in anyone."

"Do take care of Margaret until I return," Clarissa added, with an affectionate look at her sister. Looking uncertainly around, she asked, "Is Stewart all right?"

Margaret nodded emphatically. "We sent him home," she said, emphasizing the word 'home.'

"Stewart—Stewart Russell—he's home?" the officer asked, coming to attention. "We'll need to question him. What's his address?"

Margaret blanched. "I don't know, actually. I just know he went home," she said again with that same emphasis, looking at Clarissa.

The officer eyed her strangely but shut his book. "We'll find it. Oh, er, were you involved in what happened earlier?"

"They just arrived," Clarissa volunteered. "They're on their way to visit me, you see."

"So how do you know where Stewart is?" he persisted.

"He left earlier today," Margaret said, her heart fluttering with the lie. "I don't know for certain where he is now. When we saw him at the library, he was fine."

The officer pulled out his notebook again and a pencil. "What is your name?" he asked.

Clarissa, in her old, impatient tone, cried, "Officer! If you need me at the station, we must leave now. I don't have all day! And I warrant you, Margaret was not involved!" Her eyes widened at her use of the word, "warrant you," but she waved them off.

The officer surveyed Clarissa, nodded, and then put away the book.

The following morning, Margaret rose with an uncustomary heaviness of heart. Stewart was in the past. She ought to be ecstatic, for he was out of danger. And yet…yet…What if he was lost somewhere in time? And if he had reached 1819, what if he ran into trouble? A man without an identity or means of support…he could not get by on his own.

St. John, who had no choice but to spend the night since he no longer had the tallit, did not share her concerns. "He shall be fine. The tallit is divinely directed, recall. I have no doubt he is with Claire at my home as we speak."

Clarissa had returned ninety minutes after they'd reached her apartment the day before, and now agreed with him. "Remember that when I arrived here, I was at the right place, I had the right clothes, and even money when I needed it!"

"My only concern," added St. John, "is that he has my means of going home. But let us go and see this woman, Freida, Lady Ashworth called her, at her shop. It must be open today."

"May I come along?" asked Clarissa.

An hour later, following a quick breakfast and a cab ride, they stood on the pavement in front of the store. The sign "Curiosities" was unchanged, the only difference being that now the sign at the door read, "OPEN."

The three entered, setting off a bell that jangled pleasantly. A sweet-faced woman with curly grey hair came their way. She was wearing a shawl over her dress, the tassels of which told her visitors that it was no doubt a tallit. "May I help you?" she asked, with a smile.

"Are you Freida?" asked St. John.

"I am," she said, her eyes brightening.

"Lady Ashworth was here recently," he said, looking at her to see if she recalled the unusual visit from a time traveler.

Freida nodded with a little smile. "Oh, yes, I remember."

"Excellent. She said you have a special tallit for us. Do you know the one I refer to?"

"I do." She looked around as if searching for someone.

"I have come to purchase it," St. John said. "If you will be so kind—"

Her smile faded. "*You* wish to purchase it?"

"As soon as possible, if you please," St. John said with an edge to his voice.

She pursed her lips. "I'm sorry. But you are not the man I can sell it to."

Margaret could not contain herself. "Great Aunt Ashworth said he is! Lady Ashworth, that is. She said you *told* her he is!"

"You must be Margaret," she said with a kind smile. "Your Great Aunt was worried about you." Turning back to St. John she said, "I told her I can only sell it to the man it was meant for. I am sorry, but that man is not you."

"Who *is* the man you can sell it to?" Clarissa interjected.

Freida shook her head. "I don't know his name yet. I'll know him when he comes."

The threesome looked from one to the other in concern. Margaret gasped. "Lud! It must be Stewart!"

"Margaret, how vulgar! Do you still say that?" Clarissa turned on her. "Why can't you just say, 'pon rep,' as other young women do?"

"I beg your pardon, Clarissa," Margaret said, though not the least repentant. "There are more important things to occupy us just now!"

"Indeed," St. John said. He turned to Freida in consternation. "Stewart is in the past—with our tallit, and I have no idea when or if he'll return. Two of us here need very much to get home. Is there another shawl—perhaps for Margaret? Our problem, to begin with, was that the tallit would no longer transport us both."

"I've been thinking about that," she said, moving behind the counter to put something down. She faced them from there. "The tallit worked for you and your bride for quite some time, did it not?"

He nodded. "For the past three years."

"Mm-hmm," she said, unsurprised. "And Margaret is not your wife."

"No. She's a distant relation by my marriage to Claire."

Freida laughed. "Distant—quite." She rubbed her hands together. "Here's the thing. Your tallit brought Margaret here but will not take her home, correct?"

"I haven't tried to go home without Mr. St. John," Margaret explained. "But we tried to leave together numerous times, to no avail."

Freida nodded thoughtfully. "I think it's clear you are to return by another shawl." She asked, "Is there something between you and this Stewart person?"

Margaret blushed furiously, but Clarissa said, "There is," with a smile.

Freida smiled too. "I think when Stewart returns, he will come here for the shawl, and you will get back home together. In case you didn't notice," she added with a sparkle, "the tallits are for matchmaking!" Smiling, she shook her head. "One might think that if a mere mortal is given a chance to see or dwell in another time that some great thing would be changed. An assassination prevented, for instance. But no!" She smiled again. "My tallits are for matchmaking!"

"But should I not be able to purchase it, then? If it is meant for me as well as Stewart?" Margaret motioned with her arms. "And here we are, in the right place! Surely, this is providential."

But Freida shook her head. "I can only sell it to the man it was meant for."

It was like a tired refrain, Clarissa thought. Positively robotic.

Margaret's brow turned stormy. "In this day when women have such freedoms, I am still constrained to wait for a man to buy it?"

Freida said gently, "It has nothing to do with that. I have sold many special shawls to women. In this case, for what reason I do not know, the recipient is a man."

"What you are telling us," St. John put in, "is that we are stuck here in your time unless Stewart finds it convenient to come back."

Freida nodded sympathetically. "If this Stewart is the right man, I can assure you, he will return. He must." She smiled.

Clarissa asked, "You make these by hand, do you not?"

"I do."

"Can't you make one for Mr. St. John? His first child is to be delivered at any hour! And then he can send Stewart back for the new shawl."

Freida shook her head firmly. "I could make a shawl, but it won't be special. It won't meet your needs. I do not determine who to make the special ones for. I do not choose. The recipients are chosen by the Spirit."

St. John crossed his arms. "What do you suggest we do?"

Freida thought for a few seconds. She looked up and met his eyes. "Pray!"

> "Even in our imperfection, good things—even great things—are accomplished with God's help."
> Richelle E. Goodrich

Chapter 23

The two glasses of sherry were empty, and a tea service with an empty teapot, the result of Claire's sipping while listening to Stewart's tale of woe, were the only signs to reveal the passage of time as he spoke. Claire had let him ramble on with unnecessary details because he also gave the pertinent ones, and she loved hearing how Margaret had made inroads into his heart. Not that he'd put it in those terms or even meant to reveal it, but Claire had no doubt, after hearing him out, of his affection for the girl, and it warmed her to him.

After he'd finished, he slumped in his seat, suddenly exhausted. Claire was very much reminded that here was a 21st-century man, for no gentleman of her day would sit that way in company of a lady.

"Do you know," Stewart moaned, "I don't think I've been able to really relax since I overheard that deuced conversation!" He stopped short, sat up, and grinned. "Wait. Did I really say that? 'Deuced conversation?'" He rubbed his chin. "'Tis a shame Margaret isn't here; it would delight her." But then he stared, wide-eyed, at Claire. "I said *'tis*! I never say that! What's happening to me?"

Claire giggled. "Do not be alarmed. I believe it means, sir, that you are meant to reside in this time. Clarissa, you know, when she arrived in your time, lost her British accent and spoke like an American!"

He shook his head. "That seems fantastic. Unbelievably so."

Claire nodded. "What's more, every single time I arrived here from Maine, I was dressed in perfectly modish fashions of the day, and I spoke like a Brit, as I do now!"

Stewart glanced at his clothing. "I arrived in these perfect clothes. They're much better than the costume I wore in New York."

Claire smiled approvingly. "As fine as my husband's, I daresay."

Stewart said, "I wish he could see me now. The day I first saw him with Margaret in the library he looked down his nose at me and I knew he despised my outfit." Stewart had found his costume on the rack in a store that catered to movie costuming needs.

"He has an eye for well-tailored clothing," Claire explained, which implied, of course, that he also recognized the poorly fitted.

"The question is, what do you suggest I do now?" Stewart asked dejectedly.

Claire surveyed him and saw that his eyes were shadowed and recalled how he'd slumped in his seat. "Sir," she said. "The first thing you must do is allow me to offer you a guest room so you may take a nap."

"Sleep?" he asked, with one brow raised. "When we don't know how your husband and Margaret are getting on?"

She rose for the bellpull with a calm smile. "I feel, somehow, that they are safe. I don't believe the tallit would have worked for you if it meant leaving them in real danger." She yanked on the brocaded fabric and turned to face him. "Get some sleep, Mr. Russell. We'll discuss what you must do next once you're rested."

In his handsomely furnished guest room, Stewart first admired his Regency finery in the mirror, marveling at how transformed he appeared. Wearing this impeccable clothing almost made him feel like a different man. Besides the jacket, shirt and creamy cravat, he wore trousers, not breeches, as he had in New York, and black shoes. His hair was different, too, with a rather rakish cut of the day. He had more height than before on top, and curled tendrils over his forehead. A sudden image of the woman in the carriage staring at him with as much curiosity as he'd stared at her and her equipage, crossed his mind, and he realized that, for a Regency gentleman, he looked good. It brought a pleasant feeling.

He could not bear to undo the cravat, knowing he'd never tie it again as nicely, and so he lay down with it on. He removed the shoes, but when his head hit the pillow, he felt the usual sense of dread come over him. He remembered, then, that he had no reason for it here. It was due to the black suits, but they were now—think of it!—more than 200 years away!

And suddenly his exhaustion hit him full force, the burnout from having to anxiously look over his shoulder everywhere he went, not knowing what evil lurked around the next bend. But now he felt as if he were lying upon a king's bed, rich with soft pillows and secure within and without as if sentries stood guard at the door. Yet the mattress wasn't any softer than his own, and there were no sentries. He simply felt safe. He hadn't felt that way since the day in the botanical gardens. His muscles relaxed, his brain ceased its worries, and he fell into a frazzled sleep.

Margaret, Clarissa and St. John hailed a cab after leaving Freida's shop but rode in subdued silence. At length, Clarissa tried to cheer them by pointing out there were worse places to be stranded than New York City. She suggested they behave like tourists—after all, St. John and Margaret *were*—and why didn't they go to the top of the Empire State Building? Or see the Museum of Natural History or the Metropolitan Museum of Art, both of which, she assured them, they would find astonishing. They could see a play on Broadway, stroll through Central Park and taste a 'bona fide' Sabrett hot dog from a street cart (this brought curious looks but no comments). Or, she could try to get tickets for a boat tour around the city, or—

"I'm afraid I'm not in mind of being a tourist, Clarissa," said Margaret. "I should enjoy exploring using your com-puter, though."

"I can't believe you two!" Clarissa exclaimed. "There is no shortage of diversions here that you will never see elsewhere."

Margaret said, "If Stewart gets his tallit and I am to travel home with him, then why should I not also return with him, as Claire has often returned to Maine with Mr. St. John? I will have other opportunities. For today, I should like to borrow your er, laptop."

This seemed extremely dull to Clarissa who offered, "Even if we only go shopping you will find the stores here full of items you've never dreamed of! You'll find it mind-blowing."

Margaret's face creased in concern. "Mind—what?"

"Fascinating," she amended. "You'll love it!"

"*Love* shopping?" Margaret sputtered a laugh. "I suppose one can *adore* shopping as one adores a favorite bonnet, but one does not *love* it. Love is reserved for mother and father or one's siblings or spouse. Besides which, shopping has never been of great interest to me—"

"Oh, never mind, Margaret!" Clarissa cried. "You're still a bluestocking, I see," she added crossly.

"Now, now, ladies," interjected St. John. "You were doing wonderfully, let's not ruin it now. I'd never seen such sisterly accord between you if you must know. I rather liked it."

Margaret eyed her sister, and her resentment subsided. "I did, also."

Keeping her eyes on the passing street, Clarissa said softly, "In fact, I did too." A silence descended while they waited at a long traffic light.

St. John said, "Why do we not purchase a car?"

Clarissa chuckled. "You would detest driving in this city! You like speed."

"Can we not leave the city?" he asked, nonplussed. Then, remembering something Claire had told him, "What about a helicopter tour? I've never been in one."

"What is a helicopter?" asked Margaret.

"I think it would terrify you," Clarissa said, without explaining what it was.

"It won't terrify me," said St. John.

"But think of Margaret," Clarissa said.

"Leave me at your apartment and go without me," Margaret said. "'Tis what I prefer."

Many hours later, back at Clarissa's apartment, Margaret was engrossed in *The Sketch Book of Geoffrey Crayon* by Washington Irving and up to "The Legend of Sleepy Hollow." She couldn't wait to tell Stewart her opinion that Irving had borrowed the idea of the headless horseman from Walter Scott's, "The Chase."

She'd started out researching inventions as she'd originally intended to do. She thought about the huge lower classes and wondered if there was something she might hasten to "discover" for their sake but came across an article about Ignaz Semmelweis, a physician who recommended hand washing to doctors for better hygiene. (*Hand washing for doctors!* thought Margaret.) Other doctors maliciously attacked him and eventually, he was committed to an asylum. It turned out his ideas were correct. Margaret would pay more attention to handwashing. But she was no martyr. Best not to introduce anything controversial.

Continuing to search, she turned to cookery, intrigued by the simplicity of perhaps introducing a new libation when she noticed a drinking straw in an online image. She realized shortly that it was the very thing to answer! A simple device, this drinking straw was sure to become an enormous success in her day. Her version must needs be made of metal, for plastic did not yet exist, so she would use silver. Silver was expensive, and only the upper class could afford it. It would be a luxury, therefore, and much coveted. *And she would be an inventress.*

Stewart's words ran across her mind. "You're smart enough to come up with your own invention," and, "You don't need to invent something." But she guiltily kept up her plan. She sketched a straw horizontally and vertically, and emblazoned it on her brain, for she would have to draw a blueprint for the ironmonger first, and then take it to a silversmith.

Stewart, after all, was gone. Just because he'd thought her lovely didn't mean others in society would. And then she realized that unless she got back home, she might not be a part of that society any longer. And in the present day, drinking straws were no novelty. She was worse off than ever. Stuck in the present, leaving a father sick at heart to die of mortification, friendless save for her sister and Mr. St. John—*please, Stewart,* she thought, *come back!*

As her mind continued to ruminate about him and what unhappy misfortunes might have befallen him in 1819, Clarissa and Mr. St. John returned. Clarissa looked utterly fagged, but Mr. St. John seemed his usual keen-eyed self.

"How was your helicopter?" Margaret asked, politely.

St. John was going toward his guest room but stopped. "Excellent, thank you. I'm trying to convince your sister to purchase one."

Clarissa said dryly, "Spending over $1,000 today so he could take the tour *four* times was nothing next to what that expense would be." She sighed, looking at Margaret as if for help. "I've tried explaining to him that purchasing a helicopter is out of the question."

Margaret was amazed to see a small grin on Mr. St. John as he continued past. He'd only been teasing!

"I daresay he's quizzing you, Clarissa!"

Clarissa surveyed her and then gave a little smile herself. "Of course. How silly of me."

"Did he indeed take the tour four times?"

She nodded. "He did indeed. I accompanied him only once. And I daresay there is nothing more plaguing than waiting upon a tourist to get his fill of a novelty. 'Twas quite boorish of him to make me endure it."

Margaret said, "Only think of how very plagued he is with the uncertainty of returning to Claire. I am sure he would never have asked so much of you had he not been in need of a diversion to keep him from thinking upon it."

Clarissa, who had put down her purse and removed her shoes, came and sat across from Margaret in an electric recliner where she made herself comfortable. She was barefooted, wearing slacks and a summery white blouse, and Margaret found herself staring. There wasn't a drawing room in England that wouldn't be scandalized at such an attitude, such supreme lack of manners. Nor a lady who wouldn't give Clarissa a set-down for how she was surely destroying her figure and would be doomed to poor posture for the rest of her life. And yet…Clarissa looked comfortable.

"Do you mind if I call Adam?" she asked. "I haven't heard from him since last night."

"Not at all," Margaret replied, happy for the chance to finish her book. When she returned home—*if* she returned!—*The Sketch Book* wouldn't be available to her. It hadn't been published yet. She ought to have faith that of course Stewart would have the sense of mind to return to them. He was an honorable man, wasn't he? But each hour that ticked past weakened her trust.

"Hello, darling," Clarissa said into her phone. "No, fine, what about you?" There was a pause. "Good, good. Oh, wonderful…"

Margaret tried to drown out the sound and focus on her book, but it was like trying to ignore a guest in your drawing room to speak to another, only the first guest wouldn't take the hint and be quiet.

St. John passed again, straightening his jacket. He put a hand into his pocket and pulled out a cellphone similar to Clarissa's. "Here," he said, giving it to Margaret. "We stopped on the way to pick them up. 'Burners,' Clarissa called them. If Stewart shows up, you must contact me immediately."

Margaret stared wonderingly at the little device in her hands. Her own phone! "I should adore doing that! Only how is it done?"

St. John demonstrated how to make a call, but admitted, "Clarissa will have to show us how to connect our devices so you can notify me."

"Are you going somewhere?" Margaret asked.

"The library. 'Tis where the tallit brought us first and where it returned me to when I came back. I suspect the same will be true for Stewart."

Clarrisa was just saying, "Alright, darling, stay in touch. I love you, too."

Margaret's cheeks burned. Was love spoken so easily now? Astonishing!

"Give me your phones, both of you," Clarissa instructed. "I'll put my number, and then each of your numbers in them. You'll be able to call me or each other." St. John gave her the paperwork from the store and Margaret watched while she did.

"Do you indeed call them burners?" she asked. "I thought they were sell-phones."

"They are; but these are disposable." She looked up at Margaret. "You can discard them when you're done using them."

"I shan't discard mine!" declared Margaret.

When Clarissa had handed back the phones, St. John thanked her and said he'd be off.

"It's nearly time to eat," Clarissa said.

"You in America eat your evening meal far too early," returned St. John smartly.

"I know you're anxious for Stewart's return," Clarissa said, "but going to the library won't hasten it.' She paused. "Please, Julian. Wait here with us. If Stewart returns, he'll come here, I'm certain."

Margaret said, "But if Stewart returns, he may be in as much danger as ever. There may be new men after him, now." They had been happy to learn that the two men who had chased them in the alley the day before had been apprehended. Clarissa herself had seen them march by at the police station, handcuffed, stone-faced, and accompanied by three officers. But this gave Margaret little reassurance of Stewart's safety. Whoever those men worked for would only send more in their place. How would Stewart ever be safe again? Unless he stayed in the past.

"He ought to stay in the past then," said Clarissa carelessly. She realized instantly her mistake, for St. John's eyes had narrowed. She hurriedly added, "*After* he returns to get his own tallit, of course."

For the next few hours, the three contemplated what might be hindering Stewart's return. Clarissa had ordered out for dinner. Upper-class ladies in the Regency never did their own cooking, and she was not about to start. But her hired chef was off.

"He knows his danger and is letting time pass in order to make his enemy consider him vanished," St. John said, reasonably. "But I'll wring his neck if he waits over long. If I miss the birth—"

"He wouldn't be so unfeeling as that," Margaret put in loyally.

"Not intentionally, perhaps, but incidentally, I fear."

They considered where he might have 'landed' in England, and the dangers rampant in parts of London to a man unfamiliar with the area.

Clarissa said, "The tallit never yet brought any of us to a random place without purpose. Stewart has your tallit, and it always took you to South Audley Street, so why should you think otherwise for him? He must surely have gone to your home, and Claire will not allow him to stay overlong. She will be as anxious to have you home, sir," she said to St. John, "as you are to be with her."

St. John nodded but with quiet weariness that was unlike him.

Poor Mr. St. John, thought Margaret. *His troubles are all on my account, for I plagued him to bring me here!*

"Allow me to fetch you a glass of port," Clarissa offered.

He looked up. "Splendid."

Clarissa was tempted to have the time travelers watch a movie—what could be more diverting, more likely to help them forget their dilemma? Margaret would adore the experience, for Clarissa would pick something fun and whimsical; but when Margaret returned to the past (and Clarissa felt sure she would) she would never forget the thrill of it. She would be made unhappy with her life there. Clarissa herself would find it a punishment to return on account of her modern life, the technology behind only her husband in importance. So she proposed a game of piquet. She hadn't played the game in ages, as nobody played it now.

Margaret was amenable, and St. John became amenable when Clarissa pointed out that there was no better way for him to pass the time since nothing he could do would get him home to Claire. Why not spend the evening in a pleasant occupation?

But piquet had lost favor even in the Regency, and St. John suggested they play whist.

They'd played only one rubber when Margaret frowned and cried, "I cannot play any longer, I am sorry." When the others looked at her expectantly, she explained, "I can play this game at home. While I am here, I must do things that I can only do here."

"Do you mean, you wish to go out and explore the city?" Clarissa asked.

"No. Only give me your laptop again, and I will entertain myself until kingdom comes!"

And then the doorbell rang.

All three froze, staring at Clarissa. She ran to the intercom.

"Who is it?"

"Lady Ashworth," came the dignified, surprising answer.

Things never go the way you expect them to. That's both
the joy and frustration in life.
Michael Stuhlbarg

Chapter 24

When her ladyship arrived at the door, she was met by three
questioning faces, though no one dared say, "We were hoping you
would be Stewart. Why are you here and not he?"

Clarissa welcomed her Great Aunt warmly, took her shawl, or
rather tried to, but Lady Ashworth stopped her, saying, "That is the
tallit, my dear, and I must use it to get home."

St. John said, "It is my tallit, if you please, and I daresay I must
use it to get home. Do not say my wife has already borne our
child."

Lady Ashworth stopped to receive an embrace from a suddenly
emotional Margaret, who had realized, as she considered having to
stay in the future, that she'd been afraid she'd never see the woman
again. It was on the tip of her tongue to burst out with, "How is
Mr. Russell? Is all well with him?" but she was too well-mannered
to interrupt St. John's conversation with her great aunt. Her
ladyship sat across from him now and said squarely, "No, sir, but
she is more than ready, however, I should say."

He breathed a sigh of relief.

But her brows knit together and she asked, "Which is why we
are both wondering what makes you linger here? Have you not
purchased the new shawl yet?"

He explained quickly that he was not the man who could, and
that Mr. Russell (who had indeed gone to 1819 or her ladyship
would not have the shawl)—must be the one who would
successfully make the purchase, and, until he came back, St. John
and Margaret were stuck here.

Margaret felt she was holding her breath.

Lady Ashworth nodded her head rather low. "I see. So he must
needs return to you. I am come on his behalf." Her eyes twinkled

at St. John. "I commend you, sir, for having the goodness to give him the tallit."

"'Twas merely a loan," St. John amended.

"He comprehends that, I warrant you, though we thought you would obtain another for your use. Mr. Russell, as you know, is in danger here. He is willing to return, but Claire and I both thought it best, after considering the matter, for me to come first and see if we might discover whether his danger has passed." She turned to Clarissa. "The men who chased him yesterday?"

"Were arrested," Clarissa confirmed.

"But there will no doubt be more to follow in their footsteps," Margaret hurriedly added. "We do not know who sent them and therefore we cannot say whether he is any safer now than heretofore."

Lady Ashworth nodded. She accepted an apéritif from Clarissa with a short smile, took a sip, and said, "Then he is still at sixes and sevens."

"As are we," said St. John heavily, "unless he returns to us and procures the new shawl."

Lady Ashworth smoothed her gown. "I see now that he must. I shall finish this little drink, if you please, and be on my way." She hesitated. "Pity that Freida did not trouble to inform me that you were not the man to purchase the new tallit."

"She didn't know," put in Clarissa. "She said she has to see the man to know him."

St. John had been thinking. "Perhaps you can stay," he said to Lady Ashworth, "and I shall go and see to my wife. I'll return for you and Margaret, make no doubt."

"I daresay you would, sir," said Lady Ashworth. "Only I insist upon your staying. Margaret may need you. If your wife is delivered of her child betimes, I shall be there to assist, and I can do more for her than you."

Margaret cried, "But Claire made him promise! And I shall be safe with Clarissa."

Lady Ashworth nodded kindly at her. "Claire and I discussed it. She shares my sentiments on this. We both think it best to settle the matter entirely." Looking at St. John she added with a sparkle in her eye, "Though she does pine for you, Julian."

St. John rubbed his chin. "I'll return as soon as you send Mr. Russell our way."

Lady Ashworth emptied her little glass with a last, delicate sip.

"By the by," said St. John as she rose from her chair, "when Mr. Russell arrived, did he appear in my library as you and I do?"

Her ladyship thought for a moment. "Claire said he arrived just outside the house."

"Happy arrival," murmured Margaret, who saw how silly she'd been to worry so.

"When you return, send him to us immediately," said St. John, impatient as ever.

"Oh, I shall send him, but you shan't see him immediately," she warned. "I had to hail a cab to get here from the New York Public Library!" She rubbed her chin. "I should let him sleep tonight, I think. He was utterly worn out, according to Claire. I arrived at your home after he'd retired, you see." She eyed St. John ruminatively. "Expect him in the morning."

They all stood, while Lady Ashworth readied the shawl to drape over her heart.

"How did you know where to find me?" Clarissa asked, for her great aunt had never visited her apartment before.

"Stewart told me." She paused and looked around at the Georgian-style rooms. "Very well done, my dear," she said approvingly. Then, with a kind look at Clarissa, "It was prodigiously good to see you."

"And you, my lady," said Clarissa warmly, with a smile.

Surveying Clarissa more closely, her ladyship added, "I daresay the future agrees with you."

"We all think so!" cried Margaret.

Then, looking at each of them in turn, Lady Ashworth raised the tallit. "Adieu, my dears!" She drew it close about her chest and vanished.

Stewart slept all that day and woke early the following morning. As soon as he began stirring, a maid appeared, curtseyed, and asked if she could get him anything.

"Coffee, perhaps?" he asked hopefully. She blinked, curtseyed again and disappeared. Minutes later, she reappeared with a pitcher of water and filled the ewer on a stand in a corner, leaving him a fresh bar of *Pears' Transparent Soap*, (which he knew because it plainly said so) and a clean cloth. She came again and added a surprisingly sturdy ivory toothbrush but with coarse-looking bristles, and a tin of white powder which he decided instantly against using.

As she curtseyed and was about to disappear again, he said, hesitantly, "Ah, any chance of getting that coffee?"

"Cook's workin' on it, sir." She paused. "Shall I tell mistress you're up, sir?"

"Certainly, if you like." She turned to go. He said, "Er, excuse me, but is the mistress up?"

The maid smiled. "She be up early every day, now, sir." Confidentially she added, "The movement of the babe wakes 'er."

He checked his cravat in the mirror and felt that, by giving it only a tug here or there, it was quite presentable. He donned his finely cut jacket and was just putting his shoes on when a servant scratched again at the door.

"Come in."

This time a man appeared who looked with some surprise to see Stewart fully dressed.

"I'm come to help you, sir," he said. "Can I be of service?"

"What sort of help do you provide?" Stewart asked with a disarming smile, hoping it would make up for his ignorance.

The man entered and bowed. "I'm Arthur, sir, Mr. St. John's vallay."

A valet, of course! Stewart stood before him self-consciously. "Er, in that case, how do I look?"

The man looked him over head to toe. He came up and touched his cravat. "Let me do a new one for you, sir. And if you'll kindly remove the trousers, I'll give them a good hot iron, sir."

Stewart looked down at his pants. They looked fine to him. "Will that be necessary?" he asked, fearing that he'd be waiting for some time before he could go down for breakfast. And he was very hungry after his long sleep.

"Won't take me but a minute, sir. Iron's all hot, y'see. And I'll just get hold of one of Mr. St. John's cravats—he won't mind, sir." But as he removed the creamy cloth he murmured, "This is very good cloth, sir."

"Thank you," said Stewart, though he felt undeserving of the compliment. He removed his trousers, doing a double take at the pair of drawers on his person, which seemed rather loose.

"Arthur, er, where do I…? That is, where can I?"

"Ah, we 'ave a watering closet nearby, sir, or, if you prefer, there's a bedpan right 'ere," and he motioned under the bed.

"The watering closet, please," said Stewart.

After Lady Ashworth had vanished from their midst the night before, St. John came to his feet and began pacing the room. Clarissa watched him for roughly sixty seconds and cried, "Julian, this will not answer. You will have us all on edge if you keep that up."

He came to an abrupt halt and looked searchingly at her and Margaret, almost as if he'd forgotten their existence. "I beg your pardon." He frowned, then. "I wonder if I should make my way to the library in the morning. Her ladyship arrived there, as we did, and no doubt Stewart will as well. Perchance he may fall into trouble before he can reach us. He may suffer harm, and the shawl will be lost."

Margaret rose from her seat. "Oh, dear, I fear you may be right!"

"Both of you, sit down!" ordered Clarissa in a formidable tone. "You are better off staying here where Stewart knows to find you." St. John's lips turned up at being ordered to do anything by Clarissa, but he obeyed, as did Margaret.

An hour passed. Clarissa had Margaret tell her everything that had happened to her since she and St. John first appeared in New York, with particular interest in anything concerning Stewart. St. John sat by, ostensibly reading a magazine, but his ears perked up at the mention of Stewart also, for he could not help but be interested in young Margaret's admirer.

Margaret left out their having kissed, for she was too mortified to mention it, but she told everything else since she'd found herself alone at the hotel without Mr. St. John. She explained that the JASNA conference was how she had met Stewart, and that she had become a part of it without meaning to. She told what she'd learned about Miss Austen, and the library's wonderful Pforzheimer Collection, and how Stewart was studying women writers of their day. This, she assured them, had sparked many a delightful conversation, but her brow darkened when she reached the point at which she learned the men in suits were shadowing him. The men seemed more threatening each time they saw them, she said, until it was clear, "yesterday, as you recall," that they meant no less than to kill Stewart.

Her audience listened appreciatively.

St. John said, "It seems the tallit had some purpose in bringing us to New York after all. I don't suppose you have considered how Mr. Russell will find a place in society."

Margaret's face puckered in thought. That was a problem, indeed. Clarissa looked like Clarie's twin, so that when Claire left for the past, Clarissa was able to assume her identity seamlessly. As for Claire, she had been claimed by Lady Ashworth, a marchioness, as her granddaughter. Though her ladyship's pedigree had raised brows in society when first she married the marquess, the initial skepticism had long passed. She was popular for her forthright manners and familiarly aristocratic airs— unbeknownst to them by-products of being raised in modern

America—so that her granddaughter was also accepted. In addition to this, Claire was married to Julian St. John of an ancient family line and utter respectability. But Stewart had no lookalike or noble relation in 1819. He had no identity at all.

While she pondered over these disturbing thoughts, St. John came to his feet and bowed politely at the ladies. "As we are to remain for yet one more nocturnal watch, I bid you goodnight." He paused. "I trust my wife will be so kind as to hold off the birth of our child until the morn."

The ladies bade him goodnight, but neither had a reply to his snide remark about Claire and the birth. They felt his angst, but what could be said? It was in God's hands.

After subjecting himself to the ministrations of a valet for the first time in his life, Stewart felt more than prepared to face Claire at breakfast. Lady Ashworth sat across from her in the morning room when he entered, and he bade them both good morning with a fine bow.

He was served a made-to-order breakfast of three eggs, bacon and toast, as well as coffee.

"Now," said Claire, after he'd had a chance to start his breakfast and after asking how he'd slept, "Here is what you must do. Her ladyship went to New York last night while you slept."

He hated to be rude, but Stewart could not contain himself. "Is Margaret all right? Are they all safe and well?" His eyes were tormented.

Her ladyship smiled kindly and even reached across the table to pat his hand. "They are well!" she assured him heartily.

Stewart's relief was palpable. His heart had flown into his throat, it felt, but now returned to normal.

"But here is the thing," said Claire. "It seems you alone are the man who can procure the new tallit."

Stewart's brows rose. He was about to inquire how he might do that, and what made them suppose he was the man when he had no idea how to get one, but Claire continued speaking and he meant not to interrupt her again.

"You will return to New York and bring Margaret back with you. My husband was unable to procure another tallit because you must do it, you see, and so when you return, you will give him this tallit—" she motioned at the shawl, draped over a chair at her side—"and procure the new one for yourselves."

Stewart nodded unhappily. He'd found that he quite liked 1819 and wished he could stay to experience more of it. He had no assurance that he could "procure" a new tallit, nor did he believe that he was guaranteed return passage if he did.

But he knew he must go back. He could not be the cause of leaving St. John or Margaret in the future when they belonged here. But he felt sure that to go back to the future meant certain death. Nevertheless, he nodded with false bravery and grim acceptance. He would do what was best for his friends.

"Have no worries," Claire continued as if reading his mind. "We are convinced you are meant to stay with us here in our time. You arrived in proper clothing, your speech is already beginning to mirror ours, and both these facts indicate that you are meant to stay and live here. The tallit only does that for people when it's going to transfer them in time, you see."

Lady Ashworth added as if for good measure, "The tallit for your return trip awaits you at Freida's shop. Go to Clarissa's apartment to fetch Margaret; obtain the shawl, and then you are safe!"

He felt no such confidence. Frowning, he said, "I understand the shawls only work for one person. How will a new one get us both back?"

Claire said, "Julian and I have traveled to and fro numerous times with two halves of one. I have no doubt the same will work for you and Margaret."

He nodded, still unconvinced, but with a dawning hope. The crazy scheme might work.

"How will I get one?" he asked.

Lady Ashworth spoke up. "I shall tell you exactly where to go and to whom. You will tell her we sent you." She paused and took a sip of coffee. "If you need to—Freida is prescient in mysterious ways. I expect she'll know you the moment you walk into her shop." She paused, thinking back, her eyes unseeing. "Only she did not know that St. John wasn't the right man to buy the tallit, which I wonder at. When I first bought my tallit, she knew my name, though I'd never mentioned it."

Stewart nodded, chewing. Despite the hopefulness in the two women about him, he was still beset by doubts. This fantastic, unbelievable jaunt into the past was too wonderful and surely could not recur. It was to be a fluke, something he would never experience again even if he lived to see more days. Meeting and loving Margaret was another fluke. He couldn't be lucky enough, or blessed enough, whichever way you looked at it, to have a lifetime with her here. He'd never been lucky before.

As he finished his meal, he continued his dismal thoughts. By now, the thugs had had enough. They would be ready to kill him on sight. Even if the police had managed to capture the two that had been on his tail all week, the man behind it, the one who had sent them, would send more. He'd send more, and then more, and keep sending them until he knew Stewart was dead.

Stewart laid down his napkin and looked around wistfully. "Would you mind if I took a quick tour of the place before I go?" He shook his head. "I appreciate your confidence, but I can't help but feel I shall never return." He looked at Claire apologetically.

But she had come bolt upright and put a hand to her middle. "Oh, dear!" she said.

Lady Ashworth put her cup down forcefully. "Have the pains begun again?"

Claire gulped out a breath. "Yes! And this one was strong."

Stewart rose to his feet, suddenly feeling almost panicked at having to face the black suits again. "I'll take the quickest look about, I promise you, and then send your husband back!'

Lady Ashworth pursed her lips. She took the tallit from where it hung over the arm of the empty chair where Julian normally sat and where Claire had placed it.

"Why, certainly," she said, coming smilingly toward Stewart. "One of the servants can take you around." He came to his feet, and she threw the shawl around his shoulders, closing it across his chest. When he vanished from sight she added, "Just as soon as you return to us, Mr. Russell."

She turned and looked at Claire, who nodded, wincing in pain. "Thank you. I don't think we have a minute to spare!"

Lady Ashworth hurried to the bellpull. When Grey appeared in a moment, she said, "Grey, fetch Mr. Wickford! It's time!"

The fruit falls from the tree when it gets ripe.
S. Vivekananda

Chapter 25

Clarissa's chef was back, and though the next morning found the time travelers noticeably on edge, (only Clarissa was her now usual placid self) St. John had been able to eat a breakfast of eggs Benedict despite his growing unease at his separation from Claire. Margaret had tried it out of curiosity but found it much to her liking and finished it as well.

They were sipping coffee afterward and considering the day ahead when suddenly the bell rang. They snapped to attention. St. John jumped to his feet. Clarissa rose hurriedly and went to the intercom. "Who is it?" she asked.

"It's Stewart! Hurry! I'm being followed!"

Clarissa buzzed Stewart into the elevator hall, while St. John rubbed his hands impatiently.

When the young man arrived a few minutes later on the 29th floor, it was to find three faces peering out in concern from Clarissa's doorway. Stewart still wore the beautiful Regency garb he'd found himself in when he arrived in the past, but his hair was askew, and he looked harried. "Here!" He threw the shawl at St. John. "There's not a minute to lose! Your wife is in labor!"

St. John said, "Obliged." Without another word, he was gone.

Margaret couldn't help but smile. "To think, they'll have a child by the time I return!" But Stewart had shut the door to the apartment and was busily locking the two locks.

"I'm sure I was followed," he said. "I expected any moment to be kidnapped and never seen or heard from again! I'm not sure what made them leave me alone. Too many people about, I suppose." When he turned back, his eyes fastened on Margaret and he clasped her hands within his own. "Thank God you're preserved unharmed! When Lady Ashworth told me she'd seen you" —he blinked and swallowed and resumed, in an almost apologetic voice, "I was dreadfully worried, you see."

Margaret saw the earnestness in his eyes and knew it was mirrored in her own. "I was equally concerned for your welfare," she admitted, but with shining eyes.

"Come into the parlor," said Clarissa, who had never before called her living room by that name. She had her phone in her hand and thumbed a number into it. "I'll call the police."

"Wait!" Stewart cried. "If you call them, they'll want me for questioning. Then they'll release me and I'll be in as much danger as ever. And what if the black suits succeed in getting their hands on me and I'm not here to purchase that shawl?"

Clarissa nodded. "Very well." She raised her phone again. "My husband will know who to call. I daresay we need body guards." Even Clarissa, who was hugely unflappable, had no desire to find herself at the end of a gun again, for Stewart's sake or anyone's.

"They can escort you to the shop where you are to purchase the tallit. Margaret and I will wait here," she continued while waiting for Adam to pick up.

"I have to go with him," Margaret objected. "We can try the shawl together. If it only works for him, I will need one too. And I maintain, I will not leave that shop of curiosities until I am certain of being able to get home!"

Stewart sat down heavily. "I'm still trying to fathom how it is that *I* must buy the shawl. Your great-aunt told me, but I can scarce believe it. I never dreamed—!"

Margaret came smiling and sat beside him. She'd noticed that his speech was more like her own. This, she felt, was a very good sign. Freida had said her tallits were matchmakers, and that the two who were matched would be future partners for life—*and* could travel together by means of one shawl. She said it was exceptional that the tallit had brought her with St. John when she was not his wife, but that it had a purpose. More and more she believed in that purpose, and she told Stewart so.

He took her hand. "Margaret," he said seriously, gazing with his lovely blue eyes at her darker ones. "I have nothing to offer you in your day. If I go back with you, I'll be no one, penniless, and with no prospects."

She nodded. "I comprehend that." With a sad smile, she met his gaze. "I, too, will have almost nothing once my father is gone. We shall be equally matched," she said gently.

Clarissa had been speaking to Adam, but she clicked off and turned to them. "What is this nonsense about having nothing? My father will endow you with a gift before he is gone. You must see that he does."

Margaret shook her head. "We both know it will hardly suffice."

Clarissa surprised her with a smile. "I have thought about it, you know. I'd almost forgotten. I have a small fortune in the funds on 'Change, which I shall never have need of, nor access to," she explained. "You must use it in my place."

"A small fortune?" asked Margaret, astounded. "But how did you come upon it?"

"My father's brother, before he passed, knowing our plight as women and having no offspring or wife of his own, transferred what assets he could, to me."

"But how is it I never knew about this?" asked Margaret, in amazement.

Clarissa shrugged. "When it happened, you were too young to understand. Later on, if I had told you, it would only have been on account of wanting to gloat about it. Be happy I never did." She looked at Stewart. "But again, my father will behest a gift upon you when Margaret asks him to; for he takes no pleasure in knowing she will have no inheritance from him."

Stewart's brows creased. "But will he indeed willingly bestow a gift upon a penniless man?"

Margaret smiled again at how differently Stewart was speaking since his return.

Clarissa continued smoothly, "When he learns you are to marry his daughter, he will."

"If he does not have apoplexy first," Margaret interjected.

"You will remain with him on Red Lion Square until he is gone, and that will alleviate his reluctance to accept Stewart."

But Stewart's frown only deepened. "He will as like not grant permission for that marriage, considering me a fortune hunter, or at the least, a lazy-shanks!"

Clarissa was silent, for she knew what he said held truth.

"That will indeed be a bridge to cross," said Margaret, "although he can hardly call you a fortune hunter since I have none to his knowledge. He never mentioned anything of Clarissa's funds to me. But, aside from all this, first we must solve the problem of getting safely to the shop of curiosities, and then back to 1819!" She looked at her sister. "Were you able to procure the guards you spoke of?"

"Adam is sending men. It might take a few hours, but they should arrive by late afternoon. He has a private plane, but there will still be the trip from New Jersey they must make to get here."

There was silence as they contemplated that. "Let us hope then," said Stewart, "that we have no trouble before they arrive." He looked sadly at the ladies. "If they force their way in, you cannot make me vanish this time. The tallit is now 200 years away."

I think everyone is just trying to get home.
Charlie Mackesy

Chapter 26

When St. John arrived in his library, he thrust the tallit back into the little drawer where they kept it and hurried to his wife's bedchamber. He found her looking breathless, red-cheeked, and with Mr. Wickford standing nearby. Lady Ashworth sat by her side.

"Oh, my darling!" Claire cried upon seeing him. He rushed to her free side and sat beside her, taking a hand and kissing it.

Lady Ashworth said, "Well done, Julian," as if he had accomplished something great by his return or had entertained a wish not to.

"How is she doing?" he asked Mr. Wickford.

"All is well, sir," he said, nodding his head. "Thus far."

At that moment a birth pain overtook Claire. "They're—coming—faster!" she panted. Lady Ashworth placed a cold cloth on Claire's forehead, while the doctor consulted his timepiece.

"I almost wish she could go back for the birth," said Her Ladyship confidentially to Julian. "She does only what she pleases, I'm afraid!"

"Grandmamma—please!" Claire cried between gritted teeth. And then she could speak no more until the grip of pain ebbed off.

"Where did you wish her to go for the birth, ma'am?" asked Mr. Wickford.

A look of alarm swept across Lady Ashworth's eyes but was conquered in a moment. "To *my* residence, sir," she answered evenly. "Every comfort is there, and how it would have pleased the marquess, God rest his soul, for a birth to take place in that house. There have been no births there, you know," she added, "since before the marquess was born. Not since 1731."

"This bedchamber is as fit for childbirth as any, I warrant," put in Mr. Wickford expansively. He smiled condescendingly as if pitying the unlearned woman who thought a different room might somehow help the process.

Looking peaked, Claire lay back, gulping air. "Tell me," she gasped. "About Margaret. What is she doing?"

But Mr. Wickford said with a scowl, "Ma'am, this is no time for conversation." To Julian he said, "You see what your presence does. She must save her energy, sir."

Julian leaned low and kissed Claire's cheek. "Margaret is perfectly fine. I'll explain everything afterward," he whispered. As the minutes ticked past and the pains increased in frequency, Claire, though she was no screamer, groaned. Julian struggled with unease each time he saw her wracked or writhing in pain, but the groan seemed to deplete him of color.

Seeing his face, Lady Ashworth said, "Julian, I daresay that having you in the house is sufficient. Wait in the library or your study. You aren't equal to this."

"My thought exactly, ma'am!" piped in Mr. Wickford.

"I'm the one—who's not equal to it," gasped Claire. She peeked at her husband, though she was hardly able to focus. "Stay, please!"

"I will not leave you," he said firmly. He kissed her hand again, murmuring endearments until the wave of pain had passed.

After another hour passed with agonizing slowness, Mr. Wickford told Julian, "The first birth is the most difficult, sir. After this, once the passage has been opened, succeeding deliveries are generally easier." Three long hours later, when the pains were very close, Mr. Wickford dug in his bag for a jar of something and a medieval-looking instrument. "Leeches, sir" he said, proudly holding up his jar of the black creatures. "To apply after the birth. Relieving the humors does wonders to prevent inflammation."

Claire overheard this and turned in horror. "Never, sir!" she panted, while gulping in deep breaths against a wave of pain. "Never—leeches—upon—my body!"

Mr. Wickford compressed his lips and looked to St. John, who shook his head, no. With sad resignation, the physician put his jars and instrument away. Shaking his head, he reflected that Mrs. St. John had always been a strange case and he was therefore little surprised by this foolish refusal. What had surprised him was Mr. St. John's marrying her at all, considering how very befuddled the lady was when Mr. Wickford had examined her for amnesia three years ago.

Twenty minutes more and he held up a mottled red, squalling infant. A shock of dark hair the color of St. John's lay wet and flat against the scalp.

"A boy!" cried Lady Ashworth, beaming.

"A fine boy," affirmed the doctor, who was hurriedly drying off the newborn with a cloth. "I'd say he's six, perhaps six and a half pounds," he said. "Congratulations, sir. You are the father of a son."

As the child was given to the exhausted but elated mother to put to her breast—another astonishing practice for an upper-class woman in Mr. Wickford's estimation, who had asked to see the wet nurse only to learn there was none—St. John kissed her and peeked at the red-faced, puckered little human that was his son. His relief was intense.

"Julian Richard Loudon St. John the Second," smiled Claire, but she knew her husband would object. They'd had this discussion and his preference was to name a son after the marquess, his former guardian and only affectionate adult male in his formative years.

"Richard Loudon Julian St. John," he said, still poking the blanket aside to get a better glimpse of his offspring. "And not the prettiest of children, I think?"

Claire, who had fallen instantly in love with the new arrival, frowned. "He's beautiful!" She looked up at her handsome husband. "All newborns look this way." She smiled fondly at her son and his fine dark hair that would no doubt grow to look just like Julian's. She nudged him at her breast, for he was already slacking off in favor of sleep, then smiled as he latched on afresh and took hearty pulls as if he'd been doing it for ages.

Julian kissed her forehead. "You've done marvelously. You've made me quite proud. I adore you." To Lady Ashworth, he murmured admiringly, "Was she not a champion?" He'd heard that women screamed in childbirth—some women, that is. Apparently, not all.

He took a closer peek at the astonishing little human while Claire smiled gently. His son! Fatherhood seemed to have instantly expanded his male pride, as though he'd grown a foot taller or added hair to his chest.

Afterward, Lady Ashworth said, leaning over Claire and peering affectionately at the child, "You need rest. Shall I take him?"

"No, please!" Claire cried. "I want him with me while I rest." She closed her eyes, snuggling the baby against her.

And suddenly Julian felt as if he'd been under great strain, as if *he* had just suffered birth pains. The doctor, seeing his pale cheeks and brow said, "Sir, your wife and child are fine. There's nothing you can do here. Go and get some refreshment."

With relief, Julian thanked the man for his assistance, kissed his wife and then, tenderly, his son, and excused himself. He headed hastily for the library. A stiff drink was his goal. Lady Ashworth declined the offer of joining him, though she wished him much joy in his new child.

Seated with a libation in the library before a blazing fire, he considered the situation. What an awful, wonderful miracle childbirth was! And his wife was well, nursing their child. It was a mercy, he knew, that he'd been here to witness the birth. He might easily have been stranded in New York when it happened. But he'd been here and he was a father! He had an heir! Again, his chest and heart seemed to inflate with new pride, but also a sense of humility, for he was responsible to raise this little fellow properly. He and Claire.

As he relaxed further, his mind fell to Margaret and Stewart. His only concern now was to see them return safely. He wondered if his assistance might be needed to that end in New York— perhaps to help guard Stewart's safety? But he was not prepared to leave at once to find out. No, he was surprisingly weary after the birth. He must trust the young couple to their fate. And to the mystery of the tallit.

It rankled that he'd not yet had the chance to question Stewart about his prospects, his family background or education. The problem of what to do with him when he arrived, in fact, suddenly weighed upon him, as if, having been delivered of the weight of care associated with the birth, he had merely exchanged it for a new worrisome load.

St. John reasoned, rightly, that the young man would lose any credentials or associations he possessed when he came to the past, which meant that his current prospects mattered not. Still, he felt responsible to some degree for Margaret, and wanted to see her well-matched. Her father had never displayed much interest in her, for his heart had ever been on Clarissa. But how would the old man react were he to discover that his one remaining daughter wished to marry a man with no pedigree or fortune? To be in such a state was to be socially doomed.

Which meant that Margaret was, too.

Everything is more beautiful because we're doomed. You will never be lovelier than you are now. We will never be here again.
Homer

Chapter 27

To Margaret's relief, there was no trouble that day, though Clarissa noted the presence of two suspicious-looking men loitering across the street, sometimes sitting on a park bench, other times pacing. They weren't wearing dark suits, but that didn't assure Stewart of their innocence. He peeked carefully around a curtain to get a glimpse just when one of the men looked up at the building. He drew his head back quickly.

Clarissa said he ought to wear contemporary clothing to be less conspicuous when he left the apartment. Stewart hated to abandon his Regency finery, but to be safe accepted more of Adam's clothing to wear. In fine jeans and a Madras shirt and tennis shoes, he looked chipper, Margaret thought. She wore the jeans and shirt she'd borrowed previously.

They spent hours waiting for the men to arrive in the parlor. Clarissa allowed Margaret to monopolize her laptop, and Stewart joined her. He led her through news sites, history blogs, bookish blogs, and an interactive world map intended for fifth graders. Margaret was fascinated.

At 2 p.m., they stretched their legs and had a snack. When Margaret saw that the men across the street hadn't moved on, she said, "Cannot you call a magistrate to complain?"

Clarissa said, "We don't have magistrates or charleys, only the police. And they won't come unless there's been a crime."

Margaret muttered, "Well that isn't very helpful, is it?"

Adam's men came at 3 p.m. on the dot. Clarissa knew to let them in because her husband texted her to do so. Their names, the others learned upon introductions, were Ben and Mark. Clarissa told them about the suspicious men hanging about, and they each took a good but furtive look from her high front windows before preparing to leave with Margaret and Stewart.

Clarissa drew Margaret aside. "We'll have to hurry," Margaret said fretfully. "Freida's shop closes promptly at five."

"I know," Clarissa said. She looked deeply into Margaret's eyes. "This may be goodbye for us, dear sister, as I am not accompanying you."

Margaret blinked in surprise. "You have never called me 'dear sister' before." She put a hand to her heart. "But I must say," and here she hesitated, looking with real affection at Clarissa, "that you are become a dear sister as well! I am sorry we were not such to each other when you were home."

Clarissa drew her into a hug. "I am sorry I was so odious to you then. It's my fault, not yours, as I'm the elder sister. I'm so glad you came and gave me a chance to do better."

She had the look of one about to cry and Margaret hurriedly kissed her cheek. "And so you have. You've been wonderful! To Stewart as well as me," she said softly into her ear. "Thank you."

They clasped hands and smiled at each other. Margaret said, "If all goes well, and if Stewart's tallit is like Mr. St. John's, I shall be back to see you again!"

"I hope you will. And that Adam will be here so you can meet each other."

"Yes!" agreed Margaret. "I should like that. God bless you, dear Clarissa!" And with that, she went to join Stewart who was waiting patiently with Adam's men near the foyer.

Before they opened the door, Ben said, "Okay, listen up. Mark will walk first; you two stay right behind him. And I'll be behind you. In the cab, he and I will sit at the windows." She and Stewart listened closely and watched while they checked their weapons one last time—each had a gun—then nodded at each other.

Ben checked the hallway, then held the door while the others walked through. Clarissa came to the door to see them off and Margaret looked back at her with a sad smile until they turned the bend for the elevator.

When they reached the street, they saw that the men who seemed suspicious were no longer there. Hailing a cab took ten minutes, and, once they started down 5th Avenue, traffic was snarled as badly as during "rush hour," Stewart assured them.

Margaret felt every minute must be rushed lest Freida's shop should close and they be put off for yet another day.

Finally, they pulled up in front of the store with its large sign.

"Is this the place?" Mark asked.

Margaret, the only one of their company to have been there previously, said, "It 'tis."

They left the cab with Ben, but Mark stayed in it so the driver wouldn't leave. Ben said, "I'll wait outside until you're done, and then we'll take you wherever you're going."

"Much obliged," said Stewart. Ben raised an eyebrow but said nothing.

Margaret held back a grin. There was no doubt that Stewart was becoming suited for the past. *Her* past!

The door, to her relief, held its prominent "Open" sign facing out. Freida was near the door, and when she saw Margaret she opened it for them.

"So this is your young man," she said with her calm smile as she watched them enter. She faced Stewart squarely then as if examining his features.

"Is something wrong?" he asked.

"Mm, hmm!" she said softly. She closed the door and motioned them to follow her to the back of the store. She stopped in front of the glass case holding the special tallits. "Nothing is wrong, Mr. Russell," she said while withdrawing a key from a pocket and turning to unlock the case.

He looked uncertainly at Margaret, but she smiled broadly. Freida hadn't known the name of the gentleman the tallit was for on their last visit, but now called him Mr. Russell. Margaret was certain she'd only referred to him as Stewart in Freida's presence. This reassured her that the tallit truly must be his!

Freida deftly picked out a shawl that was sandwiched between two others and drew it out, turning with a smile to show them. "This is meant for you," she said. "It's 100% wool." Stewart reached out a hand for it, but she drew it back with a smile saying, "Allow me to bag it for you."

"May we not see it, first?" Margaret asked.

"Of course." She unfolded it so they could now see it was ivory with dark green stripes. There was no colorful embroidered edges, but the top bore an embroidered strip of material that Freida explained would go about his head if Stewart were to wear it to pray as the shawls are traditionally used. "That is the atarah," she said, staring at it admiringly. "Not all tallits have one."

"This is the handsomest tallit I've seen," said Margaret, as if she had seen a thousand. In fact, she'd only seen Claire and Mr. St. John's and merely glimpsed the folded garments in the shop at her earlier visit. But the embroidery of the 'atarah' was striking.

They followed Freida to the front in silence. Margaret was feeling very much relieved—she had to admit she'd been harboring a secret fear that Freida would say, "No, this is not the man I can sell it to." And then she and Stewart would be in the same predicament only with less hope than before.

At the counter, Freida eyed them calmly. "That will be $1,000."

Margaret and Stewart stared, horrified. Stewart said, "I don't have that kind of money. I'm a student."

Margaret realized she'd left her reticule at Clarissa's apartment, and that even if she had it, one thousand dollars was not in it. But the card of credit was. "I left the card of credit with Clarissa!" she moaned.

"In this case, it must be cash," said Freida. She smiled kindly. "I'm sorry."

Why had they not thought of asking about the price earlier, Margaret wondered! Why had no one thought of it?

"Wait!" she said, suddenly remembering that she had a 'burner' phone. Let me call Clarissa!"

Clarissa listened patiently and said, "Put me on the phone with Ben. He or Mark will have to come here to get that much cash." Dryly, she added, "You would think the tallit, being divinely directed, would know who may afford one."

"But we can afford one," said Margaret happily. "Because of you!" In a more sober tone, she added, "Thank you, dear sister."

Stewart reached for the phone. To Margaret's surprise, when he spoke his voice was choked with emotion. "I don't know how to thank you," he began. "This is so much. A thousand dollars! I'm sure I can never repay it!"

Margaret could hear Clarissa saying it was nothing, nothing at all, and would save his life, and he very much needed to be saved, for he must marry her sister.

Margaret felt herself blushing but was too pleased to mind.

They begged Ben to hurry to the Majestic and back so they could purchase the tallit before the shop closed. Then they waited, sitting together on the floor with their backs against the counter. Even Mark came inside and stood where he could watch the street.

The store clock read 4:45 p.m. by the time Ben returned. Breathlessly, Margaret paid for the tallit and watched while Freida placed it, along with a receipt, into a bag. Margaret was bursting with curiosity to discover whether it would truly work for Stewart *and* her and wished to try it immediately.

Freida held the bag toward Stewart, studying her. "You're in a hurry," she said.

"We are!" Margaret replied, reaching for it.

"Yes, he's in danger. I know. Here." She handed it over.

Margaret took the shawl eagerly from the bag. She and Stewart admired it together. "Shall we try it?" she asked.

"Right here?" he said.

Freida stood watching with a little knowing smile.

Margaret suddenly realized that with only one tallit, only one of them could be transported. She turned back to Freida in alarm. How could she have been so frightfully stupid not to think of it sooner?

"Do you have one for me?" she asked. "Or," she added, studying Freida, "will this take us both?"

Freida shrugged. "Why don't you try it?"

Margaret turned away to do so, but something told her that Freida knew more than she was allowing. "But you know, do you not, that it shall not work for us both?"

Freida turned to her with a patient look. "I expect not."

Stewart said, "We must try. If only one of us goes back, we'll return immediately."

"But where will we return?" wailed Margaret. "To the library, as before?"

She turned wistfully to Freida. "We need two pieces! If you do not have a tallit for me, then I must have half of this one."

Freida, staring at the tallit, nodded thoughtfully. "I suppose so." She glanced at the clock. It was five minutes to five.

Margaret cried, "Please! Do you have a scissor?"

But at this, Freida's face blanched. "For you to butcher my work? No."

Margaret's face fell. She threw herself into Stewart's arms. Tearfully she said, "I am afraid we are—we are—to be parted!" Stewart nodded, stroking her hair.

"I shall have to let you go," he agreed, "and take my chances here."

Freida, looking on, softened. "Did I not hear that the other tallit came apart?"

Margaret looked up. "My sister tore it during a fight."

Freida nodded. "It's not usually possible for fabric to come apart. As I think about this, even though it didn't tear cleanly, I think that tallit was meant for two. For Mr. St. John and his bride." She motioned at Stewart's tallit. "Perhaps yours is as well."

Margaret and Stewart stared at each other, thunderstruck. "Let us try it!" he cried.

As they each took one end, a little cry burst out of Freida, whose natural protectiveness for her workmanship overcame her generosity. "Wait! Wait! Let me think!"

But it was too late. Margaret pulled with all her might, and Stewart pulled with all of his, and then, without anything more than a mild "fsssss" the tallit split in two, cleanly and easily.

Freida was open-mouthed, but a smile curled her lips. "I am learning more about these shawls from you people! May I see the pieces?"

Margaret and Stewart handed them over. Freida examined them, noting that the embroidered pattern around the top of the garment was already forming at the new edges. As she watched, the pattern fully emerged. "Look!" she cried, holding it up.

In less than a minute, the new edges were neatly and beautifully patterned and seamed. Frieda turned, smiling, and almost reluctantly handed them back. "That saved me a lot of work," she said with a chuckle.

Margaret was nearly speechless with joy but turned questioningly to Freida. "Why did this not happen for Claire's tallit? When it tore, Claire said it made a terrible sound as if it were injured, and the edges were not neat and pretty, but jagged."

Frieda put a hand to her chin as she thought about it. "I believe this one split cleanly because it was meant for the two of you. Which means, the other tallit would also have split easily had the two it was meant for pulled it apart." She smiled. "Miracles never cease!"

At that moment, Ben came inside. Looking up, Frieda called, "Please turn my sign around for me?" He turned the sign to say CLOSED, and then came toward them, but Freida motioned to him to stop. She headed toward the door. "Come. Let's give them a minute."

He nodded and followed her. She looked back at Margaret and Stewart meaningfully. "They only need a minute," she repeated carefully.

Ben was fine with that. He'd wait out front. But he turned to glance at the couple before he left and saw they'd moved. No, they'd gone. He started looking around. "Where'd they go?"

Freida turned, saw their absence, and her manner became brisk. "Have a good day, sir," she said to Ben, now herding him gently out the door. "I'm afraid I'm already closing late today."

Ben's eyes narrowed. "You have Stewart and Margaret in here."

"That young couple?" She shook her head. "I think you will find they have gone."

"We're standing at the door," he said, heavily, beginning to feel suspicious of this woman.

Freida looked at him almost pityingly. "There are doors everywhere, my good man. Some you see, some you don't."

With that, she tried to close the door on him, but he put his hefty bulk in the way, insisting that he'd scour the store corner to corner before leaving. He opened the door and waved at Mark to join him, quickly explaining that he'd lost sight of the pair.

Freida sighed and allowed them to search. About ten minutes later, they returned to the front. Mark scratched his head, while Ben said, "They're not here. But I didn't see a back door. Do you have one?"

Freida hesitated. "No."

He looked at her squarely. "How did they leave?"

Freida leveled a steady gaze upon him. "I wasn't watching. I'm afraid it's a mystery."

Ben's patience snapped and he glared at her. "But you're not surprised. You're in on this!"

Now impatience tinged her voice. "In on what?"

"We're supposed to protect them," he said. "I need to know where they are."

"I suggest you call your employer and tell him you lost them."

Ben and Mark exchanged heavy looks.

"I'm taking another look," Mark said. "I would have seen them out front if they left."

"Wait," Ben said. "I'll call Clarissa. See what she says." As he thumbed his phone to call, he added, "We'll let her tell Adam."

When Clarissa picked up, he'd only launched into his explanation when she interrupted him.

"They've gone and you can't find them, is that right?"

He hesitated. This was hard to admit. "Yes."

"That's fine," Clarissa said, to his great surprise. "I only wanted you to get them there safely. I'll let Adam know you've done your job well. Thanks for that."

Ben's features had puckered into a puzzled frown as she spoke, but he thumbed off, looked at Mark, and shrugged. "If she don't care what happened to them, we don't have to care."

Freida, smiling again, closed and locked the door behind them.

It is part of the human condition,
and a recurrent feature of human history,
that what we find is not always what we were looking for,
and what we accomplish is not always what we set out to do.
Wilfred W. McClay

Chapter 28

Margaret and Stewart found themselves right in front of St. John's home on South Audley Street when they left Freida's shop, much to their delight.

"Exactly where I was brought last time!" Stewart exclaimed. Margaret could hardly contain herself for joy. They had made it back together only minutes after all had seemed lost!

"Look at us!" she exclaimed. "Our proper clothing is back!"

He took in her pert little bonnet with its smart ribbon down to her very genteel silk slippers. "You look wonderful," he said earnestly, every bit the young man in love.

"So do you!" she returned, blushing with pleasure, not only at his compliment but because Stewart looked most handsome in his superfine tailcoat, stirrup trousers and shoes.

At that moment, Grey opened the door of the townhouse. "Quickly, let us inside," she said, still in high excitement. She hurried ahead of him to the door. Her insides were all aflutter and she felt as light as one of cook's exquisite tea biscuits.

Grey, that usually placid establishment of a servant, greeted them with, "Why, Miss Margaret! How good, how very good to see you, ma'am."

"Hullo, Grey," she said happily. "You know Mr. Russell, I presume?"

Grey bowed politely and received their things.

Margaret could not hold off her curiosity. "Is there a new little master or is it a mistress?"

Grey tried unsuccessfully to stifle a smile. "A young master, ma'am."

Margaret clapped her hands. "Oh, joy, for Claire and Mr. St. John! Let us meet the little fellow!" She paused only to ask, "I expect the new mother is still abed?"

But Grey shook his head, his brows revealing perplexity when he admitted, "No, ma'am." The servant privately thought his mistress unwise not to follow Mr. Wickford's prescription of complete bed rest for a fortnight. Mrs. St. John had refused and had been seen in the morning room and parlor already. None of the servants understood it.

No sooner had Grey spoken, when Margaret grabbed Stewart's hand and was off before the butler could say another word.

She led Stewart first to the best parlor, but it was empty. Stewart hadn't seen the room before and took a swift admiring glance at the formal drapes and circle of stuffed furniture around a hearth before being whisked on by Margaret.

She queried a footman in the corridor who informed them that the family were all in the second parlor. "Shall I announce you, mum?"

"No need," Margaret said, breezing aside the usual protocol. She skipped to the doorway, knocked, and opened the door the second she heard St. John's, "Yes?"

"Hullo! Hullo!" She cried, still in the clouds. She hadn't realized how very much she missed her old life, her friends, and what was familiar. She even yearned to get home to Papa and give the old man an uncustomary effusive kiss!

Lady Ashworth spoke out some greeting, expressing her pleasure and relief that Stewart had come back as well as Margaret. "Of course, I knew you would," she added with great self-satisfaction.

Claire was smiling up at them ecstatically, the baby in her arms.

St. John, smiling, came and took Margaret's hand—for she had stopped in rapture at the sight of her dear, dear friends—and led her to Claire and his son, motioning to Stewart to come also. Margaret kissed Claire's cheek and then looked down for her first glimpse of the new young Master St. John. "What a fine boy!" she exclaimed. The baby's hair, dry now, was fluffy, and surprisingly thick. His little cherub cheeks were a downy pink, and she could see one tiny, fisted hand, peeking out of his wrap. Looking down fondly at the little chap, she added, "Why, I feel almost like an aunt!" She blushed instantly, for she was not that close a relation and feared she had sounded presumptuous.

"But you must be that!" Claire exclaimed. "Aunt Margaret it 'tis." Margaret bit her lip to hide how pleased she was.

"He's sleeping," Claire said, "or you'd see at once that his eyes are like his father's." She dragged her eyes off her son and looked searchingly up at Margaret who was positively aglow with happiness. "I am so glad to see you!" she cried. "You look quite well after this misadventure; indeed, you look above well. I can scarcely wait to hear all about it!"

"And I shall be pleased to tell every bit of it!" Margaret replied, sincerely.

Stewart admired the baby as best he could, not being the baby-admiring sort himself. But the new parents were blissfully unaware, pleased enough for their own sakes that no other admiration was necessary.

When the newcomers had been admonished to sit down, they told how they'd been able to return, showing the tallits. Everyone noticed that Stewart's was different, for it had the atarah. But both were a wonder and so Margaret allowed her half to make the rounds from person to person, though Claire refused to touch it for fear it might whisk her from her child. She looked at it with interest, however, and was duly impressed with the finished beauty of it, remembering all too well how her tallit had not received the same tailored finish after Clarissa tore it.

Then suddenly St. John realized that Stewart was there to stay, but without prospects, family or fortune. He leveled his gaze firmly upon him while speaking for the benefit of the room at large. "May I ask, sir, what are your plans, now you've arrived?"

Stewart shifted uncomfortably in his seat. "I—I daresay I've wondered about that very thing, sir." He looked apologetically at Margaret. "I suppose I must—" He scrounged his brain for an answer. Looking for employment was out of the question if he hoped to marry Margaret, for a respectable gentleman did not work. "That is, I can seek to earn a commission, or—or study to enter the church." These occupations, he knew, were the standard fallbacks for second sons and men who were reputable but without means.

Margaret came loyally to his rescue. "My sister informed me that she has a small fortune in the funds, sir," she said, speaking to St. John. "I mean to put it into Stewart's name. My father remembers nothing of it and will be none the wiser."

"A small fortune?" He cleared his throat. "How small?"

Margaret took a breath. "'Twas ten thousand pounds, sir, when last she had word, which was before she left our time."

"Per annum?" he asked, his brows raised, for that would be a vast fortune, indeed.

"No, sir. Though it does draw a nice annual interest."

Lady Ashworth said, "I daresay I can add to that sum. The marquess, God bless his soul, was generous enough to leave me more than I need."

St. John began pacing, one hand to his chin.

Margaret said, "My sister also said I must tell my father to make me a gift of ten thousand pounds before his estate is passed to my cousin."

St. John looked up. "Can he do that? Does he have the ready cash?"

Margaret was not entirely sure whether he could, having never been graced with much knowledge of her father's financial affairs, but she counted on her sister's confidence and said, "Clarissa said he could."

St. John nodded appreciatively. "This begins to take shape nicely for the two of you." He added, still pacing, "There is still the problem of pedigree—Mr. Russell has none."

Stewart had been thinking and suddenly said, "Do you know, I believe I have ancestors here in England? My family is broken, but I do recall that I am part English, and, I believe, part Austrian."

St. John shook his head. "That won't answer. We need to present you shortly. There's no time to explore your family heritage. I think it will be best to say you are from America, that your fortune is from…." And he fell silent. In fact, a thick silence blanketed the room, for no one knew how to account for Stewart's having a small fortune.

"From the funds!" exclaimed Stewart. "We have them in America, too, you know!"

St. John stopped and pointed a finger at him. "That's it." But his eyes wandered to Margaret and the look on his face was not encouraging.

"What is it, sir?" she asked anxiously, searching her mind for what the problem could be.

"Before we put a single penny into Mr. Russell's name," he said, turning to Stewart, "I need to know your intentions toward our Margaret."

Margaret detected a hidden smile playing at St. John's lips, but Stewart saw it not. He sat up. "I—I have nothing of my own to offer her, but…"

"Yes?"

"I do not deserve anything of this generosity, and I have no guarantee, not even an assurance, that I could even begin to pay any of it back, but…"

"Yes?" persisted St. John.

Margaret was at the edge of her seat.

"I may be pitiful in society, a bumbling bookish lout, but—"

His eyes were unhappy, but these words brought a smile to Claire who could see already the makings of a fine gentleman in Stewart. He was tall and almost elegant in his Regency attire, and would never put Margaret or any of them to shame.

"Yes?" This time Margaret had asked.

"Yes?" echoed Lady Ashworth.

Stewart shook his head miserably. "I lack—everything—I mean, everything! That a good man in this day should possess, but…"

"YES?" The whole room spoke in chorus.

Stewart stood and went to Margaret. He fell to one knee and took her hand. "But, if you can excuse all that, and forgive me my failings, and have faith in me to improve, then, I beg you dear,

dear, Margaret; Margaret who I adore—will you have me for your husband?"

Margaret bit her lip, tears popped into her eyes, and she exclaimed, "Yes! With all my heart, yes!"

He kissed her hand and then drew her to her feet, and he kissed her cheek, first one, then the other. A sudden reserve, or shyness, or perhaps it was due to the customary manners of the day, but he had no thought of taking her in his arms as he had done so easily in the library. Things were different here and he instinctively felt it.

Meanwhile, the others were congratulating them, and Claire said he must stay at South Audley Street until they could introduce him to Mr. Andrews, Margaret's father, and then some time must pass so that he and Margaret could be said to have a normal period of engagement before their wedding. Lady Ashworth began planning a dinner party, and Claire spoke of a rout, and then a ball. St. John said he'd arrange a few hunts after teaching Stewart how to carry himself and use a rifle, and of course he'd need riding lessons.

Margaret's head was spinning with delight. All of this, for her and Stewart's sake?

This, indeed, was family. This was happiness.

She had been a wallflower headed to spinsterhood, a lonely bluestocking who felt herself an outsider, yet all along she had had these warm, generous people in her life. Somehow her trip to New York had revealed this to her, and really had changed everything, far more than she ever dreamed possible.

She had gone looking for an invention but had found things that were infinitely more valuable. She was betrothed to a man who adored her, a sister that now loved her and was loved in return, a sense of belonging to this circle of relations as she'd never had before, and above all that, a new appreciation of herself. Stewart thought her forever lovely, but he'd said that lovely or not, he found her delightful. Lovely or not!

Margaret had thought the future must hold her key to happiness. Since she'd found Stewart there, in that sense it had, but only in that sense. She'd found her heart's contentment and it wasn't in the future.

It was right there, right now.

Notes
Facts and Fiction in the Book

The actual NYC JASNA Conference was held at the New York Marriott at the Brooklyn Bridge in 2012. My characters had no business over there, so I kept them close to the New York Public Library, moving the location of the conference to accommodate the story. I kept the conference theme ("Sex, Money and Power in Jane Austen's Fiction") and many thanks to JASNA for it. I am especially grateful to Miss Austen herself, who must be perpetually laughing in heaven at (and for the most part delighted by) all the fuss, scholarship, and spin-offs created about her and her work.

Margaret does not recognize Jane Austen's name because her publications to date (to date for Margaret, that is) did not bear it. While *Emma* was published in December, 1815 (although the title page says 1816), the author is given as, "By the author of *Pride and Prejudice*." During her lifetime, none of Jane's works were published under her name, though she was becoming known as the author by an increasing circle of people. (I saw one website claiming that her name was known by 1814, but this is very unlikely to have been true for the general public, including Margaret.)

The James Hotel really was formerly The Carlton, which is chiefly why I chose it for my characters, both of whom were familiar with the Regent's London Palace, Carlton House. I had to delete a humorous breakfast scene unfortunately, because I wrote it before choosing the hotel, and the James does not offer a free breakfast buffet.

When Margaret and St. John are admiring the view from the James, I gave them a better view than their room actually offers. While their "Empire State View Room" would have indeed allowed them to see the golden pyramid top of the Empire State

Building and some of midtown, I wanted readers to feel the effect of looking down upon New York with a fuller view, such as from the Observation Deck of the famed Rainbow Room (which I featured in my contemporary romance, *One Cinderella Night*). I felt it would be a shame to set a book in the heart of Manhattan but not do its beautiful skyline justice. And finally, I added a small refrigerator to the room for the fun of having Margaret discover refrigeration.

The details of The New York Public Library and its surroundings are as accurate as I could make them. My last visit to that museum was in my teens, so I had to go with internet research. **The Pforzheimer Collection**, room 319, is in the library as shown in the book and really does house the collection of literary criticism for early women writers.

In chapter 5, Stewart is offered a toothbrush that some may feel (based on films such as "Lost in Austen,") were not available then. But toothbrushes, though much coarser than modern ones, were available as early as 1780, when they were mass-produced by one William Addis, of Clerkenwald, England. Most upper-class Regency homes likely were using them.

Doctor/Mister. A reader asked about the physician, Mr. Wickford, wondering why he is addressed as "Mister" and not "Doctor." Only a doctor who had studied at University (and most had not!) was addressed as Doctor So-and-so. The others, surgeons or apothecaries, were *referred* to as doctors, but *addressed* as misters.

Glossary

Ape leader: An old maid; their punishment after death for not having offspring ("neglecting increase") was, it was said, to lead apes in hell.

Bibliothecary – Keeper of a library.

Bluestocking – Academic female.

Comb, give a comb—a scolding; to give a comb was to scold or reprimand.

Modiste – a dressmaker or milliner; a seamstress who deals with ladies' fashions.

"My father" (or "my mother") During the Regency it was standard usage for siblings to speak of their parents as "my" father or mother, not "our."

"Pluck to the backbone" – brave, bravery.

About the Author

Linore Rose Burkard is a serious watcher of period films, a Janeite and hopeless romantic. An award-winning author best known for Inspirational Regency Romance, her first book (*Before the Season Ends*) opened the genre for the CBA. Besides romance, Linore writes young adult apocalyptic suspense. (*The Pulse Effex Series*, as L.R. Burkard).

Linore has a *magna cum laude* English Lit. degree from the City University of New York, which she earned, she says, while taking herself far too seriously. She now resides in Ohio with her husband and five adult children, where she owns two cats, a Shorkie, and more teapots than any one human should possess.

Linore is President of the Dayton Christian Scribes, and active in the Middletown Area Christian Writers Group (MAC), and CAN, Christian Authors Network.

Get a free Regency "flash fiction" tale, "The Highly Sensitive Bride" (the quickest Regency romance you'll ever read) from Linore by joining her mailing list at LinoreBurkard.com/newsletter.

Other Books by Linore Rose Burkard

The Brides of Mayfair
Regency romance with heart and humor!
Miss Tavistock's Mistake
Miss Fanshawe's Fortune
Miss Wetherham's Wedding

The Regency Trilogy
Award-winning, heartwarming, inspirational romance!
Before the Season Ends
The House in Grosvenor Square
The Country House Courtship

Forever in Time Series
Forever, Lately

Contemporary Romance
One Cinderella Night
Falling In (Love!)

The Pulse Effex Trilogy
(as L. R. Burkard)
PULSE: World Gone Dark
RESILIENCE: Into the Dark
DEFIANCE: Battle the Dark

Novella, Historical Romance
Three French Hens

Other Books by Lilliput Press

Seasons of Her Soul
Christian Drama/Romance
Tammi Ector
Second-chance love follows domestic abuse and
heartbreak, but who would have thought Lee's first
storybook perfect marriage could turn out so wrong?

The Accidental Spy
Christian Adventure Fiction
Tom Rattray
An ordinary high school teacher on a pleasure sail
discovers a major threat to the U.S. East Coast—and
nobody knows it except him! Can he avert disaster
before it's too late?

And from Lilliput Classics

Quality Street: A Regency Romantic Comedy in Four Acts
by J.M. Barrie
A little-known delightfully humorous play by the
beloved author of Peter Pan!

Printed in Great Britain
by Amazon

32227097R00138